PENGUIN BOOKS

LIES WE TOLD THIS SUMMER

Emily Barr worked as a journalist in London but always hankered after a quiet room and a book to write. She went travelling for a year, which gave her an idea for a novel set in the world of backpackers in Asia. This became *Backpack*, a thriller that won the WHSmith New Talent Award. Her first YA thriller, *The One Memory of Flora Banks*, has been published in twenty-seven countries and was shortlisted for the YA Book Prize. *Lies We Told This Summer* is Emily's ninth YA novel. She lives in Cornwall with her husband and their children.

Books by Emily Barr

THE ONE MEMORY OF FLORA BANKS

THE TRUTH AND LIES OF ELLA BLACK

THE GIRL WHO CAME OUT OF THE WOODS

THINGS TO DO BEFORE THE END
OF THE WORLD

GHOSTED

THIS SUMMER'S SECRETS

A GIRL CAN DREAM

THE OTHER GIRL

EMILY BARR

LIES
WE
TOLD
THIS
SUMMER

PENGUIN BOOKS

PENGUIN BOOKS

UK | USA | Canada | Ireland | Australia
India | New Zealand | South Africa

Penguin Books is part of the Penguin Random House group of companies
whose addresses can be found at global.penguinrandomhouse.com

www.penguin.co.uk
www.puffin.co.uk
www.ladybird.co.uk

First published 2026

001

Set in 10.5/15.5pt Sabon LT Std
Typeset by Six Red Marbles UK, Thetford, Norfolk
Printed and bound in Great Britain by Clays Ltd, Elcograf S.p.A.

The authorized representative in the EEA is Penguin Random House Ireland,
Morrison Chambers, 32 Nassau Street, Dublin D02 YH68

A CIP catalogue record for this book is available from the British Library

ISBN: 978-0-241-77720-6

All correspondence to:
Penguin Books
Penguin Random House Children's
One Embassy Gardens, 8 Viaduct Gardens, London SW11 7BW

For Adam – thank you for always being there

Prologue

I'm alone in the house. Just me, the cat and you, my imaginary listeners.

It's time to do it.

Do you hear that? . . . Exactly. There's no sound. Except this . . .

That *clink*. It's me taking the key off its hook. The key has a label on it, saying ET. ET. Like the alien, but not, in this case.

I'm leaving the kitchen. Walking through the entrance hall.

Everyone is out. I can see them on Find My Friends. They're fifteen miles away, and heading further every time I refresh it.

What the fuck am I doing?

Walking up the stairs. That's what. Honestly, I wish you could see this place. The staircase is massive. Stone, but carpeted, and the carpet's squishy under my bare feet. Still brutal, though, if you fell. The air smells of polish and summer. I know my way around this house – when I arrived here I would never have imagined that. I'm getting a feel for its secrets. Its ghosts.

I'm upstairs. And here we are, in front of the door.

This is it, people. Yeah, I feel quite stupid talking to what is currently no one. Still, I have faith that one day you'll be out there, and knowing that you're listening is the only way I can make myself do this. First: is it the right key?

My hand's shaking. This is where we find out what's behind the door. At least, it could be. There we go. The key's going straight in. I don't feel great about myself for doing this. They invited me into their home and here I am, creeping around.

Should I turn back?

I should.

. . .

I'm not sure if you can hear that. It's the sound of the key turning.

You definitely heard that creak. Wooden door, opening inwards. They probably heard it creaking down in the village.

It smells musty. Like no one's been in for a while. But here we are.

Let's do it.

I took a deep breath and stepped across the threshold.

PART ONE

1

Cornwall

Six weeks earlier

Josh was wriggling around in my arms. I didn't want to
get up so I lay back and pointed at the sky. The grass was
muddy, and I knew it would stain, but I wasn't going
anywhere. No one would see.

'Look,' I said to Josh. 'Birds!'

I wasn't going to start feeling jealous of the birds
freewheeling across the sky. Swooping to wherever they
wanted to go. That was an insane cliché. They did look
happy, though.

'Run, birds!' said Joshie.

'Birds don't run. They fly,' I told him.

'No! Bird run,' he said, and I couldn't be bothered
to argue with a one-year-old. He turned over on to his
tummy and grabbed something from the grass. I tried to
pull him back.

'You're right,' I said, giving up. Some birds ran. Road-
runners, if they existed. 'See the birds running across the
sky?' He turned back and looked up. I wondered whether

I could make a recording of me and Joshie talking about birds. I wasn't allowed to listen to podcasts around the babies any more, but there were no rules about *making* them, and in fact I needed to make one this summer. I had to, and I had to do it in secret. It was hardly going to be true crime, given my boring life. It might as well be me and Josh talking about birds.

Josh had something in his fist. He moved it towards his mouth. I reached out and intercepted his arm and we had a little struggle as he tried to pull away.

Everything had kicked off a few days ago when I had been (not through choice) entertaining Joshie and Mia while listening to the season finale of *Serial* on the portable speaker. The babies hadn't minded because they were too little to understand, but when Mum appeared in the room unexpectedly, just as the recap of the murder was going on, she certainly had. I had hoped for a while that I was going to be banned from unpaid babysitting, but no: I was banned from listening while they were with me instead, and my life had become even more boring.

I prised his fingers apart and took out a snail. My little brother was constantly trying to eat snails. Maybe one day he'd go to France and try them properly. I put the snail as far away as I could reach and wished it a happy life. Time to go inside.

'Oh, Cat! Thank goodness.' Mum was in the kitchen with Mia, Josh's twin – the smaller of (can you believe it?) *two* sets of twins in our house – on her hip. Mum was arranging the nice tea things on a tray with one hand.

'Sophie and Owen are here! They just . . . dropped in. They want to talk to you. To both of us, but "*mostly Cat*", they said.' She shrugged. 'About watering the plants, I guess.'

Mum hated unexpected visitors. She considered dropping in on someone to be an aggressive act. If she knew someone was coming, she'd tidy for half a day, and now she'd been caught out. Because she was stressed, it was, as always, my job to step in and keep things going. This was not the mother I'd grown up with, the one who used to tell me I could do anything and go anywhere and make my own decisions. The second set of twins had been too much for her, had broken her, and now I seemed to be trapped.

'They're not the housework police.' I didn't bother to try not to sound pissed off. 'It's Sophie. Your friend. Do you want me to do the tea, or talk to them?'

I saw the answer on her face and held out my free arm for Mia. With a baby on each hip and a pack of biscuits in one hand, I set off to talk to Sophie and Owen, delighted that they were here. I'd been planning to drop in on them later, to see if we could use their pool.

Sophie had lived my dream career as a radio producer and was a former BBC radio commissioning editor. 'You remind me of me,' she sometimes said, though that was clearly not true because she was glamorous and fun. I guessed she meant the part about being interested in media. She and I talked often. It was Sophie who had recommended that I apply for the media course at Queen's University in Belfast.

The Allens had moved here six years ago, 'escaping London', coming to our part of Truro because Sophie and Mum were old school friends. They lived in an old manor house and had a swimming pool, and they had big parties, inviting everyone. Also, they always went to France from July to September, because they had an apartment there, and when their house here wasn't lent to friends they allowed us to use their pool. So, of course, we all loved them. Kitty and I followed their bougie summers in France avidly through Instagram.

I hesitated before going into the room. Sophie would definitely ask about my plans, now exams were over. It was good to get that one out of the way because Mum would start to spiral if she heard me airing any ideas that didn't involve staying at home to babysit.

I took the toddlers into the living room and dumped them into the playpen, ignoring the protests.

'Hi, Sophie,' I said. 'Hey, Owen. Mum's getting tea. She'll be here in a sec.'

When they visited, it felt a bit like finding film stars sitting in your living room, pretending not to notice that the sofa was covered in crumbs and stains. Sophie had glossy dark hair. Owen was a bit older than her but still looked OK. They were our friends, but they were from a different world.

I pulled my T-shirt straight and sat on the chair opposite them, crossing my legs to try to appear ladylike, aware of the mud stain down my back. Everything in their house was designed and beautiful. Everything in here, on the other hand, was from the Heart Foundation shop. It was tattered and second hand, and generally covered in snot, vomit, dribble and worse.

I also knew it didn't matter. Were Mum's stresses starting to infect me too?

'It's actually you we wanted to speak to, Cat,' said Sophie. 'As well as your mother and Bill, but primarily you.'

It was a small thing, but I always appreciated them saying 'Bill' rather than 'your dad'. Lots of people called Bill my dad and he wasn't. He was better than my dad had been, but that wasn't the point. You could tell by looking at us that he wasn't my father, but that didn't stop people saying it.

'Yeah,' Mum said. 'Bill's at work right now. Is it about watering the plants?'

'You've finished your exams,' said Owen. 'Is that right?'

'Last week.' I wasn't going to think about them until results day on August the fourteenth. It was weeks away and I was dreading it, because that would be crunch time. It was the day on which I would have to make a decision. I imagined Queen's, Belfast shimmering on the horizon, then pulled myself back into the room.

Sophie was leaning forward.

'And what are your plans for the rest of the summer, Cat?' she said. 'What are you doing between now and results day?' I had never seen someone with an actual twinkle in their eye, until now. I watched as she flashed a quick look to her husband, a tiny smile, and then her

9

attention was back with me, and I felt sick at how disappointing my answer was going to be.

'Umm . . . basically I'll be here?' I tried to inject a bit of an upbeat tone into my voice. I looked over at the whingeing twins. They'd be OK for a few more minutes. 'Helping with these monsters. And the others. So yeah, if you need anything doing at your house, then . . .' Listening to true-crime podcasts and pining for an adventure I wasn't allowed to have. That was the basic summer plan. Making a few token attempts to record something. Anything.

All my friends had interesting summers ahead. They were at least going camping, or to festivals. Working holiday jobs, meeting new people, trying things out.

'If circumstances were different,' said Owen, indicating the babies with his head, 'then you'd want to get out into the world and do something fun, right?'

'Oh God! Yes!'

'And you have your place at Queen's?' said Sophie. I nodded, glancing quickly towards the door. 'You need to make a summer project for that?'

I shrugged. 'Ideally. I'll do something.'

'Well – we've come to you with a proposal,' said Owen. 'A proposal, and a solution. As you know, we summer in Antibes. And we've been thinking about you, Cat, and your . . . situation.'

Sophie took over. 'Your siblings are adorable darlings, of course.' She stopped and grinned at the babies, who looked guilty. 'But you have ambitions and passions, and

I think we could help. I feel strongly that a change of scene could work for you and . . . well, we want to make it happen.'

I had no idea what to say.

'Cat,' said Owen. 'We'd love you to come with us to Antibes for the summer. What do you say?'

I stared at him. I stared at Sophie. I swallowed hard.

I knew their Antibes world. Their apartment there had balconies and sea views, and just like their house here, it was rented out and lent to friends when they weren't there. Sophie had invited Mum many times, but she'd never been. I'd followed their summers to the point where I felt I knew all their friends out there. The people who walked around wearing the best clothes, who swam in the sea and went to cafes and restaurants, looking beautiful. I had pored over the pictures, had matched them up with the Instagram accounts of people I didn't know. I was familiar with their friends the Thorpe family, and the glamorous Eva Santoro, the artists called Anthony and Alonzo . . . It generally formed an embarrassingly large percentage of my summer entertainment.

The Thorpes were my favourite. When Isabella Thorpe made her Instagram private last year, I'd taken it personally. Her brother, Jonathan, was good-looking. Very. I'd studied his picture way too much.

Sophie and Owen were looking at me. I looked back. I felt my face starting to smile.

'Seriously?' I said. '*Me?*'

'Seriously,' said Sophie. 'You.'

There was an awkward thing that I didn't want to say, but I knew I had to try. 'I mean, I don't have any savings really and I don't think that Mum and Bill can –'

Owen was so put out by that that he stood up. He waved his hands around, cutting through the air in a 'stop that right now' gesture.

'Absolutely not!' he said. 'We will not hear of it. We are inviting you as our guest, Caitlin. For the whole summer. We go next week. You can join us whenever you're ready.'

I opened my mouth to say something, but nothing came so I didn't.

'You'll like the apartment,' said Sophie. 'You'll have your own space, of course. Your own bathroom. Your room doesn't have a sea view, I'm afraid, but it has a balcony with a lovely vista of the hills.'

Am I going to have to start saying things like 'lovely vista'? I was sure I could do that if I tried. I smiled at them both, looking from one to the other and back as if we were at a tennis match. I'd never been to a tennis match. Maybe they had them in Antibes.

'And,' Sophie continued, leaning forward, speaking confidentially, 'I thought you might like to record your impressions. I could help you make it into an audio series about your summer. Show you how it's done. To get you off to a head start with your studies. And, of course, your career.'

I couldn't help myself: at that I let out a little scream.

'Oh my God,' I said. 'Seriously?' She nodded. 'If you're sure – I'd love it so much! I can't even ... But ...' I looked over at the playpen. Joshie and Mia had gone quiet, but that was because they were on a joint mission to push and pull each other over the fence, which they had just done. They rampaged over to us, looking for biscuits.

Sophie reached over and opened the packet. She handed one to each twin. That was why the Allens were so great. It was why I could imagine spending the summer with them. They were thoughtful and generous. Even if Sophie was way too well dressed for me, and Botoxed and tanned in a way that made me feel that we came from different species, I was comfortable with her. And she was offering to *mentor* me.

'You're worried about your family, of course,' said Owen, pulling Joshie up on to his lap. 'Well, fear not! We have a proposal for your mother and Bill. A friend's daughter who's coming down to house-sit our place for most of the summer. She's training in childcare, actually, as a Norland Nanny, so she's very trustworthy. Summer. She loves it here and has a girlfriend in Cornwall, so she's going to take care of things while we're away. Summer's keen to help your mum and Bill out with childcare, and all they have to do is to write her a reference at the end of August. So we've found a way of getting you to the Riviera, Cat, with no adverse effects at this end.' He looked extremely pleased with himself.

Mum was going to hate this. She'd hate everything about it.

Was that my problem?

Mia scrambled up on to my lap. As I put my arms round her gorgeous squishiness and smelled her lovely hair, I felt a pang of jealousy over the fact that some posh girl called Summer – a Norland Nanny, whatever that meant – might spend the summer with the babies. My siblings. They were mine, not hers.

It passed instantly.

Mum came in carrying a tray with a teapot and four cups on it. She looked around the room, smiling vaguely.

'Can you clear that table, Cat? So – what's going on? What did I miss?'

2

'Hello, and welcome to *Cat's Hot Summer*. I'm Cat, your host. It's not me that's hot – it's the summer. Temperature-wise. Not yet, but soon. So you join me today as I leave home, against my mother's wishes, I might add, and head to . . .'

I stopped. Deleted. That had been shit. How did people know what to say? Who was I supposed to be? What was my podcast voice? It wasn't that one. That was for sure.

I tried again. I took a deep breath, dropped down to a lower register. I would try to be husky and cool. I'd lose the *Hot Summer* stuff as that was embarrassing. I had to look round the hallway and check that no one was anywhere nearby. No one had heard me say that.

I tried again. Sensible voice.

'Hello, and welcome. You join me today as I leave everything I've ever known and head to the French Riviera for a summer of fun. I'm Cat, I'm seventeen, and I've never done anything like this before. I'm passionate about podcasts, but so far as a listener. This is my first recording, and it's also my first trip abroad. I've never been to London, let alone France. I had to get a passport for this trip.

'I'm travelling with family friends Sophie and Owen. They have an apartment in Antibes, and that's where I'll be living for the next six weeks. I'm about to set off. Wish me luck! And come along for the ride!'

I paused. Was that enough? Should I be a bit more open? What if I said *exactly* what was in my head?

I'd try that.

'Here's the thing: I'm excited. This is everything I wanted to happen. Up until a couple of days ago, I was walking on air. Then it caught up with me and now I'm . . . not so sure. Scared out of my skin. We're heading into the world of rich people in the South of France, and I'm feeling like Alice in Wonderland. I one hundred per cent don't have the right clothes for this shit. I don't know how to talk or what to say. I have twenty-three pounds fifty in the bank. So . . . let's see what happens. Find out if I can fake it till I make it.'

I switched off the recording and took a deep breath. I was jittery in anticipation of Sophie listening to everything I'd just said, but I had to do it. I'd left this first attempt to the very last minute, and now it was time to leave. I forced myself not to delete this one.

I double-checked the bag again. I had my brand-new passport, stiff and unused. Everything else was on my phone, so as long as the phone and charger were in the bag I was basically fine. Phone! Where was it? I panicked for a second before finding it in my hand.

I took a deep breath and walked into the living room.

I'd been putting this off, but it was time to deal with Mum. Dash and Ethan were out on a play date, so I'd said goodbye to them already. Mabel was at her mum's. The only people left were Mum and the babies. She was on the sofa with a little twin on either side of her, watching *Hey Duggee*. She didn't look up when I came in.

'Hey.' I sat on the sofa next to Mia, who climbed on to my lap, grabbed a strand of my hair and stroked it while sucking her thumb. Mum still didn't look at me.

'I'm off,' I said.

Her face was tight. 'I'm sure you'll have a wonderful time,' she said to the television.

I buried my face in Mia's hair. 'Mum,' I said. I didn't know how to do this.

Mum had plummeted since we'd told her. She'd kept it together with Owen and Sophie, and then she'd turned on me. She'd told me I wasn't allowed to go because she needed me.

But I was going anyway, and now my own mother appeared to hate me. She was furious with Sophie. With the posh stranger who was going to help with the kids, and with Bill for siding with us. She said we'd played her.

'Just go,' she said.

'I really didn't plan this.' My voice was small. 'I didn't know. But, Mum, it's Antibes. I can hardly *not* go.'

She turned to me then and there was fury in her eyes.

'Guess what – you don't have to go. She invites everyone! All the time! You're not special, Cat.'

I felt my own fury rising. 'Right. Got it. My own mother says I'm not special. Thanks. I already knew that.'

She actually rolled her eyes at me.

17

'I know you've been planning this for months. A mother can tell. I've known for ages that you were up to something. Great job. You pulled it off. Enjoy your holiday.' She paused. 'You could have gone for a week, you know. Two. It didn't have to be the whole summer.'

'I . . .' I wasn't sure what to say. Yes, I had been hiding something from her. But it wasn't this. It was university. Not now: I rode my anger instead. 'I'm seventeen. I've finished A levels. I'm sorry, but I'm out of here.'

'You said you'd be here. I needed you. But no. Get a better offer, and abandon us to lie on the beach. Off you fuck. I thought you were better than this.'

I stared at her. Mum never swore, particularly not when the babies were in the room. She glared back. Outside, Bill beeped the horn. I felt as if I was moving through fire as I stood up carefully from the sofa. I kissed Mia and Joshie on the tops of their heads, walked out of the room and slammed the door.

Kitty was standing in the hall. I could see from her face that she'd heard.

'Never. Having. Kids,' I said.

'Same.'

When Mum and Bill got together, they'd both already had children (Mum – me; and Bill – Ben and Jim, all grown up, then Kitty and Mabel), but decided to have one more to seal the deal. That one had turned out to be twins – Dash and Ethan, now five years old – and then a few years later they'd had an accident, which had also been twins – Mia and Josh.

No thanks.

'Dad's waiting.' Kitty's voice was gentle.

I looked at the living-room door. Towards Mum.

'I can't leave like this. You heard. She said *fuck*. She actually told me to fuck off.'

'So?' said Kitty. 'She'll regret it and you'll be gone. I'll keep an eye on everything here. Go.'

I took a deep breath. I looked at my stepsister. Kitty, and Cat. No parent would have done that on purpose, but Kitty and I had met for the first time when we'd been seven and eight so there was nothing anyone could have done about our matching feline names. We were a year apart, the best of friends.

Kitty was awkward and gorgeous, currently smelling of vanilla perfume and lip gloss, constantly trying to find her own style as well as navigating the complexities of growing up mixed-race in a very white corner of the country. Her aesthetic changed every week. Today she was doing nineties US teen movie. She wore a bubblegum-pink playsuit she'd found in a charity shop and was shivering. Her hair was in its natural Afro and she looked utterly gorgeous.

I followed her into the kitchen. She put the kettle on.

'Or I'll go for you.' She struck a pose. 'You stay here with a million kids. I'll head for the Riviera. You need to go to my politics class at eleven, b-t-dubs.'

'Nah,' I said. My heart lifted. 'Actually, you're all right.' There was no way I was letting Kitty step in and have this adventure for me. *She* was going to be the one in politics class. I was done with that stuff.

She hugged me. A little hug, a very Kitty one. Light and barely there but sincere.

I pulled my case out of the house, put my head down and ran through the rain. I had tried to make my hair look nice, though it never did what I wanted. It just hung there. Today, I'd put a flower clip into it and attempted to make it look cool. By the time I reached the car, that had gone. It was rats' tails around a wet flower. Classy.

Bill jumped out, head down, and put the case into the boot, while I slid into the front seat with two damp tote bags on my lap. The rain pounded on the windscreen.

Bill gave me a sideways look as he indicated and pulled out.

'OK?'

I shrugged.

'Your mum's gonna be fine,' he said. I looked away. It was hard to speak.

When I looked back at the house, Kitty was waving wildly from the upstairs window. I waved back.

'You better have a great time,' said Bill, as he drove. 'If you spend one second worrying about us back here, that's a second wasted. We'll be fine, Cat. You need to make the most of every moment. I need you to promise me that.'

I nodded. Bill didn't say any more (that had been a long speech for him), and in the end I swallowed hard and said: 'Thanks. It's hard to leave Mum when she's so . . .'

Bill put the windscreen wipers up a level and indicated to turn left, on the road down towards the station.

'I know,' he said after a while. I waited, but there was nothing more.

Bill pulled into one of the dropping-off spaces outside the station building, and I prepared myself to step out on to the wet tarmac, to run into the ticket office, ready to catch the train to London, then the Heathrow Express and then the plane to Nice. Mum was right: I could have gone for a week or two. Why wasn't I doing that?

I stepped out of the car.

I was hardly ever alone and I felt weird. Inside out. Wrong. I kept looking around for children who needed me, and there weren't any. What was I going to do without them?

The station was on a hill, on the side of a main road that led down into central Truro. Cars and buses trundled past, splashing through the rain. Other people were getting out of cars. They had backpacks and suitcases. Catching a train was a normal thing to do. People did it all the time.

Bill gave me a hug and stood to watch as I scanned my phone to get through the barrier. It closed behind me. We waved, and he turned away to head to work, and that was it.

I was on my own and on the move.

I was fucking doing this.

Cross the bridge to platform three, and wait for the London train. It was due in fifteen minutes: I had plenty of time. I regulated my breathing. I was doing it! I was getting away. My own mother hated me, but, on the plus side, I wasn't going to see her for weeks. I was having an adventure.

The journey to London was long and I spent the first hour swinging between excitement and guilt. When I settled in, I started to wonder about my podcast project. Sophie had been so enthusiastic and I knew it was going to give me a head start on my course. A bit of a calling card. I wanted it to be good. 'You can look at Antibes with an outsider's eye,' she said, 'and I'll help you edit and show you how it all works. The recording quality doesn't matter since we're not doing it for broadcast. Just record your impressions and speak from the heart. We'll set up interviews with people out there if you like. That could be fun.'

I took out a notebook and started jotting things down. I didn't write much, but still lost myself in the planning. At one point the train track ran alongside the ocean, and I stared through the drizzle-spattered window at the sea and the smudged horizon. I looked at my notes and put my earphones in, turning my face sideways and keeping my voice quiet.

'Um. Hi. So I'm on the train to London. Being on my own is weird: I keep trying to check up on kids who aren't here. Out of the window, right now, is the sea. There are people on the beach, walking their dogs. Some are swimming. A few people are lying down reading, though it's about to rain on them. And here I am, speeding past. On my way to the South of France.'

No one spoke to me except the ticket woman. The seats were less comfy than I had expected them to be, and I kept changing positions, eventually kicking my shoes off, pulling my legs up on to the seat and curling into myself.

I barely thought about the argument at all.

I didn't text Mum and she didn't contact me.

don't control

3

'I'm at Nice airport, straight off the plane. First impression: it's evening but it's hot. Views from the plane were amazing. I was a mix of scared and excited all the way and haven't felt relaxed in forever, but hey. I'm here so better work out how the hell you get out of an airport. More later.'

I put the phone into my pocket. I was getting used to this. Leaving voice notes felt good: it was a bit like having a friend. Even though I was telling my news to no one, I was still sharing things.

I couldn't think about home. I was looking forward instead.

I followed everyone into the building. When I reached the front of the line at passport control, I saw my hand shaking as I pushed the pristine document under the Perspex screen. I was suddenly certain the impassive man on the other side would find a reason to detain me and send me home, but he scrutinized it for a while, scanned it in a machine and finally stamped it.

When he passed it back, he gave me a surprisingly nice smile.

'*Bienvenue*,' he said, and I managed a *merci*.

Then I was waiting for my bag. I'd seen this scene on TV, and it was exactly the same in reality. Most people from the flight stood around staring at an empty carousel.

I knew from the telly it would take ages, so I ducked into the ladies.

A few minutes later, I was washing my hands next to an older woman who had bright-orange hair and wore a green sundress. I looked down at myself. My jeans, bobbly T-shirt and fleece looked shit. I was dressed for Cornwall, not the Riviera.

The woman caught my eye in the mirror and smiled, and I realized I knew exactly who she was. I'd seen her on Sophie's Instagram. In fact, I'd stalked her quite a lot. I was standing next to the fabulous Eva Santoro, and she was taller than I'd expected.

'English?' Her voice was husky. I laughed.

'Is it obvious?'

The woman shrugged. 'You're on vacation?'

She didn't know me, of course, and I tried to make myself look as if I didn't know her either.

She had an Italian accent, which I should have expected. I knew she was Italian and lived between New York, Italy and her home here, somewhere between Antibes and Cannes. She was often pictured in bars with Sophie.

'I'm here for the summer,' I said. 'I've never been here before. Or anywhere.' For a moment, I wanted to bolt back to the plane and ask the pilot to take me home. I could run back to my mother and say sorry.

25

She grinned widely at that. 'Welcome! You'll have a ball. The best place in the world. Usually, anyway.'

When I got back, the carousel was moving and after a few minutes my suitcase appeared, casually gliding round as if it had lived in the Riviera all its life, and I managed to drag it off. Then I was walking through customs, certain that I was somehow smuggling drugs and was about to be caught and jailed for life, but it didn't happen and then I was in Nice airport arrivals and Sophie was running up to me.

She swept me up in a huge hug, and my face was full of her hair and her perfume.

'Cat!' she said. 'Oh, darling. You're here. Wonderful. Let me take that. How was the journey?'

I tried to say all the right things as I followed her out of the building. The sky was a velvety dark blue, but it was a million times hotter than home. I wished I wasn't dressed in dorky stuff: Kitty and I had agreed that it was a practical travelling outfit and that the fluffiness of the jacket cancelled out the horror of it being a fleece, but when I looked at Sophie in her floral jumpsuit and strappy sandals I knew I was going to have to up my game. Not only that, but I'd met Eva Santoro and she was spectacular. And her first impression of me was as a person who wore a fleece.

I had a suitcase full of summer clothes, but none of them were game-upping. Nothing was in the realms of the floral jumpsuit, the gold strappy sandal, the silky green dress. I thought back to Eva Santoro. Could I dye my hair orange like hers?

'The journey was great,' I said as we walked across the car park. 'Everything worked. I was a bit … anxious. It was hard leaving home. But now …' I paused. 'Now I'm totally up for it. Thank you, you know. Again.'

She turned and flashed me a lovely smile. 'You're totally welcome,' she said. 'Did you record your impressions as you went like we talked about?'

This made me feel shy, but it was also my opportunity. 'Yeah, a bit,' I said, glad that she wasn't looking at me and couldn't see me blushing. 'I did one on the train, and at Paddington, and at Heathrow. I didn't do one on the plane because someone was next to me and I was embarrassed. But I did one as soon as I arrived.'

Sophie laughed, and I knew she wouldn't have been embarrassed in that position. 'Fair enough,' she said. 'We can look at them tomorrow and I'll show you how to edit them together. Here we are. This is us.'

She pressed a button on her key ring and a car beeped and unlocked itself. It was a small blue Renault. We put my case into the boot and I went to get into the passenger seat.

Sophie laughed.

'Other side.'

I looked in at the window and saw that, yes, I'd been going for the driver's side. I walked round the car and got in.

I took out my phone to text Mum to tell her I'd arrived safely. Then I remembered, and messaged Kitty instead.

Sophie set off into traffic that made me glad I couldn't drive.

'Even though it's dark,' she said, swerving lanes casually, 'we'll take the coast road. I want you to see it at its best, and it's a starry night so the water should look lovely.'

There were lanes and lanes of cars, all driving on the other side of the road to home. There were road signs I didn't understand, cars with bikes on the roof and boats on trailers. There was honking and sudden bursts of speed, and more traffic jams. A little boy stared at me through the back window of a car in the next lane, and when I waved he poked his tongue out and I thought of my four little siblings and smiled.

And then we were out of Nice, on the open road, and there was the Mediterranean Sea looking dark blue and brooding, the moon reflecting off it, the stars scattered above. I thought of the stretch of train track in Devon that had run beside the reddish sand and the muted greys of the Atlantic. This was a gorgeous version of that. It was like a painting, a vibe. I felt the excitement unfurling inside me. This was everything.

'Oh, there are boats!' I said it without thinking. There were sailing boats, a whole flock of them, anchored out at sea.

'We'll get you out on the water,' said Sophie, 'if you like. There's always someone going out.'

Sophie indicated, changed lanes, and put on a burst of speed to pass a row of three Fiat 500s.

'You must be a great swimmer, darling.' Sophie was turning to look at me, which made me tense as she didn't slow down at all as she did it. 'I mean, growing up in

Cornwall. Your family are forever piling into the car with all the beach stuff.'

'I mean, yeah, I can swim,' I said. 'But I'm not one of those people who ploughs up and down pools. I'm not brilliant.' I cast my mind back to school swimming lessons. 'We learned to swim at school, but it was just for half a term now and then. I do swim in the sea, but mostly I've got at least one kid with me.'

'I love to swim in the mornings,' said Sophie, looking back to the road just in time to swerve past a van. 'Will you come with me, Cat? What I do is I wake as early as I can, maybe six, and then by six twenty I'm on the sand, and at six twenty-one I'm in the water. I promise you it's different from the Cornish ocean. It's like stepping into silk. And it's warm, and it doesn't have waves. A day that starts with a swim is a perfect day.'

I did not, in fact, fancy getting up to swim at six. Swimming: yes. Six o'clock: no. But Sophie wanted me to go with her so I had to.

'I'd love that,' I lied. 'Mum used to go sea swimming before she had the boys. All year round. I never went with her in winter, because, well, the obvious reason. Freezing!'

'Well, you'll love this. It's glorious. And when we get back Owen always has breakfast waiting. Loves popping to the *boulangerie*. Honestly, darling. I'm so glad you're here. Welcome, welcome, welcome.' She paused. 'Was your mum OK in the end?'

'Yep,' I said, because it was easier. 'She was fine.'

'I know she's struggled lately. Anyone would. And seeing you going away must remind her of when she was young. When she went through all that stuff.'

I turned to her. 'What do you mean?'

There was a pause. What had happened when Mum was younger? Before she had me?

Sophie hesitated, then shook her head slightly.

'Don't worry. Have you let her know you're here?'

'I messaged Kitty.'

There was a brief pause.

'OK. I'll check in with your mother. Don't worry.'

A sign welcomed us to Antibes. The indicator was clicking. There were buildings on either side of the car and many more ahead, lit up by street lights.

Sophie drove through the town until we were in a car park right beside the water. There were boats on the left, hundreds of them, and a town made from honey-coloured stone on the right.

'OK,' she said. 'So. This is as close as we get to the apartment. It's just down there. Welcome!'

I stepped out of the car into the warm night. We had arrived.

4

The air was hot and the sky was filled with stars. I stood for a moment and stared at them. Millions and billions of distant suns above us. I could have watched them for hours. Instead, I pulled myself away and followed Sophie to the back of the car, and then I was dragging my suitcase across the car park, and bumping it across uneven pedestrianized streets.

A couple of minutes later, we were at a wooden front door in a stone building, and Sophie was searching her bag, looking for her key.

I had the dizzying sensation of being in a world I already knew. I had stepped through a portal, and felt that I was now living inside my phone. Every part of me was buzzing. I had studied this place on Instagram and Google Earth. I'd seen the stone buildings and the little streets.

And now I was here, and it was real. I reached out and touched the wall of the building. It was warm and rough under my fingers.

I heard the clip of shoes on stone, and someone called: 'Sophie! *Bonsoir!*'

Sophie turned and waved. I looked too and saw ...
Eva Santoro. She was hurrying along, a denim jacket over
her green dress. She recognized me too and did a comical
double take.

'Hey!' she said, slowing down. 'Oh, you're Sophie's girl!'

'Hi, Eva!' said Sophie. She looked at me. 'You've met?'

'In the loos! So glam! I'm dashing, but we'll catch up
soon!' called Eva. She was walking fast away from us, the
sound of her shoes echoing in the night. When she was a
little distance away, I saw her turn round. She took a few
steps back towards us.

'Actually, I wanted to talk to you, Soph,' she said. 'You
around tomorrow?'

'Always! Message any time. And, Eva? Cat here's a
budding podcaster. She's making a piece about her summer
out here. Maybe she could interview you? Nothing heavy.
Just about Antibes life.'

Eva laughed. 'Literally what I wanted to talk about.
Everyone wants interviews. Anyone would think I was
interesting! But yes, Cat. Of course! Ask me anything. I'll
ping you, Soph! *A domani!*'

'Impressive,' said Sophie as she opened the heavy front
door. 'You've been here five minutes and you've made a
friend. And we've arranged an interview. Eva's a darling.
Great first subject.'

The apartment was on the top floor. The building had
twisting spirals of stone stairs and also, luckily for my
suitcase, a tiny lift, which just fitted me, Sophie and the bag
as it juddered up. When we reached the fourth floor, the

apartment door was already open and Owen was standing there, a glass of red wine in hand, casual in shorts and a faded Radiohead T-shirt.

'Caitlin!' he said. 'Welcome.' He stood back and gestured for me to come in. 'I knew you were in the building.' He looked at me and fake whispered, 'I track her phone.'

We stepped in, and I gasped. What had been three separate rooms in my head was actually one big living space, with terracotta floor tiles and rugs and squashy sofas. Instead of a television, all the furniture pointed at a fireplace containing bouquets of dried flowers, which had a huge bright painting above it, some kind of abstract art with blues and yellows that settled into being a seascape when you looked at it for a while. The whole place smelled like food and perfume. I felt myself smiling so hard that my cheeks hurt.

'It's *gorgeous*!' I said. 'Oh wow. I'd seen it on your socials, but it's even better in real life. I didn't realize it was open plan. I love the painting.'

'Isn't it fabulous? A friend of ours painted it years ago. But come and see the view.' Sophie grabbed my hand, and so I left my suitcase right there and followed her over to the French windows and out on to the balcony. We stood under the stars and looked at the moonlit sea, stretching out to the horizon. I'd seen this view many times, but being inside it transformed everything.

'This is . . . amazing.' I wondered how many times I was going to be saying this over the next six weeks. I'd need to find new words. Gorgeous, cool, brilliant, stunning, awesome. What else was there?

'Isn't it?' said Sophie. 'Right, we need to get a picture, Cat. Is that OK? I'll put it on my story. If you're all right with that?'

I thought of her thousands and thousands of followers. I looked down at myself. If I was going to make my debut on Sophie's summer stories I would not be wearing a fleece.

'Um,' I said. 'Can I . . . well, can I take this off and put on a different T-shirt maybe?'

She and Owen both laughed and then Sophie nodded before fast-walking away.

'Don't stand still around her,' he said. 'Honestly. One minute you're relaxing in your comfy things and minding your own business, and the next a hundred people on Instagram are commenting "love the fleece, Owen". I speak from experience.'

'Oh, be quiet,' said Sophie, coming back, laughing. She handed me a kind of blazer, navy blue with gold buttons. It actually wasn't very different from my old school blazer except that it was made from lighter material and was tailored. I pulled off my fleece and put the blazer on. Instantly, I didn't feel like myself any more. Sophie arranged my hair over one shoulder and told me I looked lovely, and a minute later I'd approved a picture and there I was. On Sophie's Instagram story, wearing a blazer with a Reiss label inside it. I didn't know who Reiss was, but I was sure it was expensive.

Her caption said: 'Our lovely friend Cat @catincornwall is with us for summer fun! Let's all welcome Cat to Antibes!' I stared at the phone, wondering whether this would lead to Antibes people following my lacklustre account, which had two posts on the grid (one of the sea, one of the babies with a caption making it clear they were my siblings).

I waited. It didn't. After a moment, Sophie looked at her phone.

'Oh, Eva wants to meet tomorrow afternoon.' She looked at Owen. 'Can you believe Cat met Eva Santoro in the airport loos? Just casually made friends while they were peeing or whatever.'

I was mortified. 'Washing our hands!'

'Sophie.' Owen was laughing. He looked at home here, far more relaxed than he ever did in Cornwall. 'Soph, I can't believe you've got the poor girl on your story and planning meet-ups before you've shown her to her flipping bedroom! There's plenty of time for Eva Santoro. Come on, Cat.' He pulled my suitcase down a small corridor with wooden floorboards, and opened a door. 'This is you.'

'I'm sorry you don't have a sea view.' Sophie clicked the light on. 'But you'll see the mountains on a clear day. And you can watch the world go by from the balcony. There's a lot going on in that square down there. The queue for the museum goes along that wall on busy days, and it's always fun to spy on. Will it do?'

I stood on the threshold and looked at my bedroom.

There was a small double bed, whitewashed walls, a bunch of dried flowers in a metal jug. The window had full-length doors on to my very own balcony. The floorboards were polished and shiny in here. There was a little desk and a chair, a chest of drawers and a small wooden wardrobe.

Plenty of plug sockets, including one beside the bed for optimal overnight phone charging.

Again, I didn't have to second-guess my reaction.

'It's wonderful,' I said. 'I absolutely love it. I can't believe I get to sleep here!'

'I'm afraid you don't have an en suite,' said Sophie, and I grinned. At home I shared a bathroom with up to seven other people. 'Your bathroom is down the hall. The door on the left. It's all yours. We have our own.'

'Now, Cat,' said Owen. 'I'm sure you're exhausted, but the question is: are you hungry?'

Was I hungry? Now that he said it, I was starving.

'I hope so,' said Sophie. 'Because I made an onion tart earlier. And some salad. It's not much and it's all cold, but please humour me by having a little snack. I'm certainly having some. And a glass of wine, of course.'

Owen said, 'Soph has perfected the onion tart over the years. You have to try it.'

It turned out that the main balcony was huge, more of a terrace. Ten minutes later, I was sitting out there, barefoot but still in my jeans and T-shirt, eating what felt like the loveliest dinner of my life and sipping a glass of white wine. I didn't drink wine at home. I didn't like alcohol at all, really, though I'd done my share of drinking cider from warm plastic bottles on beaches. The wine here, though, was crisp and cold, and I thought I could grow to like it.

5

Someone was knocking on the door. I was deeply, deeply asleep. My bed was extra cosy and my first response was to pull the sheet over my head and groan at them to go away.

'Grrraaaahh,' I said, or something like that. 'Go way.'

The door opened. I heard someone laughing. Laughing! Annoying.

'I'm so sorry, Cat,' said Sophie, in a loud whisper. 'You did say you'd like to come swimming. I wasn't sure. Sorry.'

It came back with a whoosh. I was in France. Freaking France! I sat up in bed, wide awake in an instant. It was Sophie, and I'd told her to go away.

'No!' I said. 'Sorry! I'll come.' I yawned. 'I'd love to swim. I thought I was at home.'

It was warm and the apartment smelled of coffee. There were stripes of sunshine on the floor where they were coming in between the slats of the shutters. I found myself grinning as I pulled on my black swimming costume and then shorts and a T-shirt. Of course I would swim.

*

We walked down to a beach that Sophie called 'Gravette'. It was small, nestled under the stretch directly below the apartment, enclosed by stone harbour walls. I followed Sophie's lead and stepped out of my flip-flops to walk barefoot on the sand when we reached it; it was heavy and yellow, proper sand, and it had been raked recently. There was no one on the beach but us. The sun was already warm, the sea sparkling. The day felt new and clean and full of possibilities.

Sophie was going to start showing me how podcasting actually worked, to make one of my own. It had been easy to want to do it from a distance: now, close up, I was about to try it for real. Would this wild holiday experience be interesting to anyone other than me? If I was at home listening to something like this, what would I want?

I'd want a story. I'd want something to happen.

Sophie spread a rug out on the sand and dumped her basket on it – one of those wicker things that would look ugly on a stall at Par Market, but which here was somehow chic.

Then she pulled off the kaftan thing she was wearing, laughed and ran into the sea in her silver bikini. I took off my shorts and T-shirt and followed, vowing to get a tan as fast as I could.

It was exactly as she'd said it would be: like stepping into silk.

A minute later I was lying on my back, floating in the water, looking at a pale-blue sky while rising and falling on the gentlest of waves. I took deep breaths. I was going to be living here, like this, until the beginning of September. I could get up early and swim every morning.

I bobbed around in the water. There was a buoy a bit further out, and I swam towards it, discovering it was further than it had looked. My arms were aching by the time I arrived and grabbed it. I hadn't done this much exercise for ages, least of all at half six in the morning, which I was now remembering was half five at home. It felt good. My legs and arms were tingling. I decided I would swim a bit further each day.

The morning air was still. I looked out at the clear line of the horizon and tried to work out where you would end up if you swam directly out and kept going. My Mediterranean geography was hazy, but I supposed it might be North Africa. All around me the water was glimmering and still.

I turned to look back at the beach. Sophie was already out of the water. She waved, but not in an urgent way. I started to swim back. As I got closer, I saw her taking my photo, then fiddling with her phone. She'd uploaded it before I even reached the shore.

'Isn't it perfect?' she said. 'Hope you don't mind – you looked so lovely. Now. Let's talk about our plans for the day. Today, we just need to get you settled in, right? I'll drop Eva a message when it's a reasonable time in the morning and we'll meet up this afternoon. So let's talk about what you're going to ask her.'

A moment later, she checked her phone again, and smiled.

'Well,' she said. 'My friend Helena says her son wants to meet you. He saw your picture last night. I think you'll like him. Jonathan. Helena's asking if you're single. You don't have to answer, of course!'

I tried not to smile too much. 'Fully single. I'm absolutely shit at that kind of thing.'

'Well,' said Sophie. 'This might be the summer that it all changes. You never know.'

I busied myself brushing the sand off my flip-flops, unnecessarily, so she wouldn't see my face. I couldn't let her know that I'd studied Jonno Thorpe on Instagram for years. He was totally drop-dead gorgeous. I'd lusted after him from afar. Imagined meeting him, knowing I never would.

And now I was in his world. Now *he* wanted to meet *me*.

6

We had croissants and coffee for breakfast (I needed to learn to like coffee so I forced it down with lots of sugar), and then Owen cleared his throat and said: 'Soph. I just need to iron out a bit of paperwork, if that's OK. The customs stuff.'

This was code, it turned out, for Sophie and me going out so that Owen could have the whole apartment to work in.

'What does Owen actually do?' I asked as Sophie and I walked around a small supermarket together a little while later. I kept staring at the shelves and shelves of unfamiliar stuff. The fruit looked big and juicy. There were loads of strange brands of chocolate. The crisps were different.

'Oh, he imports art and things,' she said vaguely. 'From Latin America, mainly. That kind of thing. Sells it to dealers and what have you.' She picked up three different types of cheese, none of which I'd seen before, and tossed them into the basket. 'He does well, but he is a mad workaholic, even when we're out here. So you can see why I need company. Since I went freelance, I've been taking the summer off and I need someone to talk to or I end up bothering Owen all the time. He'll take his work into the bedroom if we need the apartment, but he's much happier spreading everything over the table and shouting into Zoom in bad Spanish so I leave him to it when I can.'

She shot me a lovely smile. I returned it.

'It's so kind –'

She cut me off and picked up a huge tomato, raising it so we could both admire it. 'Please – don't keep saying it, Cat. You're sweet, but you don't need to thank us all the time.' The tomato went into the basket. 'We're happy to take it as read. Now, let's talk about your recordings. Would you be mortified to record an up-to-date impression in front of me? Would that be awful?' She looked at my face as we moved to the pasta and stuff. She saw her answer. 'Tell you what, I'll finish up here on my own. You run along and make a recording in private. Turn left, under the archway, past the museum, and then look out at the water and record a few impressions. Talk about what it's really like, rather than just saying it's pretty. Be real. OK? I'll come and find you there and then we'll talk about the next stage. What cereal do you like?'

I couldn't help myself. 'The chocolate ones?' We never got that at home.

She grinned. 'You got it. Oh, and we are meeting Helena and her kids. Jonno, remember? And Izzy. They're out on the boat today, but we're going to see them for lunch tomorrow. I haven't heard back from Eva yet, but we'll try to see her this afternoon. Now, off you go.'

I stood outside the shop. It felt strange to be standing on a street in the French Riviera on my own. Now I was here, and I was a part of it, I was going to do everything I could to fit in.

I followed Sophie's directions and found myself looking over a low wall, high above the sparkling sea. There were boats out on the water, and a figure floating up and down on the waves below me. The whole scene was perfect and peaceful. I tried to think of ways to describe it, since Sophie had said I wasn't allowed to say it was pretty. I looked at the birds high in the sky, the sunlight glistening on the waves. I imagined myself as the swimmer.

I put my earphones in and started talking.

'So,' I said, 'here I am. Living my hot summer. I'm in Antibes, in the old town, and I'm standing in front of the Picasso Museum, next to a statue of a person poised on the edge of the ocean, looking out at the Mediterranean. There are boats and swimmers down there. The sun is shining and there's literally not a cloud in the sky. I'm new to this world and I feel like I've stepped into a different universe. A place I knew from my phone, but I'm here. I've stepped into Instagram. You see . . .'

I hesitated. There was something wrong with that person in the water. They were wearing something floaty and it wasn't a stylish sort of swimwear I didn't know about. That wasn't it. The figure was moving with the small waves, rather than on their own.

'Sorry,' I said – no longer sure who I was talking to. 'That person in the water? I'm pretty sure it's a woman, and I think she's in a dress. I'm way up above and I don't quite know if I'm ... I mean, from here you'd think ...' I stopped.

I forced myself to finish my sentence. 'You'd think she might be ... in trouble.' My voice came out quiet and husky. I hadn't really meant *in trouble* at all.

The hair was dark and waterlogged so it was hard to tell what colour it was. The fact was that this person had dipped just under the surface of the water, and I couldn't bear to think about what that meant. I looked around. It was still fairly early and there weren't many people out and about. I leaned over the wall and had to grab my sunglasses fast before they fell off my head. It did look like a person, and they weren't moving, or, at least, not of their own accord. And they did have limbs, which meant they weren't a bag or a seal. *Shit shit shit.*

Were there lifeguards here? I had no idea. There hadn't been anyone on duty at six this morning on the beach ... My thoughts were racing.

'Shit,' I said out loud. 'I need to find help. Right. I'm going to find somebody who – Oh!'

I turned round and there was a guy standing right next to me. A tall, skinny boy, not much older than me. He had wild black hair and heavy-rimmed sunglasses, and in his cream shorts and blue-and-white striped shirt, he looked totally French.

'Oh, um, *excusez-moi*,' I said. Argh. All my GCSE French disappeared. I turned to the sea instead. Pointed.

'You speak English?' he said, in perfect English. He pushed his sunglasses up on to his head. He had chocolatey brown eyes.

'In the water.' I pointed. 'Down there, I think there's someone in trouble. You see – just there? In the greenish . . .'

He walked to the wall with me and looked over. I heard him give a little gasp.

'Oh,' he said. 'I see. Ah! Erm . . . Stay here. I'll get help.'

He vanished, sprinting away with a funny loping run, down the hill. I didn't know what to do so I stayed where I was, staring at the water. I realized I'd carried on recording and clicked 'stop', my eyes set on the thing that I half hoped might turn out to be a bag that had fallen off a boat (though I knew it wasn't; of course, I did) being pulled gradually further out to sea.

I could hear the blood coursing in my ears. My limbs felt strange. I waited. Nothing happened. Then Sophie was there, smiling, her basket full of supermarket supplies, with a shopping bag that was made from stiff card with ribbons for handles slung over one shoulder.

'Fabulous,' she said. Her cheeriness was jarring. 'So, don't be cross, darling, but I –' She stopped and peered at my face. 'Are you all right?'

I nodded, then shook my head and pointed down at the sea. Sophie caught her breath as she saw it. As we watched, a little boat came out and someone in a wetsuit jumped into the water.

She took my arm.

'Oh, Cat. How horrible. But there's nothing we can do. It's in hand, see?'

I nodded. 'I saw it first.' My voice came out sounding weird. 'There was a man. A boy. He was there, and when I showed him he ran off to get help. He looked French but he spoke English.' I felt sick. I thought I was going to be sick. I held on to the little sea wall with one hand.

Sophie pulled me away. 'Everyone speaks English here. And he clearly *did* get help, and they've got them now. I pray they're OK, whoever they are. God, how awful. Come on, I've got something to show you. I don't know about you, but I'm ready for another coffee. Nothing good will come from us hanging around here.'

'The guy told me to wait,' I said. 'He said he'd be back.'

'You don't need to do that.' Her voice was firm. We both looked over the wall. Below, two people were pulling what was clearly a person on to the rescue boat, and I knew, as I'd known from the first moment I saw it, that this person was not going to cough and breathe and blink and come back to life.

I had seen my first dead body.

'There's no need for us to watch,' said Sophie, and I let her lead me away.

We sat outside a cafe, shaded by tall trees on a pedestrian street in the old town. I was struggling to breathe. Everything had changed. The picture-perfect surroundings, and the horror of a body in the water – it felt like a dream, or a Netflix drama.

Sophie reached out and covered my hand with hers. 'Darling. We've been coming here for decades, and we've never seen a thing like that. Once Helena had a nanny who disappeared and they had to call the police. I think she'd just run away, though I can't quite remember, but nothing like this. I'm so sorry this has happened on your first morning. I suppose from time to time people swim too far and tragedy strikes, even though you wouldn't think it possible in a sea as tame as this one. Or, I suppose . . . maybe that person just couldn't take it any more? Swimming out into the Med probably feels like a good way to go. If you're at rock bottom.'

Her words hung in the air. It was hard to know what to say. I let her order me a coffee: maybe this was the time I'd start to like it, now that everything had changed. She ordered something else too, but I didn't understand it because it came in a torrent of fast French.

All I could see was the body in the water. The person in the waterlogged dress.

'Sophie,' I said. I made myself say it. '*Do* you think it was suicide?'

She shook her head. 'There's no point speculating, darling. I shouldn't have said anything about that. We'll find out what's happened soon enough. We've got Eva this afternoon. Your first interview! That'll be a good distraction.'

The waiter came back with a tray that held two huge cups of milky coffee, a bowl of sugar and a plate of what looked like creamy chocolate cake, with two forks.

47

'This'll be good for the shock,' she said. 'Tiramisu. I thought it was more responsible to buy you sugar than alcohol at this time of day.'

I felt sick, but I forced myself to take a sip of coffee, which coated the inside of my mouth and was just objectively awful even with two sugars in it, and then, in the hope of taking away the taste, I stuck a fork into the tiramisu. I'd heard of it, but had no idea what it was.

'Did you know,' said Sophie, 'that tiramisu is Italian for "pick me up"? *Tira* – pick. *Mi* – me. *Su* – up. I think that's why I thought of it. You needed a pick-me-up.'

To my surprise, it did turn out to be exactly what I'd needed. The cake part was soaked in liquid, which, despite what Sophie had just said, was alcoholic. The cream was light and melted on my tongue, and the sugar hit made me feel better at once. Even the coffee flavour was nice.

I smiled at her. 'OK,' I said. 'This is amazing.'

I saw her glance at her phone.

'Good. Eat up. Now here's another distraction: I hope you don't mind, but I picked you up a present. A couple of things I thought would look wonderful on you. If you don't like them, just say, but if you do then – great.'

She passed me the cardboard shopping bag. I took it with a feeling of dread. She had bought me something and I wasn't allowed to keep saying thank you, so what was I meant to do?

I reached into the bag. There were two things in there, both wrapped in tissue paper. I looked at Sophie for confirmation, then pulled out the first one.

I unwrapped it. It was gold and white. I held it up and it unfolded itself into the kind of dress I could never wear. It was short and fitted with a halter neck. It was exposing and way too blingy, and I cringed at the idea that I could even think about wearing a thing like this.

But I was living in Sophie's world now.

I inhaled sharply and arranged my face into the biggest smile I could manage. The dress was beautiful and I knew that I had to make Sophie believe I loved it, because she had actually bought it for me and I had no idea how much she'd spent, but I was sure it was a lot.

'Oh my days,' I said. 'This is amazing. Are you sure?'

Sophie laughed. 'I'd better be. It's too skimpy for me and I don't think it would suit Owen. I have one at home almost the same, though mine is more forgiving, because . . .' She gestured down at herself. 'So this one's for occasions, and the other is just something for day to day, if you like it. If not, we can take it back. We can take either of them back. Also, while we're talking about this stuff, I think Bill's transferred you some money. He wanted it to be a surprise, but he and your mother want you to be able to have fun.'

I tried to take it all in. I checked my phone. There was a hundred pounds in my account from Bill, with the annotation 'have fun'. That message was definitely from him. Not Mum.

I looked at Sophie. I tried to mutter a thank you, but I was overwhelmed.

She took the white-and-gold dress from me so I could look at the other one.

Thank God, I loved this one. It was a sundress, fitted, with short sleeves that would cover my shoulders and upper arms. It was dark green with a camouflage pattern, and it was cool and unflashy – a summer dress I could wear every day. It even had pockets.

I would wear it tomorrow for our lunch appointment. If I was wearing this, Jonno Thorpe might like me. I hoped so.

I finished the tiramisu without even noticing. Sophie had only had a few forkfuls. I left the coffee barely touched.

'Thank you,' I said, as we stood up. I figured I was allowed to say it once and I hope that it encompassed the two dresses, the pudding and the drink. And the arranging pocket money with Bill. I'd message him later.

'I'll show you around the old town,' she said. 'It won't take long. It's tiny. Then we'll head back to the apartment and you can try on the dresses.' She paused. 'Try not to think about it, Cat. It's horrible, but these things, sadly, happen. We'll chat to Eva later. See if she knows what's happened.'

But time went on and Sophie didn't get a reply from Eva Santoro. She messaged her again, and again heard nothing.

'Her life is one long social whirl,' Sophie said. 'She'll turn up when she turns up.' But I could see she was unsettled.

We were sitting on the balcony late in the afternoon when Sophie's phone lit up with a call. I saw the word *Fred* on the screen, and she snatched it off the table. Before she answered, she glanced quickly inside. Owen was still in there, his laptop and paperwork taking up the whole dining table.

Then she looked at me. It was a quick look. A nervous one. She hesitated, then answered.

'Fred?' Her voice was low. Almost furtive. 'What is it? I thought we said . . .'

Then she was silent for a while. She put a hand to her chest and inhaled sharply. She stood up and walked around. She leaned over the iron railing and spoke out towards the sea, but I could still hear snatches of her words. '*Awful*,' she said. And, '*Eva? Are you sure?*' And, '*Where are you?*' And, '*Is there anything we can . . .*'

I didn't want to listen in, but I did it anyway. She was talking about Eva. Something terrible had happened to her and it was horribly easy to piece together what it was. My stomach was clenched. I felt sick. Eva Santoro had been the first person I'd met in France. And the second. Then we'd been going to see her today, and I supposed I had seen her today . . .

I wished Sophie had let me stay, to wait for the boy to come back, to talk to the police. It felt unfinished. I couldn't get to grips with what had happened.

She hung up the phone and turned to me, her face stricken. Then she walked quickly over and hugged me.

'You probably got the gist, darling,' she said. 'I'm so sorry. I need to go and talk to Owen.'

I heard their hushed voices from inside. I stayed out on the balcony, but moved as close to the open door as I could reasonably get. I'd only spoken to Eva twice. I didn't know her. It wasn't my tragedy, but it felt like it. The image of her body was stuck in my head.

I tried to hear what they were saying. 'I mean, she rushed past,' said Sophie. 'No – when I came back with Cat. Remember? I told you. They'd spoken in the airport.'

Then it went too quiet for me to hear. A moment later, Owen's voice was raised.

'What was he doing calling? I thought –' He broke off as Sophie hushed him. I edged closer still, trying to work out what was going on. I could only hear snatches of conversation, ending with the two of them agreeing that they needed alcohol.

Luckily, I heard Sophie saying, 'I'll tell Cat,' as she strode towards the balcony. It gave me just enough time to move away from the doorway and throw myself into my chair before she was there.

7

We sat outside a bar in the old town, a minute's walk away from the apartment, and I let Owen order a drink for me. I didn't care. The two of them talked about Eva and I began to wonder if I should actually be here at all.

'She was Italian,' Owen told me, and I pretended I didn't already know that. 'Italian-American, I think. Gosh, isn't it awful to talk about her in the past tense?'

'Dreadful,' said Sophie. 'I mean – it's Eva. Eva! Remember when she brought the board games over? Last summer, in the thunderstorm? And we sat on the balcony and played some word game and watched the sheet lightning?'

'Of course I do,' said Owen. 'She slept over and I made a fry-up the next morning.'

'You did! Cat was going to interview her today for her podcast. No better person to start with than Eva. What was it she said, Cat?'

'She said everyone wants an interview.' I heard her voice in my head. '"*Everyone wants interviews. Anyone would think I was interesting.*" That's what she said.'

'I wonder what she meant by that,' said Sophie. 'Who else wanted to interview her?'

We sat in silence for a minute.

'If you want me to go home,' I said, 'then, I mean, I will. I want to give you space. I know you were really close to her. I don't want to be in the way.'

I saw them look at each other.

'No,' said Owen. 'Absolutely not.'

'It's very sweet of you, darling,' said Sophie. 'But, like Owen says, absolutely not. We wouldn't hear of it. I'm just so sorry you were so caught up in it.' She paused. 'Have you told your mother what's happened?'

I shook my head. I kept having to swallow because my stomach was trying to make me sick. It was crowding together in my brain: the chat in the loos. The sound of her shoes on the stones. The body being pulled around by the currents. All of them with the green dress.

'I'll fill her in,' said Sophie.

At home in Cornwall, there were rip tides and currents and undertows, and it was easy to be pulled out to sea. Here, though, there was none of that.

'Do they know . . . what happened?' I managed to say. I wanted to say more. I wanted to ask, *Why did she arrange to see us today if she was on the way to kill herself?* I wanted to ask, *Were we the last people she spoke to?*

'Not yet,' said Sophie.

She and I were in our matching dresses, though my halter neck was a lot more exposing than her version. I hoped my upper arms looked OK. I was actually surprised by this dress. I loved it, once I was wearing it. It made me feel glamorous and wonderful. I'd misjudged it.

The old town was glowing in the sunlight. The shadows were long. The evening was so hot that although I'd brought a cardigan out with me it was stuffed in the bottom of my tote bag and felt about as useful as a fur coat would have been.

The waiter arrived with a tray of drinks. Sophie and I had bright-orange Aperol spritzes. I'd seen them on her Instagram, as well as at home, but had no idea what it was going to taste like. Owen had one of those amber drinks from old movies. A bit of brown liquid in a glass with an ice cube.

'Right,' said Sophie, holding up her drink. 'To Eva. The poor, poor darling.'

'Indeed,' said Owen. 'To Eva.'

We clinked glasses. I didn't know what to say.

'And,' said Owen, 'without wanting to sound callous, welcome to Antibes, Cat. We'd like to thank you for brightening up our summer. Now, in particular.'

'This is the golden hour,' said Sophie, looking around. 'And it's absolutely compulsory to be sitting outside with a drink. So – even though it feels strange right now – welcome to our summer world. I've been trying to get your mother out here for years and we're delighted to have you in her place. Cheers, Cat. Thanks for coming.'

I raised my glass again, and clinked it once again against hers, and then Owen's. Our spritzes had olives on toothpicks in them. I copied Sophie and took mine out and ate the olive. It was horrible. When I sipped the drink, though, I liked it. It wasn't what I'd expected. It was sharp and sweet, almost medicinal. It warmed me. Things felt a little less scary.

This street was pedestrianized and there were so many people walking past. Life went on, for everyone except Eva Santoro.

'Tell us about your life, Cat,' said Owen. 'I know there's college and exams and all that, but what else do you do in Truro?'

I thought about it. 'I hang out with friends,' I said, in the end. 'It sounds like nothing, but college was good for me. I didn't really like school, but once I got to college I felt like I found my people? I was only studying subjects I liked, which meant it was more fun. You call the teachers by their first names. You know? That kind of thing. For my second year, Kitty was at college too and it was great. And honestly? I love going for long walks with headphones, listening to podcasts.'

Sophie leaned forward. 'Yes! Which ones?'

'I like the ones with a story,' I said. 'Episodic. True crime most of all, but also scams, and actually anything with a good plot. There was one about the *Titanic* recently. I loved that. Even though I knew the ending.'

'Oh yes, that one was wonderful.' She nodded, and I could see that we were all pleased with the distraction. I kept talking, about nothing in particular, but I wanted to ask Sophie more about Mum. That thing she'd said in the car had stuck with me. *When she was young. When she went through all that stuff.* What had happened when she was young? What stuff? I had never thought at all about Mum's life before she had me. Now I wanted to know.

And I wanted to talk to my mother. I needed her. But we'd had that fight and she'd literally told me to fuck off.

'Our American friends will be in town in August,' said Sophie, after a while. 'Alonzo and Anthony. You'll love them. We always meet them right here. This bar, at this time, most days.'

I nodded and fiddled with the straps of my dress. Today I had become someone who sat at this bar at this time, in this dress.

I'd become someone who spent the summer in Antibes.

I'd become somebody who saw something in the water and raised the alarm.

It hit me again, the wave of sickness. I'd seen someone in the water. The first person I spoke to in France had died. I focused back on the conversation, trying not to look as if I knew exactly who Alonzo and Anthony were. They were stylish American artists who wore bright colours and appeared in hundreds of Sophie's photos, usually involving food and drink. I would *love* to be friends with them.

I tucked my hair behind my ear, and its unusual bounciness was a mild surprise. Sophie had made me sit down, sprayed it with something, and then curled it expertly with a wand and sprayed again: now I had some collapsing, but still-there, curls. I'd never had curly hair before and I loved it. Sophie had made her own hair go wavy and shiny, and hers seemed to be staying in place better than mine. She looked lovely. It occurred to me that this was the sort of thing you should say to someone if it popped into your head.

'You look lovely, Sophie,' I said.

'Oh, bless you! Did you hear that, Owen? You could learn a few things from Cat.'

Owen turned to look at his wife and sighed. 'Of course you look lovely. Do I have to say it every time? I suppose I do, or others will be saying it in my place.'

She gave him a look. I remembered the word *Fred* on her screen and wondered who he was. I didn't know a Fred from their socials.

My eyes kept being caught by the people of my own age. A group of boys and girls went past, the girls in tiny dresses, the boys in polo shirts and shorts. I caught a boy looking over at me. He gave me a little smile, raising his eyebrows, and I grinned back. That boy wouldn't have given me a second glance if I'd been in my normal clothes. This was brilliant.

I sipped my drink. It was almost gone.

Maybe Sophie was right. What I'd seen this morning and what had happened to Eva was awful, but ultimately it was nothing to do with me, and she hadn't been my friend.

I turned to Sophie. 'Can I get a photo of you two?' I said. 'To send to everyone at home?'

Owen jumped up. He had dressed for the evening in a white shirt, sleeves rolled up, and a pair of light trousers.

'You don't want boring old me in your pictures,' he said, taking out his own phone. 'You two look stunning. Like sisters. You can both put it on your story thingies or whatever.'

I leaned in towards Sophie and lifted my chin and held my shoulders back, my spine straight. I tried to pose in the way Jonno's sister, Isabella, might have posed. Owen snapped a string of photographs, and sent all of them over to me. I looked through and selected the best one. Sophie and I were smiling, the late evening sun on our faces. The dress looked good, my posture was great and my upper arms were actually fine.

I looked happy. I didn't look like someone who had seen a dead woman in the water this morning.

I sent it to the family group chat, where everyone would see it. I wouldn't tell them about Eva. Not yet.

Hearts appeared at once from Kitty and our other sister Mabel. Kitty replied, OMG SO SO jealous i hate you.

The words 'Mum is typing' appeared, but then they went and there was no message there. I waited, but nothing happened. A thumbs up from Bill (entirely on-brand), and a How's Antibes? from Ben, Bill's eldest boy. Then a You're there already? from my other stepbrother, Jim.

I wanted my mum. I wanted to revert, to cry, to feel her hugging me. I wanted to say: Mum. Oh Mum. I saw something awful. I saw someone alive, and then dead. I don't know how to deal with it. Mum. What can I do?

I wanted to say that, and just a word of communication would have been enough. It would have been something.

When she did reply, it was with a smiley face. The one that barely looks as if it's smiling at all.

8

We moved to sit outside a pizzeria for dinner and, in
between phone checks (I knew Mum had started a message,
and I wanted her to send it so I could tell her everything)
I ate a massive pizza without noticing. Owen gave me a
glass of red wine and I sipped it. It tasted exactly how
I thought it would. I didn't really like it, but I drank it
anyway. He refilled it. Every sip of alcohol made me feel a
bit better about the day. A part of me knew this was bad,
but a bigger part of me just wanted to stop seeing Eva's
body being moved around by the waves. Every sip made
the vision recede a little further.

I had never tasted artichoke hearts before, and the olive
in my drink earlier had been the first I'd ever had. I loved
the artichokes on my pizza straight away, and after eating
a few I thought I would probably find my way to actually
liking black olives rather than pretending to, since that
would be easier. Owen ordered a second bottle of wine.

My head started to spin. I drank the tap water that
was refilled whenever we needed it, but I drank wine
most of all.

I tried to listen to their conversation, but it was about Owen's business and some boring issue he was having with an importer, and then it kept going back to Eva and that made me sad, so I tuned out and watched the passers-by instead. After dinner, we went for a walk along the sea front and I stared at the sparkling water and felt the breeze on my arms and wondered if any of this could be real. I worked hard to focus on being here now. I knew I was much drunker than they realized. I tried to hide it, but I loved this feeling. The disconnect from reality was exactly what I needed. No wonder people did this all the time.

I was ready to head to the apartment and climb into my lovely comfy bed, when Owen said, 'Nightcap?' and Sophie said, 'Rude not to!' and I realized that even they were quite drunk.

The final bar of the evening had a cavernous interior with a dance floor, and although it was too early for clubbing, I watched with a bit of envy as a lot of madly confident young people threw themselves laughing around the dance floor just for the hell of it. They were, Sophie told me, yacht crew.

'Antibes is a great place for yachties,' she said. 'They bring a lot of life to the town. I mean, look at them! Fun.'

Owen came back with three drinks. His was amber again, and mine and Sophie's were clear.

I wished I could dance too. I'd dance off all the red wine, which was heavy in my stomach. The music was cheesy old stuff: currently it was ABBA, 'Take a Chance on Me'. About ten boys and girls, not much older than I was, were dancing as if no one was watching. Their laughter was infectious. The way their eyes shone and their faces glowed spoke to something deep inside me. Whatever 'being a yachtie' involved, I wanted it. I wanted to be like them. I shifted in my seat.

'Go on!' Sophie saw me looking. 'They'll be friendly, I promise. Have a dance.' She looked at me more closely. 'Are you OK, Cat? Shall we get you a Coke? A water?'

I shook my head, emphatically. 'No. No Coke, thanks. No water.'

I sensed them looking at each other, smiling.

'I got you a vodka,' said Owen, 'but maybe that's –'

'Excuse me.'

We all looked round.

A boy was standing beside our table.

It wasn't just a boy. It was *the* boy. The one from this morning, still in his pristine shorts and striped shirt.

'Oh!' I said. Our eyes met. I liked his eyes. I saw him understanding all the questions in mine.

He looked awkward, but in what I immediately considered to be a charming way. He made exaggerated 'eek' faces that made his social awkwardness feel nice, as if he was laughing at himself.

'Hello again,' he said. 'Um. Sorry to barge in. I thought it was you and so I had to . . . I went back this morning, but you'd gone.'

It hung there in the air between us. The thing we had shared.

'Oh,' I said. 'I'm sorry.'

He looked at all three of us in turn.

'Henry,' said Sophie. 'Henry – were *you* the boy from this morning?' He nodded. 'Poor Henry. I'm so sorry.' She stood up and hugged him. He was much taller than her. 'I didn't realize it was you who Cat talked to.'

'Thank you,' he said. 'Yes. Um – you're Cat, then?' He looked at me. I nodded.

'Cat, I'm Henry. Would it be very forward of me to invite you to dance?' he said. 'Only – we could talk? It was a strange experience to have shared. I'm glad I found you.'

I stood up. I looked back at Sophie to check. She nodded and raised her glass, though I could see she was unsure.

'Go on.' She paused. 'Henry – we'll talk afterwards, OK?'

I picked up my drink. My first vodka. I took a sip. It was nice. I thought it cleared my head a bit, so I took it with me. As we walked towards the dance floor, I tried to find the words.

'This morning,' I said. I stopped walking. He did too.

'Yes,' he said. 'I'm sorry you had to see that. That's all I wanted to say, really. I hardly recognized you this evening, you know. You look great, but I liked the casual look too.'

We were close to the edge of the dance floor. I touched his arm. Touching him made me feel strange. We'd shared an experience. He understood in a way that even Sophie didn't. He was, all of a sudden, the only person I wanted to talk to.

'I'm really sorry I wasn't there when you came back,' I said. 'I've been feeling bad about it all day. Sophie came and found me. She took me for tiramisu. I wanted to wait.'

He sighed and blew upwards, so his unruly fringe moved. 'Good for Sophie. That sounds like just the thing. I know she was friends with Eva. My dad was too. I mean, I can't believe she did it. No one had any idea that she was feeling that way.'

'Oh God!' I stared at him. The alcohol-anaesthesia wore off a bit. 'Did she definitely do it on purpose?' My question sounded stupid, but I kept talking. 'I don't know why, but I was kind of thinking she might have had an accident. Fallen or something. But yeah. Of course.' I swallowed hard, remembered Eva hurrying away from us, then turning back. The horror crowded my brain again. 'Did she leave a note?'

I took a big gulp from my drink and put it down on a table. The dance floor was definitely spinning.

'I don't know. I haven't heard. Cat, she was only fifty. And she had everything going . . . Anyway. Sorry. Let's talk about something else. Want another drink?'

I picked mine up and drained it. 'Yes!' I paused. 'Vodka and . . .' What did people have with vodka? 'Lemonade?' That sounded nice.

While he went to the bar, I sat down. He was back fast, and put the drink in front of me. I sipped it. It was different from the last one.

'So you're Cat,' said Henry. He smiled. 'I like that.' I believed him: I realized that I was comfortable with this boy, and it wasn't just because of our shared trauma. There was something about his manner.

'Caitlin,' I said, 'but I've always been called Cat.'

We stood up and moved on to the edge of the dance floor and I looked up at him. Henry's dark hair stuck up in all directions. It was down to his collar, curling at the ends. He was clearly happy being himself. His clothes were immaculate, though, like mine.

'I haven't seen you here before. Are you staying with the Allens?'

We both started to dance a bit. I tried to copy what he was doing, which was basically shuffling from foot to foot.

'Sophie and Owen are family friends. They invited me to come here with them for the summer. Which is obviously amazing. I arrived yesterday.'

'Where are you the rest of the time?'

'I'm from Cornwall. I'll tell you a secret – this is literally my first time abroad. And so everything is new and mostly brilliant but . . .'

'Oh God. Sorry that you . . . you know. This morning. Your first day.'

I was doing my best to dance. I felt self-conscious, but I was doing it anyway. How did you even move? What was I meant to do with my arms? My head was fuzzy and I was starting to feel a bit sick.

I nodded. There was nothing, really, to say to that, so I just looked at him. He was lovely, I decided. I thought of the boys from school. Most of them would be attempting to breakdance on the dance floor if they were here, and they'd be doing it badly while downing as much lager as they could. That thought reminded me of the vodka, and I danced closer to the table and took a gulp.

'How long do you plan to be in Antibes?' he said.

'For the rest of the summer.' I had to raise my voice a bit so he could hear me over 'Dancing Queen'. 'I'm staying in their apartment. In the old town, near the Picasso Museum. I don't really know anything about anything at all.'

We danced. I finished my drink and he got me another. Even as I sipped it, I knew this last drink was a mistake.

'Come out on the boat with me sometime if you like. It's just a little speedboat, but it's fun.'

I grinned. 'I would love to.' And I would. Even though the idea of the sea was freaking me out a bit, I decided I would go on a boat with Henry.

We just danced after that, shouting to each other over the music from time to time, and he kept getting us new drinks. At one point, I thought I heard Sophie's and Owen's voices, raised, but when I looked round I couldn't see anything.

I asked Henry as many questions as he asked me. I found out that he was half French, half British. He had grown up in Provence, a few hours inland from here, and his dad still lived there. Henry had just finished at Oxford uni. He had a younger sister who was studying art in Berlin. They sounded like the most intimidating family. He lived in a different world and yet here we were, dancing. Talking. We swapped stories. We carried on drinking. Things started to lose definition. Everything became fuzzy. I lost track of the time.

At one point, Owen came over and told Henry to be sure to walk me home soon. He gave me a set of keys to the apartment and watched while I put them in my bag, and they left us to it. Henry and I told each other stories from when we were little. It had never been this easy to talk before. He didn't feel like a stranger. He was the guy who'd shared the worst moment of my life. I wanted to tell him everything. I wanted to know everything.

I wanted to call Kitty and tell her. *I've met a boy!*

I focused on what he was saying. He was talking about his childhood.

'We had a den,' he said. 'We found that a bush beside our driveway had a space inside it, and we'd hide out there for hours. Pink flowers on the outside, the best hiding place ever on the inside. We'd take a bottle of lemonade and some cakes to escape from home.'

'We just play hide-and-seek in a crowded house. It's fun. It's weird, though.' I stopped and took a deep breath. This part was something I never talked about. 'It was just me and Mum, the two of us, until I was eight. And I loved it. My dad . . . well, that's for another day. Mum was all I needed. We were a unit. Then she met Bill and he already had four kids. And then they somehow had four more. So I went from being an only child of a single parent to having to share my mum with . . .' I thought of her, of how much had changed between us. Of everything I'd lost. 'With everyone.'

We left the club when it closed, at two, and walked together, laughing and happy, along the pedestrian street and through the back roads of the old town. At one point, I think I started singing ABBA and trying to get him to join in. After that, he put an arm round my shoulders to steady me and asked if I was OK.

There were other people around, a bit drunk, but I was with Henry and I felt completely safe. We passed an older guy with a beard, who threw his arms into the air and started lurching towards us, shouting something.

I looked up at Henry, who shouted, 'No, thanks! Go away,' in English. The man stared at us for a moment and then turned and stumbled off. I leaned on Henry, grateful.

When we were close to the apartment, we stopped. I looked up at him and giggled, though I hadn't meant to.

'It's been lovely to meet you, Cat,' said Henry, and his voice was soft and gentle. I put a hand on his shoulder, because I couldn't not touch him. I pushed my body up against his.

'You too, Henry,' I said. We were going to kiss. I knew it. I was ecstatic.

Our bodies were touching and mine was doing weird things on the inside. I looked up into his face. He looked down into mine. I saw him start to say something, then decide against it. I found myself smiling. His eyes were full of lovely things. I wanted to be this close to him forever. Maybe I loved him. Love at first sight. That was a thing. Was this it? It must be!

Then he stepped back and our bodies weren't touching any more.

'Cat,' he said. 'Oh God, Cat. Yes, but . . . not now.'

My stomach lurched. I felt dizzy and stumbled back too.

'What?' I got my balance back and leaned towards him, trying to get the touch back. He stepped away again. What was happening?

He didn't like me. Just because I was feeling something, it didn't mean that he was too.

'Cat. I've had a wonderful evening. I've loved meeting you. But we've both had a lot to drink, and I'd hate to . . .'

He tailed off. I looked into his eyes. I felt tears prickling at the back of mine.

'But,' I said, 'I want to.' I cringed even as I said it. Jesus.

His voice was kind. I could hear the pity.

'So we can see each other again,' he said. 'Soon. OK? Take it from there. Right now, I think you need to get some sleep.'

I turned, humiliated. I wanted to run away. I wanted to disappear from here forever. Without a word, I let myself in through the heavy front door. I staggered up four flights of stairs, and crept into the apartment, hoping I was being quiet. I locked the front door behind me and tiptoed to my room.

My stomach turned over, and not in a good way. I ran to the bathroom and made it just in time to throw up. My eyes streamed with tears. What had I done?

After I'd brushed my teeth and tidied myself up, I stepped out on to the balcony. Just in case he was down there, looking up. Just in case he was thinking of me. But there was no one in the square. Just that bearded drunk man, sitting on a paving stone in the shadows.

I heard Henry's voice in my head. *I'd hate to*. That was what he'd said.

I'd met a boy, got drunk and messed it up before it had even had a chance to begin, and now Eva's body was back in my head again, floating in the waves.

I climbed into bed and pulled the duvet over my head. I put my headphones in and started speaking.

9

'Oh my God, I thought I just had the best evening. I did! The best, best fucking evening. The best one ever. And then it all went . . . It all went. What did it go? Tits up. I've never said that before. Tits. Up. It started off like . . . I had an amaaaaaazing evening with Henry. We'd both been through the same thing, you see. The same thing, with Eva. Together. He's the only one who . . . but it's worse for him. He knew her. Talking to him was so, so, so, so . . . it was everything. Ev-er-y-thing. We talked about . . . so much. And I was totally in love. I was fucking flying. And then. I went to kiss him because it was like magic. Like a film. And he said no. He said he'd hate to. So.'

I stopped the playback when my past self started crying. My finger hovered over the delete button, but actually I thought I would keep this. I'd never play it to anyone else, but I'd hang on to it to remind me of last night's shitty mistake. I had got things totally wrong with Henry and now I'd never see him again. I'd fucked it up by being drunk.

When I woke, the first thought on my mind was, *Maybe I should just slink away*. I could leave a note for Sophie and Owen, and use Bill's money to get a taxi to the airport. Their friend had died. They were shaken up, and they could do without me hanging around getting drunk and throwing myself at people they knew.

It was midday, which meant it was eleven at home. If I was there, I'd have been handing out squash and snacks to the kids and feeling vaguely bored. My head wouldn't be pounding. I wouldn't be a ball of shame and regret who saw a body every time she looked at the sea. We might have walked to the playground and I'd have been pushing the babies in the swings.

I pulled the curtain aside. The room was full of light as I hadn't closed the shutters last night, which was just as well as I'd probably have fallen off the balcony if I'd tried. I looked out at the square. It was bright with sunlight and the shadows were sharp. Behind it all, I could see mountains. There was literally a Picasso Museum outside my window.

Should I do it? Should I go home?

Sophie laughed when I stepped cautiously into the main part of the apartment.

'Good afternoon, Cat!' she said. 'Oh, you poor thing. How are you feeling?'

I tried to smile. 'Hope I didn't wake you last night.'

'Don't be silly. There was no way I was going to sleep properly until I knew you were safely home.'

'Sorry!'

'Did you have a good evening? That's what matters. Bacon sandwich?'

A wave of nausea washed over me, but when it had gone

I felt . . . hungry. I'd drunk a huge amount since last night's pizza. Suddenly, a bacon sandwich was the only thing in the world I wanted.

She opened the fridge and took down a glass from the cupboard. Then I had a glass of orange juice in one hand and two painkillers in the other, and Sophie was heating a frying pan. I took the tablets and hoped I wasn't going to throw them straight up.

When I looked at Sophie, she was grinning at me.

'We've all been there, darling. What a rite of passage. If I overdo it now, my hangovers last for days, but you're young and I'm sure you'll be fine in no time.' She paused. 'I'd been thinking we'd look at some production work today, but let's sack it off. *Mañana!*'

The bacon roll was the best thing I'd ever tasted. The moment I'd finished it, Sophie reminded me that we were meeting the Thorpe family for lunch, and I felt a bit sick again because I'd forgotten all about that.

An hour later, we were walking through Antibes.

'Chin up, darling,' said Sophie as we crossed a square. 'How are you feeling?'

I stopped walking and forced an answer. 'I mean, fine in myself,' I said. It was true. 'The headache's gone and everything. But I just . . .'

Owen was grinning too. 'Beer fear,' he said. 'Right? The remorse of the morning after. Don't worry, Cat. Things are never as bad as they seem. You didn't do anything regrettable – I guarantee it. Onwards!'

I smiled at him. They were so kind, both of them. I *had* done something regrettable, though. I'd tried to kiss Henry when he hadn't wanted to. Oh God oh God oh God.

'Onwards,' I echoed. I took a deep breath. I kept remembering snippets of my evening and I wanted to curl up and die from cringe.

I barely cared about meeting the Thorpes today, but Sophie was excited about it. The casual dress she had got me was a perfect fit. This one was figure-hugging but relaxed, with a scooped neckline and short sleeves. I was wearing it with flip-flops, because they were the one thing that seemed to be universal, and as long as I didn't kick them off to reveal the word 'Primark', mine were more or less like everyone else's.

Sophie had done my hair again, but this time she'd straightened it. It was longer now, and I hadn't really registered how frizzy it normally was, day to day. Straightening it had revealed how badly it was cut (it actually wasn't cut at all: I'd attempted it myself about a year ago, following a video on TikTok, and then left it to its own devices). So Sophie had clipped it back with a couple of silver hair clips. She'd rubbed some facial sunscreen into my face, muttering about how I was lucky with my young skin and didn't need foundation, and then made me up with a bit of mascara and lip gloss, sprayed something on my face that felt like water but probably wasn't, and stood back to look at her handiwork. This was so far from my usual big-jeans and crop-top style that I looked like a stranger, but I was ready to be someone new.

'Perfect,' she said. 'Gorgeous.' When I'd looked in the mirror, the girl there belonged in Antibes, and that was fine by me. She felt like a mask.

As we approached a table, and as the people who were already sitting there came into focus as a bunch of celebs I knew from social media, I felt nothing. A day earlier, I would have been a ball of excitement and nerves.

The table was under a huge umbrella. It had three place settings on either side and white tablecloths, and lots of glasses and cutlery. I stood in the bright sun, looking at three people who had been pixels on a phone in my regular life at home. It was like being in a Hollywood movie, but feeling pissed off and hungover and weird and really wishing my mum was speaking to me.

'Here she is!' Sophie turned with a big smile and indicated me with a hand. 'This is Cat!' She had dressed for lunch in a bright-pink dress, with matching hair clip, flip-flops and lipstick. Owen was casual in a white shirt and brown shorts.

I pasted on a smile and stepped forward.

'Hi,' I said.

Isabella and Jonathan Thorpe were sitting on either side of an empty chair, which was clearly going to be mine, with a woman I recognized as their mother opposite them. There was a lot of getting up and kissing of cheeks.

'Cat – this is Hels,' said Sophie. 'Hels – Cat. We've known each other since we met at the BBC more than thirty years ago. Can you believe that?'

Helena looked at me, and I could see she was laughing in a nice way about Sophie's effusiveness. She was blonde and had a friendly face. She didn't even look as if she'd had any work done. 'Delighted to meet you, Cat.' She spoke like the queen. 'We've heard *all* about you. These two need a bit more young blood around the place. This is my daughter, Izzy,' she said, pointing at Isabella. I made myself smile at her. She smiled back. Here I was, in the looking-glass world. 'And this oaf here is Jonathan. We used to call him Johnny, but he forces us to go with Jonno these days, so I suppose he's Jonno.'

Jonno was, as I'd already known, an exceptionally good-looking boy, and if anything it was enhanced in real life. But I'd discovered I was the kind of girl who drunkenly threw herself at boys she'd just met and therefore could never have a relationship. However, Jonno was polished and almost impossibly handsome and, in spite of everything, my belly did jump at the sight of him.

'Delightful, Mother. Thanks,' said Jonno. He leaned back in his chair and looked at me, assessing me without bothering to hide it, and I wondered whether I was passing. I assessed him right back, and he gave half a smile.

He tapped the back of the chair beside him. 'Come to the cool side of the table, Cat,' he said, so I took the chair between them.

I looked at Izzy next to me. She was skinny, smaller than me, with waves of blonde hair piled up on top of her head, ribbons cascading down her back. A smaller, hipper version of her own mother. She started saying something, but Helena interrupted as she sat opposite me and leaned over.

'So you're from Cornwall, Cat? Are you there year round?'

I fiddled with the napkin on the table in front of me.

'Well, yes,' I said. 'It's where I live. I've always lived there.'

'Idyllic!' I thought of the rain and the winters and the fact that if you didn't have money life was hard, and didn't say anything. 'How old are you? Izzy's eighteen, and Jonno's nineteen.'

Jonno turned to me with a little snort, then said: 'Mother – I'm twenty. I know it's a minor detail, but you've put up with me for two full decades now. You had two full years of horrible oafish Jonathan before you were blessed with your adorable little Isabella.'

His mum gave him a look. He stopped talking, but he was grinning.

'I'm seventeen,' I said into the silence.

'Eighteen soon,' said Sophie. 'Cat's just left college.'

'Oh – you're waiting for results day?' said Helena. I nodded. 'Same as Izzy. Jonno's at Cambridge already. Soph – I've ordered white and sparkling water. Anything else?'

Jonno was drinking a beer. Izzy had something that might have been a soft drink, or a cocktail; it had a jug of water next to it and a bowl of sugar. Sophie and Owen ordered gin and tonics, and then everyone looked at me. My stomach boiled over at the thought of alcohol.

I turned to Izzy. 'What have you got?' I said.

She looked at me in a *duh* way. I could see disdain on her face.

'Er, this is *citron pressé*?' she said. She stared at me incredulously. I decided that I wasn't going to apologize.

'I've never been to France before. So I don't know anything. What's *citron pressé*?'

Jonno turned to me. 'This is your first time in France? Seriously? Where do you normally go, then?'

'Where do I normally go?' I echoed. I was about to explain where I normally went (the park, sometimes the beach) when Sophie stepped in.

'Cat has an amazing life in Cornwall, Jonno,' she said. 'You should ask her about it. Cat, I think you'll like *citron pressé* if you're sticking to soft drinks? It's lemon juice with water and sugar. Probably just the thing for you right now.'

'Yes please,' I said.

Izzy turned to me. 'Oh, you're not boozing it up all day long like they do? Good.'

'Definitely not,' I said. I looked at the waiter, cringing as I felt Izzy and Jonno's eyes on me. '*Citron pressé, s'il vous plaît*,' I said, in a crap accent.

'Nice touch, ordering in French,' said Jonno, giving me a sideways smile.

'My French is rubbish,' I said, which was totally true. 'That's about as good as it gets.'

'Everyone speaks English anyway,' said Izzy, dismissive. 'You don't need to bother.'

'So, Cat?' said Jonno. He eyed me, semi-combative. 'You have an amazing life in Cornwall and apparently I'm meant to ask you about it.'

He was ready to laugh at me. I didn't give a shit.

'Go on, then,' I said. 'You'd better ask.'

'Please, Cat. Do tell me about your amazing life in Cornwall.'

I waited for a moment.

'OK,' I said. 'I live in a little house with a lot of people.' I paused. There was no point in not being real. 'Technically, I'm one of nine children. Sophie and Owen brought me here to save me from a summer of doing childcare.' I instantly felt guilty. I didn't need saving from the kids. I loved them.

'Nine!' I felt Izzy and Jonno looking at each other across me.

Izzy was interested now. 'Where are you, age-wise, then?' she said.

'Number three. But basically the eldest. The other two above me, my stepbrothers, are much older. They've never lived with us, really.'

They wanted to know more, so I told them about Bill and Mum and the blended family and the two sets of twins. Thinking about Mum made me feel funny. I hadn't even been able to tell her that I'd seen a body. That the first person I'd met in France had killed herself straight afterwards. I was distracted, but Izzy and Jonno loved my story, and I felt Izzy warming to me in real time.

'So where did you go to school?' asked Izzy, hammering home the fact that I was in a different world. *Where do you go to school* was a question from a world in which there was any chance they might have heard of the establishment in question.

I knew where they had been to school. I knew what the fees were.

'I went to Truro College,' I said. I looked at Jonno, interested in his reaction. He was shorter than Henry, with a face a bit like a young Ryan Gosling's.

'Local sixth form?' he said. I nodded.

'Oh God,' said Izzy. I turned to her. She was wearing lip gloss like mine; even though she'd been drinking, hers somehow hadn't come off. 'Oh, Cat, you're going to hate us for going to stupid schools. Isn't she, Jonno? Don't hate us, Cat, will you? We didn't *choose* it.'

I grinned. 'I promise not to hate you for going to posh schools.'

Jonno pointed at me. 'She's left a loophole. You have to promise not to hate us for *anything*.'

'OK.' My eyes met his. All of a sudden it felt weirdly intimate. 'I promise not to hate you . . . unless you give me a *really good reason*.'

He held my gaze. Were we flirting? I mean, it felt like it. I pulled my eyes away. The drinks arrived and Izzy showed me how to manage a *citron pressé*: it turned out it was literally lemon juice in a glass, like Sophie had said. I poured in loads of sugar and it instantly became my favourite. I could recreate it at home and the kids would love it.

The atmosphere between us had changed. I'd passed some kind of test.

'Hey,' Izzy said, checking the other side of the table where the adults were all drinking and laughing, and then lowering her voice. 'Is it true that you and Sophie were the ones who spotted Eva in the water yesterday? Poor Eva. I love her. Erm, *loved* her.'

I checked Sophie too. I pushed my chair back a bit, and both Jonno and Izzy leaned in to hear me. I felt sick, but I was glad she'd asked. I needed to talk about this.

'Actually, it was me,' I said quietly. 'Sophie was shopping, and I was . . .' There was no way I was going to say that I was making a recording of myself talking. 'I was waiting for her. I saw there was someone in the water. I could see the person was in clothes you wouldn't normally swim in.' I shivered at the memory, even though it was thirty degrees.

'Oh my God,' whispered Izzy. She put a hand on my arm. 'You poor thing! So what did you do?'

I took a sip of lemon juice and tried not to wince. More sugar.

'I was looking around to get help and . . .' My heart was pounding now. I was about to talk about Henry. I relived the kiss-that-wasn't all over again. I wished I'd had a blackout. *Just tell the story.* 'There was someone near me. He ran off to get help, and Sophie took me to a cafe and fed me tiramisu.'

She heard that, and leaned over the table. 'Sugar. For the shock. We didn't find out it was poor Eva until later. She was going to come over to talk to Cat. For her podcast.'

Izzy stiffened. 'You have a podcast?'

I shook my head. I did not, of course, have a podcast.

'OK, we need to talk about that,' she said. 'Later.'

As Sophie turned back to Helena to carry on talking about Eva Santoro, Jonno said, 'So the other guy went off for help?'

'We ran into him later, actually,' I said. I made myself say it. 'Henry?'

Jonno's face changed and he said, 'Not Henry Tilney?'

I realized that, despite our hours of conversation, I had no idea of his surname. If he'd told me it, I'd forgotten.

'I don't know, actually,' I said, and Jonno leaned across the table.

'Soph – Henry Tilney?' he asked.

She nodded. 'Yes, and . . .'

Jonno shook his head. 'Henry Tilney is a twat. He used to be cool, but then he went weird.'

Before I could ask more, Sophie clapped her hands.

'You three are so young and beautiful. Photo time!'

They leaned in on either side of me, and a minute later there we were, on Sophie's story. A few minutes after that I got a message from Kitty.

OMFG!! you are hanging with J&I?? is he as gorgeous irl?

I smiled at the message, and decided to reply later. Then I thought I could manage a quick answer now. I knew she'd be looking at her phone, waiting. 💯, I wrote.

I modelled myself on Izzy at lunch, and ordered food that was easy to eat and didn't seem likely to come with weird cutlery. I had a goats' cheese salad, followed by fish and potatoes, amazed at how starving I was in spite of the bacon roll. The fish came with a fish knife, but I copied Izzy and used it like a normal one and it was fine. I watched Helena eating mussels, using shells to pull things out of other shells, and Owen casually dismembering a crab. The adults ignored us, and after a while Jonno tapped my arm.

'Let's leave them to their functional alcoholism,' he said. 'We'll get pudding somewhere else, yeah?'

Izzy agreed, and soon the three of us were walking through Antibes. I was sweating, and I was certain that my hair was frizzing up again. I felt like Cinderella at midnight: my disguise was about to melt away and my real self would be revealed. The joyous part of it, though, was that I didn't care. Antibes felt like a different place. Eva had died here. Had killed herself. And, in a much smaller way, it was also the place in which I'd made an idiot of myself with Henry. Trivial things didn't matter any more.

As we walked, I got a proper look at Izzy's hair ribbons. They were pink and purple, tied faux-casually around her bun.

'I love your ribbons,' I said.

She touched them. 'Thank you! I'm trying it out as a look. I saw a bit of this stuff, you know, in Milan? And thought I'd give it a go.'

'You were in Milan?' I said, and she laughed.

'I wish. I mean, at fashion week. Online. I've been to Milan, but not in fashion week. One day.'

'Well, it looks great,' I said. Jonno walked ahead, bored, no doubt, of hair talk. He shouted to someone up ahead, then waved us goodbye without looking round.

Once it was just the two of us, Izzy and I didn't quite know what to say. I waited for her to speak, but she didn't say anything. I glanced over. She didn't seem to be finding this awkward. She was just walking. She had great posture. I pulled my shoulders back and tightened my abs and held my head up. I basically walked around copying her.

'So,' I said, when the silence was too much for me. As I said it, though, she turned to me and started talking too.

'You go first,' we both said.

In the end, she smiled and said, 'So what's this about a podcast?'

I started to explain, and she grinned.

'OK,' she said in the end. 'This is brilliant. I needed something to stop me being bored this summer. Can I join in? You can interview me if you like, about what it's like coming here every single summer even if you want to go somewhere else or just stay home with your friends.'

We both stopped walking. We looked at each other. I was smiling, but I hoped she couldn't see that I was laughing at her massively privileged perspective. It would be such an interesting counterpoint to mine. Did I want to make my podcast with Izzy Thorpe? Of course I did.

'Er, yeah!' I said. 'Come over tomorrow? Sophie and I are going to get started.'

She nodded. 'For sure. And before that – hang on. Let me just send a message. There's someone else I've been hanging out with lately, and I think you'll really want to meet them. We can be a gang for the summer!'

And, suddenly, I didn't want to sneak off home any more.

10

Izzy's friend was older than us, maybe in her mid-twenties or even closer to thirty. She was sitting on a bench under a tree, wearing a lime-green playsuit with matching sandals, and she looked gorgeous. Her hair was short and dark, held back with sparkly hairclips. When she saw Izzy and me approaching, she smiled, and it was a smile that made me want to be her friend straight away.

'Hey!' said Izzy, sauntering over. 'Aisha, this is Cat. A new friend. Remember, we were meeting for lunch? And you said, if she was up for it, I should bring her to meet you? Well, here she is. *Voilà*.'

'I did,' said Aisha. I saw her checking me out, but in a nice way. Her voice was husky, and I thought she might be the coolest person I had ever met. 'Cat, I'm just gonna say it. You've passed the test. I suggested to little Izzy here that we all hung out together after lunch, and she said no. Just no. She thought you were going to be dorky or annoying or something. She was just gonna do the minimum of being nice to you to keep her mum and her friend happy and then she was gonna bail and come and hang out with me.'

'Aisha!' Izzy was squirming. 'Oh my GOD! I can't believe you just told her that!'

I stared at Izzy, and then looked back to Aisha. Then I looked back to Izzy and started laughing.

'Seriously?'

Izzy covered her face with her hands.

Aisha laughed too. 'Why not? It's true. And Cat's here, and that means you were pleasantly surprised. Cat, it's a pleasure to meet you. So you're staying with friends? Sophie and Owen – is that right?'

Izzy and I sat next to her, one on each side. We looked out at the water.

'That's right. I've been here two nights. It's been ... eventful already.'

'Oh, lucky you,' said Aisha. 'I've been here a week and I feel like nothing has happened at all, apart from meeting the lovely Isabella. Honestly, I don't know what I'd do without you, Iz. I'd just be moping around on my own.' She turned to me. 'Cat, I came here on impulse after a break-up because my friends were going to be here. But then they bailed. I was mooching around feeling sorry for myself when I ran into Izzy the other day. So what's happened to you that hasn't happened to me?'

'Well, you and I have both met Izzy,' I said. 'The other stuff ... how long have you got?'

'Forever.'

The thing with Aisha was that she was incredible to talk to, genuinely interested in everything I said. She wanted to know all about Eva.

'I can't believe you met her twice,' she said. 'And then . . . God, poor you. So, they think she killed herself?'

Izzy and I both gave little gasps.

'Oh, sorry,' said Aisha. 'Was that too blunt? I didn't mean to be. But that's the way it looks, right? No one gets into the water with their clothes on by mistake. Or was she pushed?'

'Well,' said Izzy. 'I heard Mum saying it was super out of character for her. She was really surprised. Said Eva was in a really good place and happier than she'd been for ages. So she didn't understand why it had happened.' She leaned out to look across Aisha at me. 'Hey, Cat? We could talk about Eva in the podcast, right?'

'Podcast? Excuse me – what?'

We sat there and talked about it, agreeing that we'd talk about Eva in the podcast, a dramatic part of our documentation of our summer.

'You were planning to interview her, right?' said Aisha. 'So she would have been one of your first subjects. Why can't she still be? This is what I'd do: I'd go in talking about your experiences with Eva. Then pan out from there to take in the whole of the Riviera summer experience.'

'Aisha's a journalist,' said Izzy. 'That's how she knows about this stuff.'

'Don't hate me!' Aisha stood up. 'Please. I'm off duty and I'm not the bad sort of journo anyway. I write about nail varnish and stuff. But I'm interested in what you're doing. Let's get ice cream and you can tell me more. So, who are you gonna interview?'

We followed Aisha to the ice-cream shop, the one that

always had the huge queue. As we discussed the flavours, I checked my phone.

There was a message from Mum:

Cat. Sophie told me what happened yesterday. You need to come home! Now! I knew this was a bad idea.

I put the phone away. I'd reply later.

The next morning, I went down to the beach with Sophie for her swim, but found I couldn't get into the water. It was too soon. When I stepped in, ankle deep, all I could see was Eva. I saw her bobbing under the surface, and I saw her before that too. I saw scenes I'd never witnessed: Eva walking out into the waves. Letting the water go over her head. Maybe changing her mind and struggling. I felt my breathing becoming ragged.

Sophie ploughed in and started swimming out, but I turned and went back to sit on our rug and waited. I remembered I hadn't replied to Mum, so I sat in the early morning sunshine and wrote:

Honestly Mum it's fine. It was shocking but I promise I'm perfectly safe and it's a lovely place to be xx

I sent it. I waited.

I ate a lot of breakfast, because it was literally impossible not to. I had a croissant, and then loads of chunks of baguette with butter and strawberry jam. And I decided coffee with a little bit of milk and two sugars was just about acceptable as a drink, as long as I had water on the side.

'The food here is amazing,' I said, thinking back through everything I'd eaten so far. 'That onion tart you made? Is it difficult?' I pulled off one more piece of baguette.

'So easy that you wouldn't believe,' said Sophie, sipping her coffee. 'Want the recipe?' I nodded. 'I'll ping it to you.'

When we finished, Sophie turned to Owen, who was tapping on his laptop while licking croissant crumbs off his fingers, and said: 'Darling? I need you to work in the bedroom, just for a little bit, OK? The girls and I are going to talk podcasts.'

He looked annoyed for a fraction of a second, but then smiled and stood up, wiping his hands on his shorts.

'Of course!' he said. 'Far be it from me to get in the way of the podcasting ladies!'

Izzy arrived exactly on time, dressed all in black in a businesslike manner, and I wiped down the table while Sophie made more coffee. We sat at the table and everything felt strangely formal for a moment. I looked at Sophie.

'Right, girls,' she said. 'Isn't this fab? It's what we're here for. Welcome to podcasting school. So, Izzy – Cat tells me you're going to join her and work together on a series about this summer? Getting out and doing some interviews?'

'That's right,' said Izzy. 'I mean, Cat's going to be the main character, but we thought we'd compare our experiences. For Cat it's something totally new, and for me it's honestly sometimes a bit of a drag.'

'Oh, this will be interesting! So here are some tips to get you started. For one thing, remember that when you're talking it's your job to paint in the scene. Your listener knows nothing about where you are. Be clear about the geography. Tell the listener what you can see, but also what you can smell, and any other impressions you have. Paint it in.'

Izzy and I looked at each other and smiled. I felt myself squirming inside. This was it. Everything I'd ever wanted. I was finding out how to make a podcast, from an expert. I had a colleague, and a story.

'What else?' I said.

Sophie put both hands flat on the table.

'Interviews,' she said. 'When you're talking to people – this sounds obvious, but ask a lot of questions. Nothing is too basic. Don't be afraid to take people right back to explain the things they think are obvious. Ask, ask, ask and you'll be surprised at what you might find out. Keep chatting and people will keep talking. Cat, send me over your recordings, or any that you're happy to share, and we'll do some editing.'

I took a deep breath and forwarded her a couple of my voice clips from my journey here. Sophie opened her big laptop, and started showing us how to edit and clean them up.

I looked at our three faces reflected in the screen. I was doing this. I was actually doing it.

By the end, even my stupid voice sounded OK.

11

'Hey everyone! Cat and Izzy here. We're talking to you from Izzy's house, in the old town in Antibes. Izzy, how long have your family had this house?'

'Oh . . . Like, forever? I don't know exactly, but I know my parents had it before I was born. We come here every summer. See the same people every year. I remember when I was little how much we used to love it. We'd be, like, swimming in the sea all the time. Playing on the sand. Going out on the boat . . .'

'You have a boat?'

'Oh, yeah. It's only small, though . . . I can show it to you sometime. If you like. It's quite boring.'

'Of course it is! Yeah, show it to me, please.'

'Anyway, how about you, Cat? Who was the first person you met when you arrived in France?'

'A woman called Eva Santoro,' I said. 'And here's the weird thing: she died the very next day.'

We looked at each other. Even though Eva's death was tragic, that intro had gone well.

I'd been in Antibes five days now, and I hadn't seen Henry Tilney again. Even though that night he'd said we would meet again and do it properly, I knew he hadn't meant it. He just said it to make me go inside and stop flinging myself at him embarrassingly. Plus, I was starting to think I'd felt all that attraction to him because of our shared experience that morning. And because I was drunk. He could have got in touch with me a million different ways, by contacting Sophie, who he knew, or by calling in at the place where he knew I was living. And he hadn't. So I was very much over that. I had Izzy and Aisha now: real friends.

Mum and I had settled into a terse texting relationship. I checked in from time to time and she generally replied with something that sounded a bit annoyed.

I clicked stop and looked at Izzy.

'Break?' I said. She nodded.

I checked my hair in the little mirror on my wall. I was wearing a red silky T-shirt Sophie had given me, insisting that it didn't fit her any more, and a short skirt she'd just come home with the other day and given to me. Underneath it was a pink-and-red bikini she'd made me get fitted for.

I'd tied my hair into a high ponytail and added ribbons. Izzy had given them to me and I was wearing them every day.

We were recording at Izzy's house, which, again, I had already known from Instagram, though I'd taken great care to appear surprised by everything on my first visit earlier in the week. They lived in a whole house in the old town, close to the Allens' apartment, and Izzy had a bedroom with a second room opening off it, which she called 'my dressing room' and which we'd set up as a recording studio. The whole house was immaculate, filled with expensive stuff and smelling of flowers and polish and a 'room scent' called 'Baies'. Who knew 'room scents' were a thing?

Izzy's phone pinged and she looked at it and tumbled down the stairs ahead of me, taking them two at a time and somehow still as graceful as a dancer. She was wearing a loose white dress, her hair in a bun, her toenails painted yellow.

'Yay,' she said. 'Aisha's here! Who fancies the beach?'

The downstairs of their house had a red tiled floor, and it was always cool underfoot. I walked in and saw Aisha lounging on the sofa, and Jonno doing push-ups with no top on. He saw us coming and jumped to his feet in one move.

'Jesus, Jon,' said Izzy. 'Stop peacocking.'

Jonno was glowing, grinning. He did look good: he was only wearing a pair of board shorts with blue stripes, and Izzy was right: there was something peacocky about him. His muscles were defined in a way that looked a bit weird, but I had started to feel comfortable around him, not least because it turned out he'd had a boyfriend until the start of the summer.

'Hey, Jonno,' I said. 'Hey, Aisha.'

She came over and kissed us both on each cheek. 'How are my podcast girlies?' she said in the husky voice I tried to copy when recording. 'I was going to come up but didn't want to disturb.'

'We're good!' Izzy was twirling around. 'We just recorded an intro, but so far so good.'

'Have you got into Eva yet?'

We looked at each other.

'We're going to interview Helena,' I said. 'She's known Eva for ages. We'll talk to her later. So we have a plan.'

'And what about the people you're living with?' said Aisha. 'They knew her too, right?'

I nodded. I was hesitant to interview Sophie about her friend. It didn't feel right.

'Maybe,' I said.

'I love the sound of their penthouse.' She paused. 'You said they let it out sometimes, right?'

'Yeah, they do. It's gorgeous.'

I had no idea how Owen's moving art about funded three houses and their madly luxurious lifestyle, but it seemed it did. Maybe their apartment rentals brought in significant income.

'Interesting,' she said. 'I'm wondering about coming back here later this year. Figure it would be an amazing base. When the tourists are gone? I may as well be sitting in a penthouse as I write my make-up reviews, y'know?'

'Oh, you should! Do you want to have a look at the place? I'll ask Sophie if you like?'

'Oh yes, please!'

I sent a quick message to Sophie. Izzy's friend Aisha's interested in renting your place in the autumn or winter if poss. Could I bring her over sometime?

Jonno was pacing around. 'This is all great, but beach now, please. I really wanna get in the water.'

Izzy was pulling on a pair of espadrilles. 'All right, Ken.'

'My job is Beach,' said Jonno, and actually he *did* look a lot like Ken from the Barbie movie.

Aisha stood up. 'Yeah, a dip would be just the thing, right? My job's Beach too, right now.'

We were heading off when my phone rang and when I looked at the screen I saw it was Sophie. This was unusual: she messaged and sent voice notes all the time, just little snippets of things that had occurred to her. A call was new. Maybe, I thought, she wanted to talk to Aisha, though they seemed pretty haphazard about their apartment rentals and I couldn't imagine she'd find it urgent.

My mind leaped to home. Something might have happened. The boys were reckless around roads. The babies were fragile and senseless. What if . . .

I answered fast. 'Sophie?'

'Cat!' she said, and I relaxed instantly, knowing from her tone that there wasn't an emergency. 'Where are you, darling? At Izzy's? All OK?'

'Just heading to the beach. Are you all right?'

'Fab. But – could you possibly pop back if you have a minute? We just need to talk to you for a second. I promise you'll be back with the others in no time. It's just a silly thing. Nothing for you to worry about.'

I agreed and hung up. 'Sorry,' I said to the others. 'I'll meet you at the beach.'

Owen was sitting at the table when I got back to the apartment.

'Cat!' he said. 'Have a seat. Thanks for popping home. We need to talk to you about something.'

I started catastrophizing all over again. Had I done something to upset them? Were they sending me home? The idea of going back now that I had settled in was . . .

'Here's the thing,' said Sophie, appearing from their bedroom. She looked different from usual. Her make-up had smudged a bit and she hadn't done her hair. I saw her making an effort and pulling herself together. Her tone became much jollier. 'Oh, look at your face! Don't worry. It's nothing bad. Not at all. It's just that something's come up and we thought we'd get everything in place right away because it's . . . irritating. That's all.'

She turned her face away for a moment. Was she annoyed with me? Worried? Owen put a hand on her back and rubbed it, and she leaned towards him so his arm was round her shoulders. I watched her take a deep breath.

'Cat – Owen and I need to travel to Dubai soon, and we'll need to be there for at least a week. It's a work thing that's come up. I'm so sorry. I don't normally have to tag along for work business, but this time it's more complicated and I just do.'

I nodded.

'So we were wondering – maybe you could go and stay with one of our friends while we're gone? I just don't think we can leave you here on your own, but you've settled in so well already, and I'm sure Hels and the kids would love to have you.'

I thought about what it would be like to stay at Izzy and Jonno's. Nice. Maybe a bit intense, but still. Nice.

'That's fine,' I said. I wondered if there was any way Izzy and I could stay *here*, in the apartment, instead. She was eighteen, and I almost was. We'd be sensible, and then I wouldn't have to be a guest in someone else's house.

'Great,' said Owen. 'Things are moving fast. Bit of a minor work crisis, but nothing for you to worry about, so we thought we'd just make sure you were going to be all right.'

I thought about it. 'When do you go?'

'Saturday,' said Sophie, an apology in her voice. 'I'm so sorry. Working on the pod with you girls is much more fun. But you can carry on with your research, and when we're back we'll pull it all into place. In fact, consider it a deadline! Oh, and, yes, if your friend is interested in renting the place out, bring her over. That's fine. Get her over before we leave and I can tell her about the logistics. We're always happy to take bookings.'

I made myself smile. I looked her in the eye. 'I will,' I said. 'She'd like that. And, honestly, don't worry about me. I mean, I could always go back to Cornwall if that is easier for you?'

I saw Owen look to Sophie, a question on his face and instantly regretted making the offer. What if they said yes?

But she shook her head. 'No. No need for that at all. Our business logistics can't ruin Cat's summer. And they won't.'

12

I joined the others on Gravette beach, right at the back in what had become our usual spot up against the wall. It was crowded, filled with holidaymakers, a mist of sunscreen in the air. Aisha was in the water, swimming to the buoy and back.

'Owen and Sophie are going away,' I said. 'For a week. They asked if I could stay at yours for a bit. I mean I guess Sophie's going to ask your mum. Would it be OK?'

Izzy leaned back on the wall and held her face up to the sun with a grin.

'Awesome,' she said. 'Stay as long as you like. That would be cool. We can work on the pod non-stop.' She opened her eyes. 'Jonno, after this we should go to Cornwall,' she said. 'Don't you think? I want to meet all Cat's brothers and sisters.'

Jonno had been lying back, making sure every possible millimetre of skin was exposed to the sun. At this, he propped himself up on his elbows.

'You know what – we fucking should,' he said. 'Cat, Soph is always trying to get Mum down there. Honestly, we never went because it's kinda far and it rains, right?'

'Right.' I couldn't argue with that.

'But now we have you!' He turned and smiled at me. I smiled back, but inside I was panicking.

'You do.' I spoke carefully. 'I wish I could invite you to stay, but ... our house really is tiny. We're crowded. We don't have, I don't know. Room scents. Antiques. We have *one* bathroom.'

Izzy waved a hand.

'We don't care about that stuff. I wasn't inviting us to *stay* with you. I just can't wait to meet your babies.' She clapped her hands, a new idea occurring to her. 'I know! Can we FaceTime them?'

I looked at the water. Aisha waved at me, then did a handstand, her feet pointing straight up in the air. I wondered whether I would ever be brave enough to do what she'd done. Just travel to a new place on my own and stay for weeks. Talk to strangers because I didn't know anyone.

Then I focused on what Izzy had just said. I hadn't seen the babies for ages.

'We could try,' I said. 'I haven't checked in for a while. Yeah, we could try a video call. See who's around.'

Izzy squealed, and Jonno shuffled backwards so he'd be able to see my screen. He moved up next to me, so I was in the middle. His shoulder was sticky with sunscreen and attached itself to me like a hot car seat on a summer's day. I wanted to pull away, but there was nowhere to go.

I messaged Kitty, who replied saying that she was at her mum's, but that she thought my mum was at home. By the time I was making a WhatsApp video call to Mum I was starting to realize that actually this might not be a good idea.

By the time she answered I was hoping she wouldn't.

Then she was on the screen, at a funny angle, looking confused. Her hair was a birds' nest, and she was wearing one of her old maternity tops. I tried to tilt the phone so Izzy and Jonno wouldn't see her, mouthing 'my mum' at them, and Izzy craned round to see the screen.

'Cat!' said Mum. 'Cat – is it a video call? Oh God, I look awful. Are you all right?'

Her voice came out loud and tinny, and I put my earphones in. Then she was in my ears and it was better.

'Hey, Mum,' I said. 'Yeah. I'm on the beach. If I cut out it's because the 5G isn't always very good.'

'5G!' said Mum. 'Oh my. How the other half live.'

I smiled at that. It was true: you never got 5G in Cornwall. 'Mum. How *are* you?'

She paused. 'Are you OK? You don't sound like yourself.'

'No, I'm really fine. I mean, I'm literally fine. I'm sitting on the beach in Antibes!'

'Let me see you properly,' said Mum.

I extended my arm so she could look at me. I was a little bit suntanned now. The bikini was nice. I knew my hair was looking good, because –

'Are you wearing hair ribbons?' said Mum's voice in my ear.

I turned my head round so she could see. The ribbons fell down to my shoulders. They were red and pink, matching my bikini.

'Do you like them?'

Before Mum could answer, Izzy leaned over so she was in shot too, and waved. She motioned for me to give her one earphone, but I resisted.

'Oh. Um.' Mum was panicking. 'Hello?' she said in a totally different tone of voice.

'Izzy says hello back. She can't hear you,' I said. 'But this is Izzy, my friend. I told you about her.'

'Cat, don't ambush me!' said Mum. 'I look a fright.' She was genuinely shaken, and I remembered how stressed she got, and how much she hated unexpected visitors.

'Sorry,' I said. 'I'm sorry, Mum. Really. Izzy and Jonno wanted to see the babies. Are they around?'

There was a bit of a strange silence. Then Mum spoke in a different tone. Clipped, colder than usual.

'Sure. Of course. Mia and Josh are with Summer. The boys are on a play date, but you probably only want the cute ones, don't you?'

I watched the random parts of our house that flashed past as Mum moved around, phone in hand. Then she was in the living room, and she passed the phone to someone.

A girl's face filled the screen. She looked confused.

'Hello?' she said.

'Hi.' She came into focus. She was dark haired, with huge dark eyes and dark skin. She was frowning at the screen. 'Sorry. Hi. I'm not quite sure what's . . . ?'

Then I heard a familiar voice. Two.

'Want phone!' That was Joshie.

'Summer read book!' That was Mia.

I grinned and passed a headphone to Izzy, who leaned in and looked at the screen. Jonno craned round and appeared on the screen on my other side. I pulled the headphones out.

'Hi, Summer,' I said. 'Sorry to spring this on you. I'm Cat, and this is my friend Izzy, and this is Jonno. We just wanted to say hello to the kids, really, but I didn't mean to interrupt you reading. Hey, Mia! Hey, Joshie!'

They both came into shot. Josh with his springy curls, and Mia with her black wisps of hair.

'Cat!' they shouted. They both tried to grab the phone. There was a tussle, and I could hear Summer laughing.

'Hey, you two,' she said, and somehow, without getting at all angry, she managed to get everything under control and hold the phone up so we could see both of them. Summer had a posh voice and apparently a magic touch with my siblings. I tried not to be jealous, because I was sitting on a beach in the South of France, but it did feel weird.

'Cat – they talk about you all the time,' said Summer. 'It's so nice to actually meet you.'

'This is Joshie,' I said to Izzy and Jonno, pointing at the screen. 'And this one's Mia. I talk about them a lot too.'

'Can confirm,' said Jonno.

'Hey, guys!' said Izzy. 'Oh my God, you two are gorgeous, aren't you?'

'Yeh,' said Mia.

'Gorgie,' confirmed Josh.

We chatted to them both. Izzy was charmed to the absolute max, and Jonno kept chuckling. By the time we started to say goodbye I felt a new warmth between the three of us.

'I love the ribbons,' said Summer, before we hung up. 'Very Milan.'

The moment the screen was blank we all laughed. I was happy, and I tried to hang on to that, but there was something inside me making me feel bad. I decided to ignore it.

Aisha wandered up the beach. 'Ice cream?' she said.

Jonno jumped up. 'I'll get them. What do we all want?'

When he'd gone, Izzy turned to Aisha. 'We just FaceTimed Cat's family,' she said. 'Oh, those toddlers are adorable. Honestly, you should have seen them.'

Aisha was polite, but I could see she didn't care at all, which was fair.

I was happy to know the kids were in good hands with Summer, who was clearly both lovely and capable. By the time Jonno appeared with his hands full of ice-cream cones, though, my bad feeling had a name.

Mum.

I thought about the way she'd said *'you probably only want the cute ones.'* And *'don't ambush me like that.'* We'd parted on a huge fight and nothing felt normal between us any more.

'So what did Sophie want before?' said Aisha, sitting next to me and taking a strawberry-sorbet cone from Jonno with a smile. She tipped her head back towards the sun. 'Was everything OK?'

I took my mango ice cream. 'Thanks, Jonno. Yeah, it was fine. They have to go away for a work thing. Oh, and she said you could come and look at the apartment if you're interested. Has to be before Saturday.'

Aisha grinned. 'How about now? I'm so at home here now that I can't bear to leave without knowing I'm coming back.'

I held my cone between my knees and tapped out another message to Sophie.

Is it OK if Izzy and Aisha and maybe Jonno come over to sit on the terrace so Aisha can chat with you about the rental? Today? Or another day? Promise we won't disturb Owen.

She replied at once.

Of course! Come whenever you want.

By the time we got back, Sophie had redone her make up. Her hair was bouncy and her eyeliner was immaculate. The terrace was shaded and the sea was sparkling. I almost managed not to think of Eva when I looked out at the water.

Aisha leaned on the balcony and looked out. 'God,' she said. 'This is beyond gorgeous. No offence to your house, Thorpes, but this view is to absolutely die for. I hope they let me rent it!'

'Of course we will!' Sophie had appeared behind us, with a tray of cold drinks. 'Aisha – I know the kids think we're all hopeless boozers for daytime drinking.' She winked at me. 'But would you join me in a glass of wine? Prosecco?'

Aisha hesitated. 'I mean, if you're having wine. Then – that sounds glorious.'

Sophie fetched a bottle in an ice bucket, and two glasses. She'd given us lemonade and glasses full of ice. She was so generous.

'So,' she said. 'What do you want to know?'

'I mean, not much,' said Aisha. 'Just how much it is, I guess. And availability.'

While they discussed 'mates' rates', Jonno, Izzy and I talked about nothing in particular. As always, it came back to our podcast.

'Sophie?' said Izzy, after a while. 'Can we ask you some questions? And record it? You can tell us how we're doing at interviewing.'

Sophie sighed. She had started to relax since she'd been talking to Aisha with her fizz.

'Go on, then,' she said. We set up Izzy's phone to record and started asking.

'When did you first meet Eva?' I asked.

'Oh, forever ago,' said Sophie. 'God. Let me see. Maybe twenty years ago? That was when we started coming here . . .'

She broke off when we heard Owen's voice from inside.

'Well, someone is trying to fuck me over!'

Sophie stopped talking and rushed inside.

When she came back, she closed the door behind her and sighed. 'Sorry about that. He's stressed with work, as you can tell. He's moving into the bedroom so it won't disturb us again. Where were we?'

'Is he OK?' said Aisha. 'Sounds –'

Sophie's face closed. 'There's always up and downs, and when the buck stops with you? Well, it makes things that much more complex.'

'What does Owen actually do?' said Izzy.

'Imports and exports,' said Sophie. 'Terribly dull. Girls, do you mind if we carry on later?' I could see she was agitated. She sat down, then stood up again and walked to the railing. 'Aisha – how long are you down for? And what do you do?' I gave her a look. She was changing the subject.

Aisha stretched her legs out and sipped her wine. 'I'm only here for a few more weeks this time. Honestly, Sophie? I'm freelance, and I'd just been through a bad break-up. I found a single room in a little hotel, and decided to decamp for a while and read books. See the sunshine and swim in the sea. Spend some time on my own. Get some perspective.'

I looked at her. That wasn't quite how she'd explained it before.

Sophie sipped her drink. 'Oh, I know. It does wonders for the soul, doesn't it? So did you already know Izzy and Jonno?'

'No,' said Aisha. 'Izzy and I got talking on my third day. To be honest, she was an angel sent from heaven, because I'd been on my own and in my own head, you know. Newly single and I was totally dwelling on everything. So I saw this gorgeous girl and made some pretext to strike up a conversation and I . . .' She looked at us with a rueful smile. 'I properly attached myself to you guys and you've been really nice about it. I know you're all younger, but it was like suddenly having real friends. So, thank you.'

Sophie leaned over and clinked her glass against Aisha's. 'Well, cheers. Here's to a bright future. Onwards and upwards.'

We stayed for ages. Aisha asked for a tour of the place, and Sophie asked if I'd show it to her. It didn't take long: I showed her the open-plan kitchen, the living area, the table that still had some of Owen's stuff on it. My bedroom and bathroom, and the outside of Sophie and Owen's room. We both heard Owen saying, 'So are you saying some arsehole is . . . ?' before we exchanged a glance and tiptoed away.

'I'll just use the loo,' said Aisha. 'Back out in a sec.'

On the terrace, Sophie looked happier. 'She's lovely,' she said. 'Poor girl. I like the idea of this being a place where people come to heal. And of you three cheering her up so much.' She looked back inside. 'Where is she?'

'Loo.'

As they were leaving, Jonno hung back. 'Cat,' he said in his usual casual tone as we stood on the landing. 'Fancy going for a drink on Thursday? Izzy has to help Mum with some stuff, but I thought it would be nice to sit in the evening sun and watch the people go by, yeah?'

'Sure,' I said. I raised my voice so the others would hear. 'Iz, you can come and join us after, right? On Thursday?'

She laughed, and said, 'I mean, maybe.'

I rode down in the lift with them and we set off through town, not going anywhere in particular. Aisha said she was going back to her hotel for a nap after the wine and kissed us all goodbye. The sun was hot on our heads, and I was with people I liked. I was starting to be a bit tanned, with hair that was stiff with salt and thus full of body. I was wearing the right sort of clothes. And I was laughing with people who were starting to feel like real friends.

'You're sure you don't mind me staying with you for a bit?' I said as we went. 'I really don't want to impose. I thought we could stay here, but Sophie said no.'

Izzy stopped and looked at me, grinning.

'You idiot! I can't wait!'

'We'd love it,' confirmed Jonno. '*Mi casa es tu casa.*'

I could stay for as long as I wanted. They liked me. I liked them.

Everything was fabulous.

13

As I walked over the warm paving stones towards the bar, I realized I was walking a bit differently. I was standing up straight, being confident. I started leaning into it, trying for a strut.

Being in Antibes was changing me and I was here for it. I would cringe forever at the memory of that first night. But since then I felt different.

I had found my way into this looking-glass world, and was bossing it even if it felt like I was slightly doing it in disguise: this evening, I'd washed and curled my hair, and dressed in my camouflage dress, the one Sophie had got me on that first day. It was the easiest thing to wear, the one I reached for whenever I wasn't sure. I'd put on mascara and lip gloss and I felt good. I'd take a selfie with Jonno and upload it, and Kitty would go wild. Kitty refused to accept that he was gay: as a more assiduous student of his social media, she'd said, 'He had a girlfriend before he was seeing Will. He's bi, Cat.' She'd immediately reacted to the two Jonno pictures I'd put on my story so far. If he actually did come to Cornwall later in the year, I'd introduce them and see what happened.

At home, if I was heading out to meet a friend, I'd never have bothered with any of the gloss. Life here was different. Intoxicating. Magical. The sun shone almost all the time. It was like being in a movie.

I tried harder to walk in a cool way, experimenting with a little wiggle of the hips. Izzy was great at walking, though she'd considered it hilarious when I'd told her that. She strutted as if she was on a runway, but in a totally unselfconscious way. It was just how she was. She said it came from sadistic ballet teachers, but I thought it was also her certainty that she was someone who could and should take up space. I tried to channel it, to imagine myself into that mindset.

When I saw Jonno sitting at a table bathed in early evening sun, I did everything in my power to walk towards him like a model. I wanted to be one of the beautiful people of the French Riviera.

And so, of course, it didn't work. Everything changed in a fraction of a second: I tripped on the edge of an uneven paving stone and the hard ground came rushing up to meet me. My chin hit stone. My bag (an old one of Sophie's) flew across the street. I felt the pain in my knees and on the palms of my hands.

Someone laughed. That was the worst thing of all.

Jonno was beside me in a second.

'Hey,' he said. 'Cat! God, are you OK? Can you get up? Actually, one sec. Just stay there.'

I looked round, afraid that he was taking a photo. In fact, though, he was retrieving my handbag. While he was doing it, I wriggled round so I was sitting up. I was trying really hard not to cry, but I felt like a child. Like Dash or Ethan, at home, when they'd tripped up on the pavement and grazed their knees. They would cry like mad, and I sympathized now. I wanted to burst into tears too. It wasn't the injuries, though my knees in particular were agony. It was the shock of it. One minute I'd been smug about the way I was strutting across the street, and then I was on the ground, and people thought it was funny.

I pulled my dress round to try to cover myself.

Jonno helped me up and led me over to the table, holding my hand. I appreciated him doing that: I was never going to take walking for granted, ever again. He looked down at my feet.

'You're not even in high heels!' he said. 'Fucking flip-flops! Ha!'

That was annoying, but I sucked it up.

'Can you imagine me in high heels?' I said. 'Never gonna happen.'

'Probably wise. Now, let's get you a proper drink, yeah? None of that "I don't like the taste of booze" stuff. Can I order you something real?'

I didn't have the strength. I agreed that he could get me whatever he wanted, and managed to ask for a glass of water too, and he went in to order at the bar.

Half an hour later, I was feeling a bit better. I'd sipped at the drink Jonno got me: it warmed me like medicine, and I appreciated him making the effort. I'd downed a lot of water too. I was trying very hard to reach a place in which

I would be able to laugh at myself for falling over and actually mean it.

'Iz and I used to get so bored here,' he said. 'It's nice having you around.'

'I will never get my head round that. The fact that you two found this place boring.'

'Does it sound bratty? Some days we just got train passes and rode up and down to Monaco. Actually, we should do that sometime. It's fun. What do you think? You and me? Or we could hire a boat? Explore?'

I laughed, but when I looked at him it stopped in my throat. Jonno had a strange expression on his face. He had to be thinking about something intense, to make him look like that, but we weren't talking about anything much at all.

He gripped my hand tightly.

'Cat,' he said, and I'd never heard him sounding like this before. 'Cat, this isn't going to be news to you, but when I said just now that it's nice having you around, I meant it. I really like you.'

'I like you too!' My voice came out too bright, sing-song, stupid. Whatever he was doing, I had to stop it.

He grinned. 'You're so good at playing it cool. I've given you opportunities, and you never take me up on them. In the end I thought, fuck it, and decided to ask you on a date. And you said yes!'

I swallowed hard. 'This is a date?'

He shook his head, smiling as if I was being funny.

'What else would it be?'

'A drink. Between friends. Izzy's coming later! And I asked Aisha!'

His face changed again. 'Izzy is not coming later. Cat, there's playing it cool and playing it cool. If you thought this was just a drink you wouldn't have turned up all dolled up.' I didn't know what to say to that, so he carried on. 'And you certainly wouldn't have been so nervous that you fell over!'

That shocked me into speaking. 'I tripped! I didn't fall because I was *nervous*.'

'Sure you didn't.'

'And I'm not dolled up. I'm just in disguise.' As soon as I said the words I screwed my face up. That wasn't what I'd meant to say at all. It wasn't even what I thought any more. Not really. Shit. Jonno gave a surprised bark of a laugh.

'You're what? In disguise? Are you a *spy*?'

I was close to tears of frustration. 'No!' I said. 'I'm not a spy. I didn't mean to say that, OK? I'm not in disguise. I just like to make an effort.'

He wasn't going to let it go. '*Disguise*. Is that how you see it? You're walking among us in your disguise? Are you totally fake? I have to say, Cat: you're obsessed with who's posh and who's not. The thing is, we don't care. I don't care how many fucking bathrooms you have. It's you who fixates on that stuff. If you think you're trying to disguise yourself as a rich person, then I have to say that's a bit pathetic.'

'You think I'm pathetic?'

We looked at each other. My knees were stinging. So were my hands and my chin. Everything was stinging.

I was, indeed, pathetic. I blinked hard. I saw his gaze, combative at first, soften. He stretched his hand out and, stupid as I was, I thought he was genuinely trying to make friends again. I reached out to pat his hand across the table. He turned his hand over and grabbed mine and somehow we were holding hands. His was warm and a bit sweaty. Mine was scraped and painful, and I had to pull it away.

'Sorry,' I said. 'Still hurts.'

'Cat,' he said. 'Sorry. Of course I don't think you're pathetic. To answer your question, I think you're gorgeous. Totally gorgeous. And real.'

He shifted his chair around so he was next to me, and then his arm was round my shoulders and he was pulling me towards him. I felt him kiss the top of my head. All the alarm bells went off at once. I needed to get out of here. Jonno was, I realized, about to attempt to kiss me.

I didn't want to kiss him.

He was doing to me what I'd tried to do to Henry.

I'd once admired him from afar, but I didn't want to kiss him. No part of me wanted that. How had I got this so wrong?

I tried to pull away, but he kept hold of me. He kissed my hair.

'You're not like other girls,' he murmured.

This was, it turned out, exactly the wrong thing for him to say, or, from my point of view, the right one. It woke me up: these words were a massive red flag. I had always hated the idea that for a girl to be cool she had to be different from other girls. I pulled away quite violently this time. He huffed at me.

'I hate that,' I said. 'Telling a girl she's not like the others. It's not a cool thing to say, Jonno.'

He put his hands up in mock surrender, which was, it turned out, incredibly irritating.

'Sorreeee,' he said. 'Message received. But I'm hardly going to say you *are* like other girls, am I? What am I meant to say?'

I picked up my bag. 'Nothing,' I told him. 'You're meant to say nothing.'

I stood up. Jonno took my arm.

'Seriously,' he said. 'You're actually storming off on me? Jesus, Cat. Sorry I said that. I didn't realize, OK? Educate me.'

I felt the anger bubbling up. I wasn't great at confrontation, and the last thing I wanted was to have a fight in public with someone I'd thought, until a few minutes ago, was my friend. I knew that Jonno had been in debating societies at school and uni, and I knew that if we started arguing he would win. He would somehow win in a way that would mean I had to end up spending the rest of the summer as his girlfriend.

Which, a few weeks ago, would have been a dream scenario. I was confused. I tried to pull away. He stopped me. I tried really hard not to cry. I failed.

'Please let me go.' My voice was quiet, catching, sobbing. I was desperate to get back to the apartment. To shut the door and cry.

'Jesus. Of course I'll let you go.' His voice was hard again now. 'I'm not some monster, whatever you think. If you're not interested, that's fine, but don't tell me you haven't been acting like you are, because you have.'

I burst into tears. I was stupid, and desperate to get away. He was still holding my arm. His fingers dug into my flesh.

'Sorry,' I said, hiccuping, hiding my face in my hands. 'Sorry if I gave you the wrong impression. I didn't –'

I stopped talking because I realized there was someone else standing at our table. Someone had appeared on the other side of me. Someone else put a hand on my shoulder. I flinched. The last thing I needed was another person here, witnessing whatever this was.

Then I looked round.

Just when I thought the evening couldn't possibly get any worse, I found I was standing between Jonno Thorpe and Henry Tilney.

14

We sat on a bench overlooking the sea. It was uncomfortably close to the place where we'd first met. My eyes kept drifting down to the water, scanning for a body that wasn't there.

'I didn't need rescuing,' I said.

He was silent for a moment. Then he said: 'I know. You were doing fine. All the same, I'm glad I was there. To help you leave. To get you away from him with the minimum of upset.'

The sun was setting and half the sky was pink and purple.

I suspected there was mascara all down my face. I knew that there was a scrape on my chin and that my eyes were puffy and red. Somehow, though, it didn't matter with Henry. I'd efficiently burned that bridge on my first night, which was weirdly freeing.

'God, I'm rubbish at everything,' I said. 'I think there's actually gonna be the *maximum* of upset there.'

'You're not rubbish at everything.' Henry paused. 'I think that Jonathan Thorpe has a very inflated idea of his own importance. If he learns a few lessons about whether or not a woman should be grateful if he decides he's going to go out with her, then good.'

I remembered Jonno talking about Henry, the first time I met him. '*Henry Tilney is a twat,*' he'd said. '*He used to be cool, but then he went weird.*'

'You two used to be friends, right?' I said.

'*Used to be* is right.' He gave me a sideways look, a grin. 'Particularly after this evening, I guess. Want to tell me what happened?'

I thought about it, and shook my head. Then I changed my mind. I took a deep breath.

'I thought we were going for a drink. Apparently I had it all wrong and it was a date. I had no idea.' Then I remembered. 'And I'm meant to be going to stay with them! On Saturday. For a week while Owen and Sophie are away for work.'

Henry was looking at me. His eyes were lovely. I knew I ought to be mortified that he'd found me like this, but I didn't have the energy for it.

He hesitated. He started to say something and stopped. Then he started again.

'Er – feel free to say no,' he said, 'but ... you're very welcome to stay with us. Nothing dodgy, I promise. We're a few hours from here so you won't run into Thorpe or any of his family. No need to answer now, but I promise it's a genuine offer. We have loads of space. My sister's home and you'll like her. My dad's not around at the moment. It's chill. You'd be super welcome. No pressure.'

I gave a little nod. Right now every part of me wanted to get out of town and far away from Jonno. But going to stay with Henry? Frying pans and fires?

Before I could even think about that, I knew I needed to clear the air.

'Um,' I said. I looked at the water. Its shimmer had gone as the sky had clouded over a little bit. It looked opaque now. There could be anything in there. 'You know before? When we went out? I'm . . .' My breath hitched and I closed my eyes. I had to say it. I didn't want to, but I forced it out. 'I'm sorry. About what I did. I was so drunk. I'd never been that drunk before, and I know I tried to . . . and you didn't want . . .'

It turned out that was all I could manage. I heard his voice again in my head. *I'd hate to.*

'Hey,' he said. I could hear the smile in his voice, even though I couldn't look at him. 'I wasn't sure if you remembered. I just – well, it didn't feel like the moment. I wanted to be sure you knew what you were doing. I didn't want you to regret things in the morning.'

I nodded. Mortified.

'I've never done anything like that before. I'm so, so embarrassed.'

He leaned towards me and butted me with his shoulder. 'Don't be.'

It was perfect. Exactly what I needed. I turned to him and smiled.

'Thank you. Um – if it's really OK to come to yours? I think I might like that.'

*

I was heading back to the apartment, plans with Henry made as long as Sophie agreed, when I ran into Aisha, sitting on a low wall in the square outside, writing in a notebook. She didn't look up until I was nearly there. Then she shoved the notebook quickly into her bag.

'Sorry!' She laughed at her own panic. 'Letter to my ex that I'll never send. No one must ever see that. Are you back from your drink? I was going to join you like you said, but Izzy told me not to.' She looked at me properly. 'Oh God – are you *hurt*?'

I closed my eyes and winced.

'Yeah,' I said. 'Turned out I had things a bit wrong.' I told her everything, and she took my less-scraped hand and walked towards the apartment with me.

'Don't worry about him at all,' she said. 'Honestly, babe. These things happen and they feel massive at the time, but actually you'll laugh about it soon, I promise. Come on. Let's get you in there. Tell Sophie about the change of plan. Don't worry! At least Henry was around to rescue you.' She paused. 'I'd have asked you to stay with me, Cat, but my wonky little room can't really accommodate two.'

Aisha came up to the apartment with me. Sophie was more upset by the change of plan than I'd expected. She almost looked as if she was going to cry. In fact, when I looked closely, she looked as if she *had* been crying.

'It was all sorted, though,' she said, and her voice wobbled. 'That was the one thing I *didn't* need to worry about and I don't think I can . . .' She stopped, and Aisha stepped in. She touched her arm and Sophie turned towards her.

'It's still sorted,' she said. 'Cat's got a new plan, and of course I don't know this Henry, but it sounds fine to me. Cat trusts him and that means a lot. And I'll be around here any time she needs anything.'

'You will?' Sophie said. She sniffed and pushed her hair back from her face.

'Absolutely. I promise. Just say the word, Cat, and I'll be there.'

'I'll be fine.' I put the kettle on. 'It's Jonno, Sophie. I thought we were going for a drink. He thought it was more than that. I can't go and stay with them after that! It'll be *so* awkward!'

I saw Sophie look over at Aisha.

'Can you imagine?' said Aisha.

'Well, yes. It does sound tricky,' said Sophie. She turned away. 'Owen?'

Owen couldn't have cared less. He put a suitcase beside the door, looked at the tea I was making and poured himself a brandy instead.

'Sounds fine,' he said. 'Cat can sort things out for herself.' He looked at Aisha. 'And it's good to know you're around too.'

Sophie sighed. 'As long as you'll be OK, my darling,' she said. 'Promise? Is Henry's dad going to be at Northanger?'

I frowned. 'Northanger? What's that?'

She looked at me, as puzzled as I was. 'Their house. Massive vineyard place. You see, that worries me a bit. You having all these plans to go there but not even knowing the name.'

'It's called *Northanger*? Like Jane Austen?'

'Oh, that was Elisabeth,' said Owen, who had popped out of the bedroom again. 'Henry's mum. Huge Austen fan. It was originally something else. North something. But she changed it. So yes – who else will be there?'

'Henry's dad's away. But Henry's twenty-one, and his sister's going to be around, and they have a housekeeper who comes in sometimes.' The idea of a housekeeper had blown my mind when Henry had mentioned her.

I saw Sophie and Owen looking at each other and making a wordless agreement. 'Well, if your mother's OK with it, then it's all right by us. You'll have plenty of space to spread out! So you'll check in with us, OK? Every day. Promise?'

'Promise,' I said. I looked at the amount of luggage that was piling up. Three massive suitcases, and they weren't even leaving until Saturday. 'So this thing in Dubai is a work meeting?'

'Yes,' said Sophie, at the same time that Owen said, 'Several.' Then they both laughed.

'Those things can require way more outfits than you'd ever imagine, Cat,' said Aisha. 'Right?'

Sophie nodded her agreement, clearly grateful.

I hadn't told Mum about the change of scene. I thought I might tell her when I got there.

I messaged Izzy to see if we could talk, but she left me on read.

*

At six on Saturday, Sophie tapped on my bedroom door and came in as I was yawning and doing my own packing.

'Right,' she said. 'We're about off, Cat. Keep your keys on you, and if you need to come here at any point, you must. Call Helena or Aisha if you need anything. I've filled your mother in. We'll be back in a week. This is your health insurance info. I put you on our policy. So if you need to see a doctor or anything like that then you'll need this.' I took a printout from her. 'And this too.' That one was a little plastic card. 'And if you have an emergency, it's not nine-nine-nine. It's one-one-two.'

I wanted to make everything as easy for Sophie as I could. I didn't know how.

'Thanks,' I said. There was a moment. A moment when the air in the room was bristling with unsaid things. I could feel that she wanted to tell me something. I hoped she would. I waited. Time stood still.

In the end, I cracked. 'Sophie – are you OK? Is there anything I can do to help?'

It was as if I'd flicked a switch. She shook her hair out, ran her fingers through it, stood up straighter and plastered a grin on her face.

'Of course I'm OK! And I'm so sorry, Cat. I was so excited to see what you and Izzy had been working on. Next week, OK? I promise we'll get it into shape. Plus this was supposed to be a perfectly relaxed summer and here we are, dashing off. But we'll be back to it in no time. This whole thing is such a drag. Now, you promise you're going to be all right? Please make it up with Hels's kids as soon as you can. Won't you? I know what it's like when you're young and things can be so volatile. I can see that a few days over at Northanger would be nice, but Hels says you're welcome back there any time. She's already made you up a bed in Izzy's dressing room. Let us know what you do, OK?'

She kept talking and I wished she would tell me what was really happening. My best guess was that Owen's work had hit a bigger problem than they were letting on. Imports and exports had to be complex. Maybe he needed her there for moral support. Practical support. It made no sense to be dashing to work meetings on a Saturday. I wished they'd trust me with the truth.

An hour later, they left, looking worried, with a million more instructions. Sophie enveloped me in a huge perfumey hug, and even Owen clasped me tightly, which was so off brand for him that, for the first time, I felt a bit scared. Also, up close he smelled of sweat, not cologne. What was going on?

But then they were off.

It was strange to be here on my own. The silence was loud. All Owen's stuff was cleared from the table. The door to their bedroom was closed, and I left it that way.

I went out on to the terrace and took my phone out. Izzy still hadn't replied and she'd also unfollowed me on Instagram, which honestly felt like an unnecessary slap in the face. I hadn't heard anything from Jonno. Now, I had messages from Kitty, Aisha and Henry.

I looked at Henry's first.

All OK? Leaving home now. We'll be there at ten. Will call from car park.

I replied to him with a quick Amazing!, and then turned my attention to the other messages. Kitty had sent a voice note: 'Oh my God, I can't believe I have to stop fancying JT. But I will! Solidarity. Fuck him, right? Everyone here says hi.'

I smiled at the phone. I had people in my life. Real people. It would be OK.

Aisha's message said, Have they left? You OK? I'm at Gravette if you fancy it before you head off?

Ten minutes later, I was back in the water, swimming for the first time since Eva. The sea was smooth and warm, the sky a deep blue. Whatever was going on, I knew I'd be OK.

PART TWO

15

Henry and his sister pulled into the car park at ten past ten. He was driving a light-blue convertible with the roof down.

'Oh nice,' said Aisha, who had helped me get my bag from the apartment. Not that I'd needed help, because I wasn't taking all my stuff, but I'd been incredibly grateful for the company. She'd made us a post-swim coffee and we'd sat on the terrace together. I was a person who drank coffee now (still with two sugars, though).

I looked at Aisha.

'Right? Where am I even going?'

'God knows, but you promise to send photos?'

They both got out as we walked over to the car. When I saw Eleanor, I took half a step back. She was the most intimidating person I'd ever met.

Although she was shorter than me, she had so much presence. She had short pink hair, a lot of piercings in each ear and in her nose, and she was wearing ripped denim shorts and a T-shirt that said *X-Ray Spex* on it. I didn't know what that meant, but it was probably a band.

'Hey!' She came up to me and kissed me on each cheek. 'You're Cat, right? I'm El. Welcome!'

I saw her look at Aisha with a question.

'This is Aisha,' I said, instantly relieved by how easy this was. 'My friend.'

While they said hello, Henry put my bag into the boot of the car, and a couple of minutes later I was hugging Aisha and we were off. El was driving, and they'd made me sit in the front even though the back seat was tiny and had no room for Henry's long legs. She beeped as we left the car park, and we all waved.

By the time we turned off the road and headed down a bumpy driveway, a couple of hours later, I felt my face beginning to hurt from all the grinning I'd been doing.

Henry and Eleanor had made me laugh all the way. They'd played loud music and we'd yelled along with it. I already knew, or hoped, that El would be my friend in the way I'd wanted Izzy to be, the way that, until the other day, I'd thought Izzy was.

El was nineteen and she lived mainly in Berlin because she was by far the coolest person I'd ever met. The only half weird thing that had happened on the journey was El looking across at me from the driver's seat and saying, 'Right. Someone has to say it. Is there something weird going on with the Allens? I barely even know them, but everyone's saying they've shut up shop and run away. And you live with them! And they've booted you out. So you must know.'

I started to say no, without thinking. *No, they've just had to go to deal with a work crisis.* But then I stopped myself. I remembered Sophie's puffy face. Owen's tight hug.

I did actually think there might be something weird going on. Now that they were on their way to Dubai, I was hoping they were OK.

'Actually,' I said, 'I don't know. They said they were going to some meetings. But yes. I think there's stuff they're not saying. I have no idea what it is. I don't know why they had to go at the weekend.'

I got out my phone and sent Sophie a quick text.

Hey Sophie! We're nearly there, at Northanger. All fine. How are things with you? Hope you're both doing OK, whatever's going on. See you next week xxx

I looked at it. That was the most I had ever alluded to the fact that we all knew this trip was more than they were saying it was. I sent it.

El was quiet for a bit. 'Dubai, yeah?'

'Yeah?' It came out as a question. 'For a meeting? A business thing?'

'But their work is South America based?'

I nodded.

I saw Eleanor looking at Henry in the rear-view mirror. Something passed between them.

'I mean,' I said, 'I have no idea what's going on with them. One minute they were just here for the summer like they always are, and then they had to go. But maybe that's what they do. I don't know. Why – what do you think's happening?'

She laughed. 'Good question. No idea. I know they've been . . .' She trailed off and shook her head.

'They've been what? You can't say that and then stop talking!'

She shrugged. 'I don't know. I think they had a . . . wobble. A year or two ago. Maritally. I wonder if it's something to do with that.'

'Oh God, really?' It had never occurred to me for a second that Sophie and Owen were anything but rock solid. I tried to make it make sense, but then I stopped thinking about it because I knew we were about to arrive.

I was delighted that their dad was away. I didn't know anything about their mum at all apart from the fact that she'd renamed the house: in fact, I was certain Henry hadn't mentioned her that first evening – *urgh!* I still couldn't think about it without cringing. I hoped it would come up in conversation at some point, but it was clear she wasn't around. All I had to go on was Owen saying she was called Elisabeth. That was it.

The drive was stony and narrow. It took us steeply uphill, and then it curved round a corner and a house appeared in front of us.

I'd expected something big, but this was *spectacular*. Enormous. A big square block of stone.

'Home sweet home.' Eleanor slowed down. 'Oh! Shit.'

'What?' I couldn't see anything wrong. Eleanor pointed to a battered-looking car parked over at the edge of the drive, two wheels on the grass. It was green, scratched and dented. A Citroën.

'Dad's here.' Her voice was flat.

'He wasn't,' said Henry, from the back, 'when we left this morning. He was staying at the coast for a couple more weeks to . . . Yet here he is, it appears.'

I sensed them looking at each other. Neither of them said anything for a moment, and then they both burst out laughing.

'It's Cat,' said El. 'He came back to meet your . . . *friend*.'

'Oh God . . .' said Henry. 'Sorry, Cat. Sincerest apologies.'

I tried not to react as I watched my relaxed week evaporating. Coming here had been the easy option. The nice, carefree one. The one that took me away from Jonno and his family, away from the awkwardness. The fact that their dad wasn't around was going to make it totally fun.

But, I told myself, it would still be fine. Henry and El were easy company. They were friendly and funny, and so of course their dad would be the same. With an adult in the house, things would be more sensible. I guessed I'd be less likely to fling myself at Henry again after a few more drinks.

I cringed at the idea. Yeah. At least that wouldn't happen. Being close to him was confusing because I couldn't help it: I liked him a lot. But I was going to be Ms Cautious around him.

El parked behind the green car, switched the engine off and turned to me.

'OK. So – Dad has a strange exterior, but he's actually fine. He'll really like you. He's a big fan of the Allens so you come pre-approved.' She gave me a little smile. 'Plus, you're much more the way he thinks a girl should be than I am. Imagine what an old Tory army guy thinks of the fact that his only daughter is *this*?' She pointed at herself.

An old Tory army guy. Oh no.

Henry opened the back door and unspooled his legs. 'Don't listen. He adores El. She's by far his favourite.'

'I am not,' she said. 'You're not either, obviously.'

'Well, I know my place,' said Henry. 'Third.'

I frowned. 'Third? Out of two? Harsh.'

I opened the car door and stepped out, working hard to keep my dress from riding up.

'Third of three,' said Henry.

'We have another brother,' El said, pulling things out of the boot of the car. 'Didn't Henry tell you about golden boy?'

I helped her. My silence answered the question. We had talked for hours, and I didn't think he'd mentioned a brother.

'Big brother's a banker in London,' said Henry. 'You won't meet him. Anyway, welcome.'

As I picked up my bag and pulled it on to my shoulder, I looked over at the green car. It didn't seem like the sort of car a Tory army guy would drive. Its boot was filled with branches and rubble. Garden waste. Maybe this was a crappy car he just used for that kind of thing and there were loads of others somewhere.

I stood on the gravelly drive and looked up.

Although the house before me was massive, it looked friendly somehow. There were pale-blue shutters at every window, and flowers in window boxes. A bicycle leaned against the wall. It was a mixture of crumbling (spiderwebs, peeling paint), and modern (a video doorbell). A creeper, covered in flowers, grew up the side of the house, and those trees with thin leaves (olive trees maybe?) stood in pots on each side of the door. It looked like a painting.

I stared around. Both siblings saw me looking and smiled.

'It never changes,' said El.

'Technically, it does,' said Henry. 'Dad's always changing things. The shutters were green before and he's been building some kind of shed in the garden, hence all the . . .' He waved at the rubbish in the green car. 'But yes. At the same time, it never changes. Even if he swapped every brick one by one it would still be the same house. Like the philosopher's axe or whatever.'

I was wondering immediately about a podcast series that uncovered the secrets of this place. A nice, straightforward podcast that didn't make me feel bad in the way that talking about Eva's death had done. I wasn't collaborating with Izzy any more after all. I could move on and do this on my own. Work on it with Sophie when she was back. I was thinking about how you would describe it using only a few words. You couldn't just say *lovely*. I remembered having that same conundrum when I first looked at the Med from Sophie and Owen's balcony.

'How many rooms are there?' I said. 'I mean, it looks huge.'

They looked at each other.

'Never counted,' said Henry. 'But –'

He broke off as the front door opened. A man stood in front of us and my heartbeat sped up. I was looking at a tall, beaming guy ... not a guy. A *gentleman*. He was wearing a baggy woollen jumper with a Christmas tree on it. He had short grey hair and a moustache.

I'd seen him before. I was sure I had, though I couldn't place him. Our eyes met and I thought I saw a flash of recognition. Then it was gone.

'Ahhh!' he said. 'Welcome. This must be Cat.'

I could see him in Henry: he had the same gangling quality, though his dad had the kind of posture that made him look as if he did a lot of yoga, but which I supposed was probably actually from the army, given what El had just said.

'Dad!' said El, and she stepped forward to hug him. 'Where did you spring from? And what the hell is this?' She pinched his jumper between finger and thumb and looked at it. 'We're in *August*. What's with the Christmas jumper?'

He looked down and huffed all his breath out through his nose. 'Ahh. Stone walls, stone floors, indolence. I was doing the crossword and I got cold so I grabbed a pullover. Didn't notice it was the festive one.' He looked up, chuckling, and his eyes fixed on mine again. I smiled and his grin widened. His eyes were dark like Henry's.

Henry stepped forward. 'Dad? This is my . . . friend Cat. As you know.'

'Caitlin Morland,' he said with a nod. 'I've heard all about you.' He stepped forward and I wasn't sure whether I was meant to shake his hand or something else, but then he was kissing me on each cheek like a French person. He smelled nice, as if he was wearing a floral cologne. His moustache was scratchy, but it wasn't horrible.

Then he stood back and smiled at me. His eyes crinkled and he looked genuinely pleased to be meeting me. That flash of mutual recognition was gone and I decided I'd been mistaken.

'I admit it,' he said. 'I came back here to meet you, Cat. Always a delight to have a house guest. Just by being here, you're brightening up my life.'

'That's very kind of you,' I said. I almost believed him.

'It gets dull when the kids are away. We're remote here and when you're old and alone, the crowds don't exactly beat their way to your door. I recently lost a dear friend, and to be honest I'm a lonely old man. So thank you for visiting. You must make yourself entirely at home. Please.'

I gave him my best smile; I was genuinely relieved that he was nice.

Then he nodded to Henry.

'I see what you mean,' he said.

I looked to Henry, but he was blushing. Henry hadn't struck me as a person who blushed and I wondered what on earth he had said to his father about me. Oh God, I hoped he hadn't told him about that first night.

And what should I call him? Mr Tilney? Some army title? His first name? Whatever that was. I hoped I would never have to address him directly.

'Come on, Cat,' said El. 'Let's be sexist. We'll let Henry and Dad sort the bags. I'll show you around.'

I let her lead me into the house and, even though I'd known it was going to be beautiful, it took my breath away.

The entrance hall was huge, with a wide staircase leading up to a gallery that ran round the edge of the hall upstairs, with doors leading off it. There were guns mounted on the walls. Actual guns, displayed. I tried not to look at them, but I wondered if they were loaded. I hoped not. No. Of course they wouldn't be.

There was also a piece of art, an oil painting of lavender fields and grapevines. I loved it. There was something familiar about it, though that was probably just the fact that we'd been driving through that landscape for about an hour and a half.

Mr Tilney was right: it was cool the moment you stepped inside and I could see how you might end up in a Christmas jumper if you sat still for an hour or so. The floor tiles were pale stone apart from the stairs, which looked a bit incongruous with their fluffy blue carpet. All the walls were thick stone.

El was smiling, watching me taking it all in.

'Come on,' she said. 'I'll show you to your room first. Then we'll have a proper look around.'

She set off up the staircase, taking them two at a time, and I followed, one at a time. At the top, she walked part of the way round the gallery, which had a wooden bannister on the side that overlooked the entrance hall, and then took a door on the right and set off down a corridor.

I felt lost at once. There was no way I was going to remember the way from my bedroom back to the entrance hall. Whenever we passed an open door, I looked in, and I saw rooms with sofas, rooms with tables, rooms that appeared to be empty, but we never paused for long enough for me to be able to see anything properly.

Then she set off up another set of stairs. The second floor was smaller; it felt cosy. El opened a door and motioned me in.

'This one OK?' she said. 'You're next to me. I love it up here so I thought you might too. It's the attic, obviously, which I think is nice. We get the view from up here.'

I walked into the room, which was bigger than I would have expected an attic to be, with a sloping ceiling, a double bed made up with a pale-blue duvet, and a red patterned rug on the floor that was probably worth more than our car at home.

I followed El over to the window. We stood and looked out. The Provençal countryside was spread out before us: fields, houses, twisting lanes. In the distance, a field was completely purple. On the horizon, there was a row of what looked like mountains. The whole thing shimmered in the sun. I watched a distant car snaking along the road. It was totally different from the bright brashness of the Riviera.

When I looked down, I could see that our bags must be in already, as the roof was back on the car and no one was out there.

I looked at El.

'This is incredible,' I said. 'I mean, I knew your house was going to be nice, but . . .'

She nodded. 'So this room's OK for you? You can have one on the floor below near to Henry's if you like.'

I blushed at the thought of Henry in a bedroom capacity, but was filled with gratitude at how completely she had accepted me as a friend, even though we'd only just met.

'I love it!'

'I'll show you where the bathroom is. You share just with me. Come on and I'll give you a tour of everything else. Honestly, the kitchen is the place where it all happens.'

El turned and left the room, and I followed.

'Here's me. Same room, other way round.'

She stepped back and indicated her room with a hand gesture. I stood in the doorway and looked in. It was, indeed, a mirror image of my room except that Eleanor's was full of stuff. A free-standing rail held an array of brightly coloured clothes. There was a dressing table covered in make-up and jewellery and bits and pieces, with Polaroid pictures of El and various other cool-looking people tucked in around the edge of a mirror.

A group of photos in frames was hanging on the wall above her bed. I stepped into the room to look at them. They all showed the same woman. She was beautiful with dark hair, huge eyes and high cheekbones. In some of the pictures, she was holding a baby, in others a toddler. She and a tiny version of Eleanor, with dark hair and a serious face, were looking at a book together, cuddled into an armchair.

El saw me looking.

'Yeah, that's my mum,' she said. There were a few seconds' silence, during which I knew I needed to say something. I cast around for the right words, but it was hard because I didn't know what the situation was.

'She looks lovely,' was all I managed.

El smiled at the pictures. 'She was the best person in the world.' We both looked at the photos for a moment. Then El spoke quickly. 'She was always leaving little notes and pictures for me. I've got a collection of them. Can I show you?'

She opened a drawer in her bedside table and took out a pile of pieces of paper. Thick paper, torn from a sketch book. They had pencil drawings on them, and words written underneath. I saw a picture of a cat, a picture of a little girl, a picture of a flower before she put them away.

'Did she . . . ?' I didn't even want to say the word.

'Died, yeah. I was thirteen. Shit age for it. I guess there's no good age, and maybe it's better that at least I remember her clearly, but . . . suddenly I was the only girl in this family of alpha guys. Or, two alphas and Henry. I think you need your mum when you're thirteen. A lot. And the years after. But suddenly she was gone.'

I thought about my own mother. She knew I was here. She'd replied to my message telling her that with a thumbs-up emoji, which I actually thought was worse than not replying at all.

I needed to talk to her. To clear the air.

'Can I . . . Can I ask what happened?'

El turned and looked at me, then suddenly smiled. 'Course you can. It was years ago, Cat. I don't have a problem with talking about her: in fact, I have more of a problem with *not* talking about her, which is Henry's approach. And Dad's. It's only me and Fritz who ever mention her. She had an accident. She tripped at the top of the stairs. The massive stone staircase? She fell all the way down it, and hit her head, and she died. Just like that, instantly. Fine one minute, then dead. I was away at school. We all came home, but it was . . .'

'Oh my God!' I put an arm round her shoulder, feeling self-conscious, but she didn't push me away. She leaned on me a bit. We'd just come up that staircase. How did Eleanor do that?

'That's why it's the only bit of the house with carpet. To stop it happening again. I drove myself crazy trying to invent time travel. I seriously did. I spent about a year figuring out how it could work, because the only thing I wanted to do was to time travel back and wait at the top of the stairs to save her. Took me ages to accept that wasn't going to happen. And we don't know exactly what happened that day. I've always wondered, but Dad didn't see, nobody did, and so we'll never know.

'I'll tell you what – it's pretty dark to find yourself wishing your mum had had a terminal illness because that way you'd have had time to get used to the idea, and to talk to her before she went. And she could have left you real letters. If she'd known she was going to die, she'd have left me so many pictures. So many words. I used to try really hard to imagine that she'd just run away. I thought she'd come back for me one day.' She pulled away and gave me a sad little smile, eyes glistening. 'Still waiting.'

'That's terrible.' It was hard to say the right thing, because everything sounded like a cliché. 'I can't imagine. The shock. Were your brothers at school too?'

'Yeah. It was awful for all of us, and then Dad didn't know what to do so he just sent us back to school after a couple of weeks. Yeah. Back to boarding school in another country, where we were supposed to deal with the fact that we didn't have a mum any more. I'd only started at Swithun's a year earlier. That's the school.'

Now I wasn't second-guessing my reaction. 'Oh my God, El! That's awful. I'm so sorry.'

She set off down the corridor and after a moment I followed.

'It wasn't quite as heartless as I've made it sound.' Her tone was lighter now. 'I mean, it *was* – losing your mum at thirteen is every bit as terrible as you'd think it might be. Worse. A horror show. But, to be fair to my dad, he did ask if I wanted to stay here. I could have lived at home and slotted back in with my old friends at the local school. In a way I wanted to, but then ... well, the idea of being in this massive house. Just Dad and me. Without Mum or the boys. In the actual place where she died. It somehow seemed worse, and the boys were going back to school and mine wasn't far from theirs, so in the end I took that. Being a few miles from Fritz and Henry, but particularly H. With dispensation from our stupid schools to see each other at weekends. We had family nearby and I did escape to see them from time to time. So this is the bathroom.'

I inhaled sharply at the change of topic, and stood next to her to look in through the door. It had a sloping ceiling and just enough floor space for a shower, loo and basin. There was a vase of dried flowers on a little table, and a pile of towels next to it, and the walls were bright white.

'Pretty,' I said.

'I know it's not bath season, but if you ever did want one there are other bathrooms you could use. One has a free-standing roll-top thing. It's gorgeous. Just shout and I'll take you there, any time.'

'Thanks.' I couldn't imagine wanting to stew in hot water. It was something I was never able to do at home, sharing one bathroom with a minimum of six other people. However, *a free-standing roll-top thing* did sound nice.

I wanted to ask Eleanor more about her mother, but of course I couldn't. She had closed the subject. A treacherous part of my brain was thinking *this would make a great podcast*. The idea of someone falling down the stairs and landing in a way that killed them instantly was terrifying. And with no witnesses. She must have tripped? I thought of the Netflix show *The Staircase*.

Then I thought of the look in Eleanor's eyes. This was her real life. I couldn't poke around her home, wondering if there was more to what had happened. Besides, it was usually the husband, and their dad was a kind, lonely man who sometimes found himself wearing Christmas jumpers in August.

Plus I was a guest in his home. Although I couldn't wait to record my impressions of this house, I needed to leave the whole tragedy thing alone.

16

Eleanor showed me around the rest of the house, and I knew I would never remember where anything was. The part I did remember, though, was that Henry's room was on the floor below mine. It was large, with two windows that overlooked a hillside covered in vines, and my heartbeat sped up as I looked at it. Henry wasn't with us, and it felt intimate and exciting to be looking into his room. The rumpled sheets, the book face-down on the bedside table. The clothes on a chair, the plugged-in charger. There was a smell of Henry about the place. I had a flutter in my stomach.

The room was gorgeous, with yellow walls shining in the late-afternoon sun. There was a lot of polished floorboard, and there were shelves and shelves of books. The next door down from Henry's was a linen cupboard, but El opened it anyway.

'Henry's cupboard,' she said. 'He used to shut himself in here and ignore us all. He'd do it for hours, with a book and a torch. He'll love that I've told you that.'

Round the next corner there was a corridor with just one door on it. Eleanor didn't stop.

'What's this one?' I asked.

She hesitated, then huffed all her breath out. 'Mum had her own rooms,' she said. 'Her studio was in there. She was a painter. Not as a career, but she did sell some. Anyway, it's locked now. Dad doesn't want anyone going in. He loved her art, and it's too much for him.' She forced a smile. 'You know, he's never got over her. He never will. We were kind of dreading the idea that he'd remarry at some point. He's had relationships, I think, but most of them he keeps secret and they don't seem to last. To be honest, I prefer not to think about it. But maybe he'll remarry one day. Who knows? It's different for men, isn't it? They can be old and still sexy, unlike women.'

'Women can be old and sexy,' I said, though I couldn't imagine finding anyone of either sex above, say, forty in the least bit attractive. Gross.

Eleanor flashed me a grin. 'Well, you know that and I know that. Anyway, we don't go in Mum's studio.' She paused. 'I have no idea if Dad does. He'd never talk about it so we'll never know.'

When we finally reached the kitchen, I saw that El had been right. It felt like the heart of the home.

There was a huge wooden table in the middle of the room, with kitchen stuff around the edge. Pans, shelves, a row of labelled keys hanging down. Henry was sitting at the table drinking from a mug that said *Je m'en fous* on it, and when I saw him I felt the smile changing my face and wondered whether I ought to try to be a bit less obvious. Whatever polite things he might say, we both knew I had blown my chances with him, but he had rescued me from having to stay with the Thorpes after being ambushed by Jonno. The one thing I had learned from both those encounters was the fact that I was shit at going on dates. Or even knowing what one was.

Henry stood up when we came in. 'There you are! Coffee? Tea? Even though we're in deepest Provence we can offer a traditional English cup of tea if you'd like one, Cat? Or a tisane? A cold drink? I'm on the coffee, but I can make you anything you'd like.'

El laughed. 'I like this version of you, H. So helpful! Cat, please visit more often.'

'A cup of tea would be lovely,' I said, hearing my voice sounding overly polite. 'If that's really OK?'

'Of course!' He went over to the kettle and switched it on, and then took a yellow teapot from a shelf, poured in a bit of hot water and tipped it away. Then he started spooning loose tea into it. I had never made tea like this, had never seen anyone make tea this way. I was fascinated. I wouldn't have asked for it if I'd known it was going to be this much hassle.

Mr Tilney came in, and so did a black-and-white cat, slinking around his legs.

'Ah!' he said. 'Making tea! Exactly what I was after.'

I held out my hand to the cat, and it came over and let me stroke it.

'You and Cat are on the same page there,' said Henry. 'It was her beverage of choice too. Cat, meet Minou. She clearly approves of you.'

'Get me a coffee?' said Eleanor.

Mr Tilney gave me a conspiratorial look and shook his head.

'Coffee's for mornings, don't you think, Cat?' he said. Minou stalked out of the door, on to the terrace outside and sat down in a patch of sunshine.

'I'm still trying to get used to coffee,' I admitted. 'I can only do it with lots of sugar. You'll probably hate this, but at home my mum has instant.'

He laughed. 'Instant coffee! It's a different drink entirely, don't you think? It has its place. Bet the Allens don't drink instant, though?'

'They don't,' I said. 'They have a machine. In Antibes and also in Cornwall and probably in ... wherever else they live.' I realized I didn't know where that was. They had a third place somewhere snowy: they went skiing there.

'They have a chalet in Courchevel, don't they?' he said. 'I think it's close to my brother's.' I nodded, pretending I already knew that. 'Do you happen to know what's going on with them right now, Cat? With the business? I keep hearing people talking about them, but it all seems very mysterious.'

He said it so casually, but I knew that, like when Henry and El had asked, he really wanted to know. I wished I could offer any kind of answer, even though it would have fed what was clearly a lot of speculation that was swirling around. But I couldn't. For one thing, Sophie and Owen had been incredibly good to me, and, for another, I didn't know anything.

'Not really,' I said. 'They're in Dubai. At least, they're on their way there. They had to go for some meetings for Owen's work, but I don't know anything more than that.'

I thought of how upset Sophie had been. I reminded myself not to gossip.

'Ahh,' he said, and changed the subject. 'So we've saved you from having to stay with the Thorpe family, have we? Pleased to be of service. I've always found them a bit dreadful.'

'They've been really nice to me,' I said. 'But then ... Jonno and I had a bit of a misunderstanding.'

'Their boy? I thought he seemed a decent chap.' My eyes met Mr Tilney's and he smiled. 'But what do I know? If he's upset you, then I will concur with Henry that the boy's an arsehole.' I laughed, relieved, and the conversation moved on.

'Cat's from Cornwall,' Henry said as he handed out the drinks.

'Dad, why have you never taken us to Cornwall?' said El. 'It sounds gorgeous. Not fair.' She stuck her lip out, fake petulant. Her father sighed.

'Because you've grown up on a vineyard in Provence, sweetheart. Excuse me for not taking you hundreds of miles – a thousand, perhaps? – to a sea-swept corner of the continent. We can't go everywhere. And you can get more or less the same effect in Brittany, and we went there, didn't we?'

I sat back and listened as they talked about old holidays. Italy, the Caribbean, Australia, California. I couldn't begin to imagine how one family could be rich enough to do all this. And to send three children to boarding school, and to send them straight back after their mother had died.

Every now and then one of them would try to include me in the conversations, but I had nothing to contribute. I hadn't been to any of these places, though when the Philippines got a mention I was able to say, 'My dad lived there.'

Henry turned to me. 'Seriously?'

I shrugged. 'I never visited. I didn't know him, really. He died about four years ago and I didn't go over for the funeral. Some of his family arranged a memorial in Devon and my mum took me to that instead. He used to send me birthday and Christmas cards, but I hadn't seen him for years when he died.'

I stopped, ambushed by the memory. Mum leaving the twins with Bill and coming to Devon with me to hold my hand while I tried to work out how to grieve for a man I hadn't known.

'So you've lost a parent too.' El's voice was quiet.

'It was different,' I said, also lowering my voice. I really didn't think of myself as having lost a parent in the way Henry and El had. 'He was an addict. He ended up over there because he was running away from things. Mum chucked him out when I was about three. I never saw him again.'

There was, weirdly, a prickling at the back of my eyes. El shifted her chair over so it was next to mine and put an arm round my shoulders.

*

Late in the afternoon, Henry invited me out for a walk in the vineyard. On his advice, I put on proper shoes, though my not-Converse trainers weren't really *proper* in the way his sturdy Timberlands were.

We walked down the garden. There was the brand-new-looking shed at the edge of a patch of scratchy grass with loose earth around it, dry and powdery.

The sun was low in the sky as we stepped over a little ditch into a field. The hillside stretched out with its straight rows of grapevines. I turned my face into the light and closed my eyes. I breathed in the plants and flowers and a musty, wineish smell that I supposed was the grapes.

'This place is amazing,' I said, opening my eyes. I knew my words were trite, but was all I could manage. 'So all this – the vines and everything – it's all yours?'

Henry smiled down at me. He shrugged. 'The vines technically aren't any more. Dad had to sell them off to keep the house running. But we still get to walk in the fields. Everyone knows everyone around here and they'd never tell us to get off their land or whatever. So it doesn't feel any different.' He paused. 'Actually, it's nice to see it through new eyes. Sometimes . . . when I'm away, it doesn't always call me back. You know? It's not necessarily been a happy place. Things have happened here. Well, one thing. Sometimes my little room in Oxford felt far more homey than this.'

I touched his arm. 'El told me, Henry. What happened to your mum. I'm so sorry.'

He nodded and turned to look back at the house, so I turned too. Two of the shutters were closed and all the rest were open.

'Thanks,' he said. I felt strange standing so close to him. I really did fancy him, but I wasn't going to let that fact make me do stupid things again.

'So you're all done with uni?' That felt like a bland enough question.

'I am! Graduation was in July. Two days after I met you, in fact.'

I winced at the memory of that night and focused on what he'd said instead.

'You flew over to Oxford and back?'

'I did.'

'You didn't say.'

He shrugged. 'It didn't feel interesting.'

'So what's next?'

I had probably asked him this that night, but, if so, I couldn't remember the answer.

'An excellent question, Cat,' he said. 'If I was doing things properly, I'd have got myself a training contract in some lucrative field, all lined up. Banking, like my brother, for example. Or perhaps I'd have a place at law school, and be ready to do a year's conversion course followed by a career as a solicitor. At the very least, I should have bothered to get myself a place on a master's course somewhere in the world. And yet . . .' He spread his arms wide. 'I seem to have done none of it. And do you know why that is?'

I shook my head, not sure whether I was actually meant to answer.

'It's because I'm lazy, Cat. I didn't want to. It was easier not to apply for things when everyone else was doing it. So here I am, standing in a field.'

'It's your field, though,' I said. 'Or, at least, the field outside your house. Which makes it different.'

We crossed through the vines. Henry stepped easily over a ditch when we reached the edge and held out a hand to help me follow. Our hands touched: I had kind of expected an electric shock between us (this was the first time we'd properly touched since that awful night), but what I got instead was warmth. A warmth that warmed me all the way through. That pulled me in. That made me want to . . .

But no. I wasn't going to make that mistake again. Still, he kept hold of my hand.

We looked at each other.

He reached out and stroked my hair. He tucked it behind my ear and looked at me with something lovely in his eyes. I held my breath. I wasn't doing anything to mess it up this time.

Our lips met.

17

I closed my bedroom door and stood by the window to message Sophie.

Arrived at Northanger, I wrote. All fine. House is amazing!!! Henry's dad is here and he seems lovely.

I sent it and looked at the message, instantly regretting the word amazing and all the exclamation marks because it might look as if I thought this place was better than the apartment. I knew the message would stay single-ticked because she would still be on the plane, so I was surprised when the ticks doubled and then turned blue.

I worked it out in my head: they might actually have landed by now.

I waited for her to reply, but she didn't.

I lay on my bed and relived my kiss with Henry. It had been the lightest of kisses, just a brush on the lips, but it had made my whole being leap to attention. Every part of my body had wanted more. Every atom was straining to get closer to him. A kiss on the lips. *Is that all?* My body was screaming at me to do more. I'd have kissed him properly. I'd have pulled him back here, to my bedroom, to carry on. But he'd just stepped away and smiled, and I'd remembered not to push it and stepped away too.

He'd kissed me on my first day at Northanger: that had to mean there was more to come. I had successfully avoided messing things up, and that was a massive win. I needed to be patient.

How did everyone else do it? Even my own mother, who was chaotic and sad most of the time, had been married twice. Yeah, my dad had been a fuck-up, but she'd got it right with Bill.

Sophie and Owen had always seemed perfect. Though Sophie had been upset to get a call from another man, and Owen hadn't liked it at all. I remembered what El had said about their marital wobble. That must have just been gossip, though. They adored each other.

I decided to record my impressions of Northanger so far. It was part of my French summer, and I could do it without Izzy, and share it with Sophie when she was back. I could talk about the house, the tea, the smell of the vines.

When I picked up my phone, though, and looked at the screen photo, which I'd changed to an Antibes seascape, I thought of Mum again. I needed to tell her I was here. I wanted to hear her voice. I thought about everything El and Henry had been through, and although they thought I understood because of my dad, I really didn't. I still had my mother and I needed to fix things with her.

She didn't answer.

I felt awful about that call from the beach: I knew it had upset Mum. I had already known that it was important for her mental health not to surprise her with strangers, but I'd done it anyway.

Ethan and Dash were five and it was school holidays now, so they were going to be rushing around like rockets, agitating to go to the park and the beach and the shops and the park again. The boy twins' lives had been turned upside down when the second set of babies arrived. Mum had lost the plot, and I'd ended up taking them to the playground all the time. They loved me to push them on the swings. They would yell: 'Higher, Cat! Higher, Cat!', and I would pretend I thought they were saying hello.

'Hi!' I'd say. 'Hiya!'

'NO! Higher!'

I'd string it out for as long as I could, then I'd slap my forehead.

'Oh! You want to go higher? Why didn't you say?'

It wasn't a brilliant comedy routine, but to the boys it had been everything. It was literally the funniest joke they had ever heard. I missed people who loved me like my siblings did. Who thought I was wonderful when I was just being myself.

I wrote a message on my group chat with Kitty and Mabel.

Hey. Either of you home? I really want to talk to Mum and she's not answering. Are they all OK?

I closed my eyes and tried to visualize them. It didn't really work, so I opened my eyes and scrolled through old photos on my phone.

I saw my little brothers as babies, as toddlers, as annoying little kids who got into everything and messed it up. I saw them in their school uniforms, smart before school and chaotic afterwards. All of them wanting the same person for comfort. Mum.

I really wanted to talk to her.

Soz. We're in Bristol w our Mum. All fine tho! you know it xx

I forced myself to put the phone down. Bill's voice was in my head. *'If you spend one second worrying about us back here, that's a second wasted.'* That was what he'd said, on that rainy drive to the station. I'd promised.

I kept my phone out, hoping she would call me back, and turned my mind to the present. I was at Northanger. I was here with Henry and he'd kissed me and we would kiss again and, even though I was trying to keep my feelings under control, I was obsessed. And I'd met El, and she already felt like a friend.

I looked at my phone screen again. A text landed but was just from Jonno.

A word of advice. Next time you're not interested in someone, don't act like you're all over them. You're not all that.

It was the fourth he'd sent me, and they were all basically the same. All 'words of advice'. I deleted it and then blocked him, trying to convince myself he was all part of my summer experience and if I was feeling brave enough I could bring our non-date into my summer podcast.

That galvanized me. I remembered Sophie telling me to be clear about the physical geography of places as I talked. I grabbed my notebook and sketched out what I thought was a floor plan of the layout of this house. I walked through the corridors in my mind and realized that my room, and Eleanor's, were both above her mother's. Almost one hundred per cent. I looked at the wooden floor, wondering whether I could lift a floorboard and look down into Elisabeth's studio.

The story about Henry's mum was awful. The idea that she had just tripped at the top of the stairs and died. Gone, in a second. Bodies were fragile.

I wondered how they could do it. How did you live in a place in which your mother had died?

I walked around my room, touching the furniture. I wanted Henry's house to absorb me. There was a chest of drawers, a sturdy wooden wardrobe, a little writing desk with a drawer. I supposed I could unpack. I opened drawers and began to put my things away. The stuff I'd brought from home looked rubbish in what was practically a chateau, but then again it had looked rubbish in Antibes too.

I nearly didn't open the bottom drawer. All my clothes had fitted easily into the top two because a lot of my things were still in Antibes. I only knelt on the floor to open the last one because it was there, because I wanted to look at everything I could. And then, even when I did open it I almost missed the piece of paper.

It was right at the back, stuck into the join at the corner: a piece of plain paper folded into quarters, ragged at the edges. I used my fingernails to pull it out, which took a while as it was properly wedged in. Eventually I opened it, then stared at the words and the picture in front of me.

The picture was a pencil sketch of a man, and it matched exactly the style of the drawings from her mum that El had shown me. The man wasn't Henry's dad (or whatever I was meant to call him). It was someone else: a younger man with thick dark hair and a clean-shaven face. He looked handsome, in a rugged and oldish sort of way.

The words were underneath it. They were also in pencil, in beautiful French-style handwriting.

Il me tuera.

I took out my phone and put them into the translation app.

I stared at the words. I read them over and over and over again.

He will kill me.

18

I couldn't show the drawing to Eleanor. I couldn't show it to Henry. I certainly wasn't going to show their dad. My heart was pounding. I had no idea if this really meant what it seemed to mean. It must have been written and drawn by Elisabeth: it was exactly like El's pictures except that where they were lovely, this was chilling. I looked around the room, trying to work out what to do with it. Should I put it back where I'd found it?

I sat on my bed and saw it shaking in my hand. I folded it up, then opened it again.

He will kill me.

What the hell? Who was this man? Whoever he was, she had said he was going to kill her. And she had died. She'd died before her children could get back from school to see her. Maybe this guy had *pushed* her down the stairs. She had known he was after her: perhaps he'd crept into the house and surprised her.

I remembered El's words: '*Dad didn't see, nobody did, and so we'll never know.*'

I was so engrossed in my thoughts that I didn't hear the

footsteps approaching. I didn't hear anything until there was a tap at the door. I managed to shove the paper under my pillow, just as Henry pushed the door open. I jumped to my feet and took a step towards him.

'Sorry to disturb!' he said. He came over and put a hand on my shoulder. We looked at each other. This time, though, I was the first to look away. 'Cat, would you care to come down for an aperitif? I'm afraid you have to. Our father does it every day, no matter who's here. Has a drink at six, on the dot. El's there already.'

I tried to find the right words to answer. My head was spinning. I needed to find out who that man was before I did anything more. And Henry was in front of me: I desperately wanted to kiss him again, and I also felt so awkward because of the note I'd just found that I could barely look at him.

Be natural. Be normal. 'Sure!' I said. 'That sounds great. Sophie and Owen drink every day too. Or Sophie does. But ...' I tailed off, feeling disloyal. Sophie had done everything for me. She was spectacularly generous. I had no business gossiping about her. 'I mean, yes of course I'll come down! Let's go!'

We sat out on the terrace with aperitifs. The sun was low in the sky across the valley, and the shadows were huge. The day's heat had calmed down and the air was warm and perfect on my arms. I ended up sitting next to Henry on a swing seat. There was space for three on there, but we spread out, which meant I wasn't too close to him. Minou jumped up and settled on my lap and I felt honoured.

'I meant to ask – what's with the new shed, Dad?' said El.

Mr Tilney shrugged. 'A man needs his shed.'

'You've got a whole house, though. If you need a man cave.'

'Well, sometimes it has to be a shed. Humour me.'

He made a great fuss of getting me an aperitif, once I said that I had barely heard of any of the fancy drinks he was offering. He reeled off a list and it meant nothing to me.

'I've only had Aperol spritz,' I said. 'Out of all those things you just said.'

'Seriously? Then you must try them all!' He beamed at me. 'Not all tonight. But let's try a different one each night that you're here, to get an idea of what you do and don't like. I say, we'll begin with a straightforward classic that you're going to love.'

Henry jumped to his feet, and the seat swung me and Minou back and forth. 'Kir royale?'

His father nodded with a smile. 'I'll have a pastis. El?'

El looked happier than I'd seen her so far. 'I don't want to be all stereotypical and girly, but what the hell – kir royale for me too, thanks.'

She was sitting on a lounger, and she lay back and closed her eyes. 'Berlin is cool,' she said, without opening them, 'but there's something about this place. It's kinda magical. I forget the smell of it. The way the air feels. It's softer here.'

'You know you can come back any time,' said Mr Tilney. 'When you get sick of the, I don't know ... drugs and graffiti. Come home for soft air and kir royale. Any time, Eleanor. You know that. It's not so much fun on my own.'

'It's not *just* drugs and graffiti,' she said, and I could hear the smile in her voice. 'I mean, it's not *not* them, but it's not only them.'

'All I'm saying is, your home will always be here. I very much hope so anyway.'

Her eyes were suddenly open. 'What's that meant to mean?'

He shook his head. 'Oh, nothing. You know it's a big house. I rattle around on my own. You know that the investment plan I was working on fell through when ... Place is a money pit. Not a place for a man to grow old in. I might not always want to have to get in the car to go anywhere. Does that make sense?' He turned to me. 'Does it make sense to you, Cat? What do you think? This is a place for a family, not a lonely old man, right?'

I hadn't expected to be drawn into this, but I nodded. 'I mean, yeah,' I said. 'It's gorgeous. It does feel like a house that should be filled with people.'

He grinned.

'Exactly. I like you, Cat. I appreciate that. When people come to visit, then of course I'm happy. I'm delighted! Particularly right now. But just me? Surrounded by ... memories? All alone?' He screwed his face up. 'Not indefinitely. But it's why I came back today. To exist in a populated house around you young people.'

Surrounded by memories. He hadn't been there, when she fell. He must have found her body.

I looked across to El and saw that she was struggling. She was blinking hard and her face was moving around in a way that she clearly wasn't controlling. I looked away, across the valley towards the sun.

'Dad,' said El. 'You can't do that. Sell the house. You can't!'

Her voice cracked on the last two words. I looked at her quickly, and her face crumpled.

I looked at her dad. He was struggling too.

'I stayed here until you were all adults. I know you want to have this place to come back to for the rest of your life. But I'm a human here. An ageing one. An ageing one who is throwing all his fucking money at this house and it's never enough. Whose investment plans have –'

'This is Mum's house! If you're so short of cash, what's with building new bits, like a fucking shed?'

The air was tense.

'I'll go and . . .' My voice trailed off as I realized they didn't care what I was doing. I got off the swing and stepped into the house, through the French windows and into the kitchen, pausing while my eyes adjusted to the relative darkness. I could still hear.

'I'd hoped one of you would take it o–' he was saying.

El cut him off. 'Oh yeah!' She was almost shouting now. 'I work in a cocktail bar and go to art school. I'll just save up for a couple of months so I can . . .'

I walked over to the far end of the kitchen where Henry

165

was tapping an upside-down ice tray. Behind me, I heard Mr Tilney's voice yelling: '*I was not asking you to buy it!*'

The kitchen was somehow enormous and completely homely. I took an inventory of everything to calm down my heartbeat from the tension outside: the pans hooked around the walls, and a branch of rosemary hanging down from a shelf. I looked at jars of flour and sugar and wondered how long they had been there. Mr Tilney didn't seem like the kind of man who would do a lot of baking, but what did I know? I remembered that there was a housekeeper called Marie, though she hadn't been in evidence: maybe she cooked for him. I was careful not to think what a waste it was, that he lived here on his own while my family was crammed into a few rooms. Life didn't work that way. Plus he hated being alone. All those keys dangling down: all those rooms. I looked at the labels. One said ET on it, which made me smile. I imagined unlocking a room and finding a little alien.

Henry looked round.

'OK?' he said. 'Is . . . everything all right out there?'

'Yeah. Of course. I just . . .' I looked over towards the terrace. 'I thought I'd give El and your dad a moment. Can I help?'

The sound of El sobbing was audible even from in here. Her dad raised his voice and then abruptly stopped talking. Henry looked at me, his expression nervous.

'Fighting about the house?'

'Yeah.'

I looked at the tray. There were two champagne glasses

containing dark-red bubbly drinks, which I supposed were kir royales. Then there was a china jug and a glass of milky liquid, and finally a glass of beer. Henry dropped two ice cubes into the milky drink.

'Don't worry,' he said. 'It's a thing they do. Dad says he's going to move to a bungalow, and El gets upset about ... about our mother. They'll be OK in a moment.'

Henry had changed into trousers for the evening, and I wondered whether dressing for the evening was a thing I should be doing. I was still wearing the dress I'd had on earlier, the green one Sophie had bought me.

'Could you grab a couple of bowls? They're in there.' He indicated a cupboard with his head. 'If they're having a moment, we could sort out some snacks.'

I opened the cupboard. There was a pile of brightly coloured glazed bowls in there. I took the top two. One was royal blue, the other bright yellow. 'Wow. Lovely bowls. Are they going to be OK? Not the bowls.'

Henry paused for a moment.

'Mmm-hmm,' he said. 'Dad and El have always gone at each other. Whatever she says, she's always been his favourite. It doesn't stop them fighting. They're too alike, though don't tell her I said that. They'll be fine, until he actually does move out. He's going to have to do it soon.' He winced. 'That will not be a good day.'

He looked so sad that I chanced a touch on his arm. It felt nice. Neither of us moved.

'Henry – this is a weird question, but what should I call your dad? I mean, do I call him Mr Tilney?'

Henry laughed, surprised. 'He'd be General Tilney, but no. Call him Fred. He'll insist on it.'

'Fred?'

My brain whirred. That phone call Sophie had taken about Eva Santoro. It had been from someone called Fred, and Owen had been annoyed about the fact that he'd called her. I wondered whether it was the same Fred. Somehow everybody I was meeting here seemed to be connected.

'Yep. It's Fritz's name too. It's just me and El who call him Fritz. He hates it. Naming your firstborn after yourself is exactly on-brand for my dad. They kind of did the same with El. Mum was Elisabeth, but Dad called her El and then they always called El that too. So you could say I'm the odd one out. The only one blessed with my own name.'

There was a lot to take in here.

'Your dad would really be OK with me calling him Fred?'

Henry nodded. 'Course he would. When you meet Fritz, you'll have to call him Fred too. He's the only one of us who could ever afford to take this place on. He won't come near it, though, so you won't meet him this week. He hates the place since Mum died. Fritz is . . . not Dad's biggest fan.'

A part of me seized on the *when* in that sentence. They'd said, earlier, that I wouldn't meet their brother, but now Henry was assuming that I would, at some time in the future. Did that mean we would continue to be friends? It made me feel fuzzy. He opened a bag of crisps and tipped them into the blue bowl. He handed me a pack of peanuts, and I emptied it into the yellow one. I was pleased that the snacks you got here were exactly the same as the ones we'd have had at home. Crisps and nuts.

'Dad needs to sell up,' Henry said. 'This place is unbelievably expensive to run. It's a constant stream of repairs. Boilers, roof, you know? I mean, of course you know. You know what *repairs* means.'

He turned to look at me, grinning, and I looked back at him. The moment grew longer. It changed. Neither of us looked away. I saw his eyes flicking from side to side, as he looked at one of my eyes and then the other, and I wondered whether I was doing the same to him.

Were we about to kiss again? Now, with a bowl of peanuts in my hand? He didn't look away. I felt I was looking into his soul. It sounded stupid, even in my head, but it was true. After what felt like eternity, he took a step towards me. He put a hand on my shoulder and then he was moving closer and then our lips were meeting. They brushed each other and my whole body tingled. Then his lips were on mine properly, and it was happening. I managed to put the bowl on the counter so I could put both arms round him.

We stood in the kitchen and we kissed properly. My universe shifted. The sun came out. All the flowers bloomed. My body yelled at me to do more. I lost myself in him.

Henry pulled away first. I couldn't stop smiling. He was grinning too. He looked like I felt.

'Was that OK?' His voice was gentle.

'Of course! Um. How about you? Because . . .' I could feel how much I was blushing. 'That first night. You didn't want to. You said you'd *hate* to and –' I made myself stop talking.

'I wanted to kiss you,' he said. 'Of course I did. But, I mean. Look at me. I'm not exactly a catch. I'm no – dare I say – Jonno Thorpe?'

I cringed even harder and shook my head behind my hands.

'Don't say that,' I said, into my palms.

I heard him breathing hard, and then his words came out fast. 'The thing I hated was the idea of you waking up in the morning and regretting it. I couldn't bear to be that guy.'

At that I took my hands away from my face and looked at him.

'I would never have regretted it. Never. I massively regretted lunging at you. I felt so stupid. I'm not exactly . . . I mean, you know it already, but I don't exactly have a lot of experience and . . .'

He put his arm right round me and pulled me towards him. He kissed the top of my head. I reached round his waist and hugged him back. I looked up. He looked down. We smiled.

He picked up the tray, and I took the two bowls of snacks.

By the time we were back on the terrace, Eleanor and her father were laughing together and everything felt wonderful. It turned out a kir royale was a very nice drink indeed.

19

'OK. New podcast chapter, and new location. I'm recording this at a house called Northanger in Provence, where I'm staying with the very wonderful and friendly Tilney family. It's a big old house surrounded by vines, and the only modern-looking thing here is a shed in the garden.

'So. I'm going to delete this next bit before anyone else hears it, but I can't not say it: I KISSED HENRY! Properly. In his kitchen while his dad and sister were arguing outside. I think this is it. Real.'

I switched the recording off. I'd sort that out tomorrow. For now I lay in bed, full of good food (which had sort of appeared out of nowhere, but which had actually been left in the fridge by the housekeeper and reheated) and happiness, and hoped against hope that there would be a knock on the door. I'd been so miserable about Jonno and *now* look at me! I had actually kissed Henry, first in a gentle way and then in a real one.

As the excitement wore off and the endorphins calmed down, or whatever it was that had happened, I started to feel a cold worry. With each minute that passed, I became less optimistic. I'd been sure he was going to tap on the door and come in for a goodnight kiss, but he would have done it by now. Wouldn't he? Maybe . . . now?

I wrote a text.

Goodnight! come and say it in person if you like? X

I looked at it and deleted the end part. I sent, Goodnight! x and waited.

And waited.

And then, just as I was giving up hope, he arrived, tapping gently on the door, waiting for me to say 'Come in' in my quietest voice.

We sat side by side on my bed, leaning on the wall, Henry's arm slung round my shoulders. We spoke in whispers because of El in the room next door.

'I'm glad you still like me when you're sober,' he said. 'I honestly didn't think you would.'

'I like you all the time. Whatever state I'm in.'

And I liked how it felt when I leaned my head on his shoulder. I loved the solidity of him. The feel of his hands on my waist. I turned and raised my face to his. He leaned down and we kissed. Again and again. We held each other. We kissed again.

When he left, it was too late to try Mum again so I plugged in my headphones and started another recording.

I kept it quiet so as not to disturb El, making sure that even if she could hear me talking she wouldn't be able to make out the words.

Still, I hid under the duvet, even though it was a hot night, particularly up here at the top of the building. I sweated as I spoke. I decided to focus on the house. I remembered what Sophie had said about keeping it real, and tried to do that.

'The thing with this house, though,' I said, 'is that although it's mind-blowingly big and beautiful, something terrible happened here.' I stopped. No one would hear this. I might as well get it all out. 'And there's something else: I found a picture. Of a man. And I don't know what I should do about it.'

I relaxed into it as I recorded all my experiences and thoughts, energized by Henry. I described the man in the drawing, and the words underneath it. I talked about everything that had happened that day. I talked about the argument between Eleanor and her dad. I talked, of course, about Henry. I'd have loads of time to edit this before Sophie heard it.

After a while, I had to stop and plug my phone in, and then someone was tapping on my door and I opened my eyes and it was morning.

'Cat?' The door opened a tiny bit and it was Henry. I sat up suddenly, aware that I hadn't even taken off the tiny bit of make-up I'd been wearing. 'Sorry to barge in! Are you OK to come out for market day?'

I had fallen asleep while waiting for my phone to charge, and I was instantly consumed by guilt. The drawing was poking out from under my duvet, though folded up and just looking like a piece of paper. Still, I moved it before he could see.

'Of course!' I said, yawning. 'When are we leaving?'

'Twenty minutes? No need for breakfast. We'll get it there. You'll see.'

I sat in the back of Fred's car with El. The boot was still filled with garden waste and smelled of soil.

'I promise I'll get this emptied,' said Fred when El wrinkled up her nose at it. 'They're not open on Sundays, or I'd do it right now while I've got a carful of helpers.'

As we drove, I looked at Henry in the passenger seat and wondered whether he could feel me looking at him. He didn't turn round, but I felt that he was aware of me. It was just something in his posture. The smile in the shape of his cheek.

Then my phone vibrated. I took it out and angled it away from El. It was a message from Henry, and it just said, You look beautiful xxx

I replied:

You look pretty handsome yourself xxx

We messaged back and forth for the whole of the twenty-minute journey to the market town.

Henry and El cheered when Fred found a parking space in a little car park by the river, and so I did too as it was clearly a victory. We stepped out on to sandy soil, and I inhaled deeply. Sun, flowers, food, exhaust fumes ... I loved it. I felt the sun on my bare legs and shoulders. I loved the feeling of energy in the air. I looked at Henry. He grinned at me and I felt the world fill with magic. He took my hand and squeezed it. I squeezed back.

The place was crowded in a way I'd only seen in Truro in the late-night shopping evenings before Christmas, when it felt as if everyone in Cornwall came into the city. That was my favourite time to be in town. I loved seeing everything so busy, and everyone so happy, even though I had no idea where all the people appeared from.

This market had the same vibe, but it was bigger and brighter and much, much hotter. When we arrived at eight thirty it was already crowded. There were market stalls everywhere, on every pavement in every street. It blew my mind: I looked from a stall with mountains of olives to another that was selling the kind of shiny bowls that we'd used last night for the crisps, to a third that had a million types of cheese.

'Wow,' I said. 'This is ...'

As I looked at everything, it occurred to me that I had turned up at the vineyard without a gift for Fred or the family. He was treating me as one of his children, and I was just accepting it. I would, I decided, find something for him here. I had enough money in the bank for that.

'Right,' he said. 'Breakfast!'

It occurred to me that I could pay for breakfast, but I had no idea how much that would be. My budget was tight: I was definitely better off getting a token gift than making a grand gesture with no price attached. I would, however, make sure I paid for myself at least.

I followed the three of them down streets lined with stalls, staring at everything as I went. One was selling wicker baskets like the one Sophie used for beach stuff, and suddenly I wanted one of them more than anything. I wanted to buy a basket and fill it with fruit and flowers and cheese and olives. We turned right down a little alley and came out in a shaded square that was filled with cafe tables with red-and-white checked tablecloths.

A man in an apron came over, and everyone kissed each other on the cheeks while talking rapid French. I felt more like an outsider than ever. I imagined the family coming here when they were younger, when Elisabeth had still been alive. They clearly knew this cafe guy, and even with my mediocre French I could tell that he was asking after their lives. 'Berlin' came up. So did 'Oxford'. I listened to Henry and El speaking their other language, and envied them their mother tongue. Literally their mother tongue. I thought of my mother, and I missed her like a limb.

Then I realized I was being introduced.

'Cat,' said Henry.

The man looked puzzled. '*Comme chat?*' he said. They discussed the name Catherine for a while, and I wondered whether to remind them that I was actually Caitlin, but decided not to bother. I liked the way Catherine sounded in French. *Catreen.* It was halfway to Caitlin anyway.

Then we were sitting at an outside table in the dappled shade of a tree whose huge branch stretched across half the square. The chairs were metal and wobbly, the tables iron under the tablecloths. I didn't see anyone ordering, but suddenly there was coffee in front of us, and a basket of croissants and chunks of baguette, and butter and jam and honey, and everyone was digging in so I did too. I spread jam on to a piece of croissant and heard my stomach rumble as I looked at it.

'Welcome to the Northanger Sunday morning,' said Henry, looking up with a grin. 'When we're all here we have to come to market and we are obliged to start the expedition by eating our body weights in pastry. It's been a while, but that makes it all the better.' I looked at each of them in turn. The argument between El and her father seemed never to have happened: she looked perfectly happy and so did he.

'You're part of the family now,' said El. 'Whether you like it or not.'

I looked at Fred. 'Absolutely,' he said. 'Please, stay as long as you like. As long as you can. Cat, are you headed to university in September?'

I wasn't sure how to answer. Mum would have learned to manage without me this summer. The babies would be getting easier. Wouldn't they? Perhaps it was going to be OK for me to stay away, after this summer.

'I really hope so!' I said. I couldn't imagine going back to Truro and settling into my old life. I longed for more adventures. Endless adventures. I was desperate to go to Belfast. 'I have offers from a couple of places, but it all depends on how I do on results day.'

'Results day!' He sat back and laughed, seeming genuinely amused by this. 'It's incredible how quickly we forget, isn't it? But, yes, the horrors of results day. I went through it three times with my three – six, if we include GCSEs – and it never got any easier. When it is?'

'August the fourteenth,' I said. 'Less than two weeks away.' Should I mention that my birthday is on the eleventh? No.

'Well, if the Allens are delayed for any reason, then please stay. Allow me the nostalgia of a fourth or seventh results day? I have to go down to the coast for a few days at some point, but I'd be sure to be back for that.'

El was looking at him with an exaggerated double take.

'Father?' she said. 'I don't remember you being a ray of sunshine this time last year. When I was in Cat's position you were *extremely* invested in the A stars, and you certainly didn't consider it whatever this is. A special exciting event of some sort.'

He reached over and patted her hand. 'That's why it's more fun when it's Cat. No offence, my dear Cat, but it's far more enjoyable when I have no personal responsibility for whatever you might decide to do next. But, of course, you'll be back with the Allens anyway. Where are you hoping to study?'

We talked in an easy way about my potential future in Belfast, which I was pleased to discover was seen as a cool and interesting place to go.

'Media and broadcast production?' That part confused Fred. 'That's a university subject these days, is it?'

'Dad!' said El. 'You don't have to do classics at Oxbridge any more. Unless you happen to be Henry, of course.'

'I did not do classics,' said Henry mildly.

'I'll probably be in London,' El said to me. 'Maybe I'll pop over to Belfast to see you.'

'Oh!' said her father, turning to her, delighted. 'You're going to go, then? And this is how you choose to convey the news to me? What happened to staying in Berlin?'

Henry rolled his eyes as they started bickering, and changed the subject.

'So, depending what you want to see or buy here, we generally split up for an hour or so, and meet back here before we go home,' he said.

'Please can I stick with one of you?' I said, meaning Henry. 'I'll never find my way around on my own.'

'Of course! And I'll save this place on your phone maps,' said Henry, holding out his hand. 'And then you'll always be able to navigate back no matter what, because however hard one tries it's impossible not to get lost. Dad – what's your plan?'

'A lovely meander. I'll see you at twelve.' He stood up, knocked back the rest of his coffee and gave us a little wave, before strolling over to the cafe interior where I saw him paying the bill. I opened the maps app on my phone, aware, as I handed it to Henry, that I was giving him a device that contained a rambling voice note from last night in which I had speculated at length about his mother's death. I held my breath, but he just spent a minute fiddling with it, and handed it back.

'There you go. I put a pin in where we are right now, so if we do all lose each other you just need to be back here at twelve. If you want to be super safe, we could link up on Find My?'

'You can just do Snap Maps,' said El, but Henry shook his head.

'I'm afraid I'm *far* too grown up for Snap.' So we all added each other and it turned out that it was just as well, since within half an hour I had wandered away to look at a stall full of crates of the reddest, shiniest tomatoes I had ever seen, and when I looked round they had both disappeared.

I looked at them on Find My Friends, and saw they were in two different places. I decided to spend a bit of time looking around by myself.

I stared at a stall full of olives, wondering if I could take some home because I was pretty sure that Kitty would quickly learn to love them. A cat wove around my legs. There were people everywhere. I felt hot and strange and foreign and lost, and for a moment I wanted to be in Antibes. I knew where I was with Sophie. The Allens' apartment didn't have any dark secrets, as far as I knew, whatever the gossip might say. I wanted to look at the sea and eat ice cream and dodge the Thorpe family, rather than being tangled in someone else's family drama, betraying them with my thoughts and my voice notes.

But I couldn't be anywhere other than wherever Henry was. That won out over everything.

I walked around, wondering what I should get for Fred. As I looked at olives, garlic, lettuces, china, tablecloths, chili plants and more and more and more, I realized I had no idea at all. I could hardly hand him a bag of vegetables. A bunch of flowers would be weird. He already had loads of lovely china. Could I get him something for his new shed? What, though?

I knew he liked alcohol, but he seemed to be stocked with everything he could possibly need. In the end, I leaned against a wall in the shade and sent a message to Henry.

> Help! Lost you, and I want to get a thank you gift for your dad but no idea at all what it should be! Any advice?? xxx

I turned the volume up and waited for a reply. It was half past ten so I still had an hour and a half. I kept walking, hoping for inspiration. What was a good present for a host? Chocolate? I hadn't seen any chocolate stalls, and that was probably because anything made of chocolate would have melted instantly. I looked at a stall of souvenirs.

'*Bonjour!*' said the woman standing behind it. I smiled and said *bonjour* back to her. I looked at the array of linen, ceramics and lavender on her stall and although there was nothing here I'd feel comfortable giving to Henry's dad, I picked up a bright yellow-and-orange mug. Mum would love this. A handwritten sign said it was sixteen euros, and even though this was a lot of money for a mug, and particularly for one that was going to have to survive a precarious journey and then live in a household filled with small children, I decided to get it anyway. The woman had a card machine so I paid using my phone, and she wrapped the mug in tissue paper, saying smiley things in French as she did so. I just nodded and smiled back and hoped for the best.

I turned round and gasped. Henry was standing right behind me. Again. He held his hands up.

'Sorry!' he said. 'I startled you, didn't I? I'm always doing that. That's what they tell me. It drives my friends mad.'

Strangely, I had never really thought about Henry having friends. He had, though, just finished three years of university, and he was engaging and funny and kind. Of course he had friends. For all I knew he could have a girlfriend. He'd never mentioned anyone.

Of course he didn't. He'd kissed *me*. Told me I looked beautiful. He'd come to my room at night.

'I thought I'd lost you,' I said.

'Here I am. There's no need to get anything for my dad, but if you did want to I am here with some pointers. Unless that was you finding something?'

'Mug for my mum.'

'Follow me.'

I ended up spending an enormous amount more than I had planned on Fred's present, but I decided not to care. I would never have thought to buy him a bag of cheese, but with Henry picking things out I was pretty sure this was going to be right. He did all the talking, asking for slivers to sample, sharing them with me, and I agreed to everything he said, and then paid on the card machine, horrified to see that I'd spent over fifty euros.

I would have to be careful with what I had left in my account, which was now less than thirty euros. I didn't say any of that to Henry, who obviously had no concept of my financial situation.

We walked together through the crowded streets, hand in hand. Henry stopped on a busy pavement to kiss me, and people walked around us. I had a bag of cheese in my hand, and he was carrying a basket that literally had baguettes sticking out of it. I felt like a girl in a movie.

Then we carried on walking. We passed through smells I remembered, notably the amazing aroma of a wall of rotisserie chickens. We passed through lavender, and raw meat that hit the back of my throat, and a wave of garlic. And then we were walking down the same alley we'd taken this morning, and somehow we were back in the square with the cafe.

'How did you even –' I started to say to Henry. The words dried up in my throat, because sitting at the same table as before was Henry's dad, and next to him was a man. A man with thick dark hair.

The man from the drawing.

20

When he saw us coming, Fred got to his feet.

'Ahh, here they are!' he said. He was being different. Performative. 'The young people return.' He turned to the other man and spoke French, which I vaguely understood as meaning that we had been gone for a while and now we were back, though there was probably more nuance to it than that. I couldn't really focus. My heart was beating so hard that I thought it had to be moving my chest. I was the only one here who'd seen that sketch. Had to be.

'Ah.' The man nodded politely, and I studied his face. Did he look like a killer? Elisabeth Tilney had certainly seemed to think so, and the fact that she had died after writing it was strong evidence, but I wouldn't have guessed it. He wouldn't have made me shudder if I'd passed him on the street. He just looked like a guy.

He was a bit younger than Fred, but still quite old, and he was unmistakably the man in the picture. It wasn't just his thick hair and dark eyes, because anyone could have had them. It was everything about him. Elisabeth had captured his features almost perfectly. His eyes were slightly hooded at the corners. His mouth was wide, and he was looking right at me, with interest. In real life, his nose was slightly longer, but that was it.

Henry walked over to him and did some perfunctory kisses on the cheeks, but the man didn't take his eyes off me. I shivered.

I didn't know anything, of course. I needed to remember that. I was not in danger. As far as this man was concerned, I was a boring stranger. A house guest.

'This is our friend François,' said Henry. 'François, this is Cat. She's from Cornwall and she's staying with us this week.'

François frowned slightly. 'Cornwall?' he said, rolling the R in a way that made my home sound more interesting. They discussed where Cornwall was in French for a bit. I smiled as I heard Henry say it was '*comme Bretagne*', and realized he meant Brittany, not Britain.

François turned to me. 'So, we speak English?' he said, in strongly accented French. He was looking right at me, all the time. I didn't like it.

I gave it a go. '*Je suis désolée*,' I managed. '*Mon français est très mal.*'

God, you'd never know I'd got an eight for GCSE. I was actually pleased that I was getting words out. The man in the picture, the man who Elisabeth had said was going to kill her, had a name. François. Suspect number one. The man who, whenever I looked up, was watching me.

As Henry and I sat down, I started planning how I'd bring this into my secret podcast. I'd already talked about the accident and how I'd found the sketch. God, I wished Izzy was still my friend. She would be as interested as I was. She'd help me work out what the hell was going on with François.

Maybe, I thought, I could message her. Apologize properly for the whole Jonno shitshow.

The cafe guy stopped beside our table, his hands full of a tray of other people's drinks.

'*J'écoute*,' he said.

'I'm just having a small beer so I can drive us home,' Henry said. 'What would you like?'

'Could I have a *citron pressé*?' Henry gave me a lovely smile, a smile that made my nerves jump to attention, and then gave the cafe guy our order. He took my hand under the table, out of sight of everyone else. I could feel his pulse through his skin.

I mainly thought about Henry and his fingers, but also listened to the conversation. I discovered that François was the closest thing the vineyard had to a neighbour, which meant he lived a mile or two away in a remote house in the valley. He had been an old friend of Elisabeth's, and I wasn't sure whether that meant he was her ex from before she met Fred, or whether he really was just a friend. I also couldn't tell if he was making me uncomfortable because of everything that was swirling around my head, or if there actually was something strange about him.

I saw the way he looked at Fred, when Fred wasn't looking at him. I didn't think the two of them were quite as friendly as they were trying to pretend.

It was giddying. The intensity, and promise, and invitation of Henry's hand in mine. The gut punch of meeting the man from the sketch. The weirdness of finding my way in yet another new world. I didn't think I'd ever done this much *feeling* before.

Eleanor appeared and ordered a drink called a *rinquinquin*, a name I found myself saying over and over again, savouring the throaty rhyminess of it, high and silly in the proximity of Henry. When it arrived, I took the sip she offered me from her glass and found it was a kind of peach wine. I immediately wished I could have one of them too: El saw me regretting it and ordered another *rinquinquin* anyway and passed it to me. I found myself giggling like a schoolgirl while the adults talked, Henry's hand on my knee. I caught El clocking it.

As we stood up to leave, Fred looked at my bag.

'Purchases?' he said. 'Do show.'

I remembered the wildly expensive cheese, and handed him the plastic bag. The smell that wafted up from it in the sun made my eyes water.

'Actually, yes,' I said. 'This is for you, to say thanks for having me. I had some advice from Henry, so it should be the right sort of thing. Hope you like it.'

Fred took the bag and looked into it. When he looked back at me his face was genuinely alight with happiness.

'Dear girl! You didn't need to give me a single thing! Any friend of Henry's is a friend of mine. There was really no ... but no. I'm not going to talk myself out of this. A collection of my favourites! The things I rarely allow myself because of the stupid doctors. Cholesterol and all that. Thank you, thank you.'

I gave a little smile, aware that I was blushing, but hoping that it was hidden by my suntan.

'It's lovely of you to have me to stay. And to make me feel so much at home.'

'While you're here, it's your home too. And ...' He paused, shook his head. 'No. Nothing. Let's head home for lunch. Henry, did you get baguettes?'

Henry patted his basket, the four baguettes sticking out of the top, and we all headed off. I tried to imagine what on earth Fred might have been about to say, but was jolted out of it by François, who was saying goodbye to everyone and who seemed to think he knew me well enough to go in for a kiss on both cheeks. I tensed up, but at least the kisses were light and quick. He smelled of cigarettes more than booze.

Then, as I was pulling away, he said something right into my ear. It made the goosebumps go up all the way down my arm. I didn't hear his exact words and I was too taken by surprise to ask him to repeat it. I knew he hadn't been saying he was going to kill me, but still ... he might have been. Later, I tried to re-create the sounds in my head, but I couldn't make it make any sense at all. It sounded like *bonsoir*, but it couldn't have been. That meant good evening, and it wasn't evening and why would he secretly whisper *good evening* into my ear?

I took a step away, and away and away. I went over to El and walked with her to the car. When I looked over my shoulder, François was watching us go. He made some kind of hand signal to me, and I looked quickly away. It had been a bit like a wave, I thought, but not quite. I shuddered.

Back at the house, we spread things from the market out across the table, and ripped off bits of baguette and got stuck into the best Sunday lunch I'd ever had. There were tomatoes, olives, meats, wine and, of course, a lot of cheese, though I followed Henry and El's lead and hung back from Fred's special ones because he really did seem to delight in them, acting like a child having a first taste of ice cream.

After a pudding of figs, yogurt and honey, produced in individual bowls by El, I yawned.

'Is it OK if I go for a bit of a siesta?' I said. 'Sorry. I'm just . . .' I suddenly, overwhelmingly, wanted to lie down. I needed to be on my own, to clear my head.

They all told me to go and rest for as long as I needed, and I yawned and stretched my way up to the attic, full of bread and a bit drunk. I was fuzzy and, in spite of François, mainly happy.

I sat on the bed and tried to assess what was happening. I wanted to think about Henry, to wonder when we would next kiss, but the memory of François whispering right into my ear unsettled me. It stopped me being able to daydream properly.

And then I didn't need to daydream anyway, because there was a knock at the door and Henry was there, politely asking if I minded him visiting for a second. And then we were kissing and then we were sitting on the bed and kissing more and I was curling up and feeling his arms round me and every other thought I'd ever had evaporated from my head.

I hadn't realized I'd fallen asleep until I woke up. One moment I was leaning on Henry with my head in his lap and him stroking my hair, and then I was waking up alone. It took me a while to get my head straight. Once I'd established that I was the only person in this room I looked at the dots on Find My Friends, and saw that El was in the house, and Henry was in a field nearby. I tiptoed out to the corridor. El's bedroom door was open and she wasn't in there, so I went back into my room, closed the door, curled up on the bed and looked at my phone.

I decided to act on the thing that had come into my mind and messaged Izzy.

> Iz, I'm really sorry. I didn't mean to mess things up like that. Can we be friends again? There's some stuff I'd really like to talk to you about at some point.

While I waited for her reply, I remembered that I should check in with Sophie and send her a quick message.

> All fine here. Hope Dubai is OK.

I paused, wondering whether to allude to the fact that everyone was gossiping about her, but realized that no one would enjoy being told that. So I just added a kiss and sent it.

I thought about Eva. I googled her, and tried to read a brief article on a French news website. They'd used a photo of her that I recognized from her Instagram, one where she was standing on the beach, her hair glowing bright gold.

When neither Izzy nor Sophie replied, I messaged Mum to see if she fancied a catch-up, and cheered up when she answered straight away.

On the bus right now but let's speak later xxx

It was immediately followed by a check-in from Aisha.

Hey Cat! You OK?

That made me feel strong. I decided to make another secret recording, and then I'd go and find Henry in his field.

I told my phone all about the meeting with François.

'I instinctively wanted to get away from him,' I said, in a whisper. 'There was just something about him. Probably because I could see that he was the man Elisabeth thought was going to kill her, but still. I don't know his surname, but he's our first and only suspect. Ladies and gentlemen: François, the neighbour. The man in the picture.'

I stopped recording. Then I started again and filled in all the background I could think of. I took a photo of the drawing. I felt a bit weird having this stuff on my phone while I was in the house so I named the files 'media coursework' and gave each a number. Then, I password-protected them all and messaged Kitty to see if she was around.

My phone instantly rang with a video call and Kitty's face filled the screen.

'Hey, Cat,' she said. 'Let's see this new place then.' I swung the phone around to show her my room. The door swung open and I tensed up, ready to introduce Henry to my sister, but it was only Minou. She padded over and jumped up on the bed. I moved the phone to show her to Kitty, who shrieked.

'Oh my God, that is a beautiful cat! And how cool – we're Cat, Kitty and a cat. Three witches. What's this one called?'

I stroked her. 'This is Minou,' I said. 'She's lovely.'

'I want to reach through the screen and stroke her. Stroke her for me!'

I did, and when Minou started purring Kitty's happiness seemed complete. I looked at the background and realized she was at our house. My house. Home.

'So, what's going on over there?' I said. 'Who's there? Can I say hello? Is Mum home yet?'

'Everyone's fine, Cat. Don't worry. Summer's just brilliant. Let's go and find them.'

I swallowed hard as Kitty set off down the stairs. It was strange to be in this massive house with its empty rooms, looking at our tiny home a thousand miles away. Everything looked small. Kitty walked into the living room, and I remembered talking to the Allens in there all those weeks ago, walking in with a baby on each hip, a pack of biscuits and no idea of the fact that my life was about to take a massive swerve.

Now the babies were sitting on the grass in the tiny back garden, with Summer. She was wearing jeans, a striped top and a white cardigan. The babies were each leaning on her while she sat up against the wall of the house and read a book, again. She'd been reading to them last time too. They loved books. I should read to them more.

This was a book with a red cover, one I hadn't seen before. I tried to see what it was called, but I couldn't. Josh and Mia were enthralled.

All of them looked up as Kitty came out.

'Sorry, Summer!' she said. 'Hey, babies. Look, I've got Cat on my phone. Right here! She wants to say hello! And she's got a *real cat* with her!'

'Hey, Cat,' said Summer.

Kitty held the phone in front of Mia first.

'Say hello to Cat,' said Kitty.

'Cat! Cat!' said Mia, and my screen filled with her mouth, all wet and glistening and dark.

'Oh, darling.' That was Summer. 'Darling, you can't eat Kitty's phone. You can't actually kiss Cat, I'm afraid.' I heard the smile in her voice.

'Hey, Mia,' I said. 'How are you doing, baby girl? Look who's with me here – a real cat.'

I put Minou back on the screen. Mia shrieked again, at least as excited to see Minou as she was to see me. Then Josh was there too.

'Want cat,' he said, and although he was probably talking about Minou, I decided that he also meant me.

'How are you doing?' I turned the phone so that Minou and I were both in the shot. 'What have you been up to?'

They didn't answer, so Summer did.

'They're brilliant as ever,' she said.

'Where Cat? Where you being?' That was Josh.

'In France, Joshie. Staying in a very big house right now. Do you want to look out of the window?'

'Yes,' said Mia. 'Window, please.'

I walked over to the window and held the phone up. There was a real gasp from Kitty and Summer, and a baffled silence from the babies.

Then Kitty's face filled the screen. 'Isn't this new place by the sea?'

I started to explain that Henry's house was a long way inland, and it took me a moment to realize that El was standing in the doorway, grinning. I wondered how long she'd been listening.

'Oh, babies?' I said, making my voice extra jolly. 'This is my friend Eleanor. It's her house. Say hello!'

She came over and looked at the screen.

'Well, hello there,' she said. 'How's Cornwall?'

There was an incoherent chorus of hellos, and when i died down, Mia's voice rang out.

'Pink hair,' she said.

'Why pink hair?' said Josh.

El grinned and touched her head. 'Do you like it?'

Mia twisted round to look at Summer. 'Mia have pink hair?'

194

'One day,' said Summer. 'When you're bigger, if you want to, then I'm sure you can have pink hair. But you'll have to grow up a bit first.'

They all talked for a while, and then we said goodbye to Mia, Josh and Summer. As Kitty returned to the house I heard them going back to what they were doing before.

'Do you remember what was happening in the book?' said Summer. 'Gina went into fairy-tale land to fix the story.'

Her voice disappeared as Kitty shut the door. 'Your mum's not home,' she said. 'She took the boys into town on the bus, to go to the library and the park. She's doing OK, though. Actually, she seems loads better. So don't worry about her, right?'

She seems loads better. That was because of Summer. It had to be. For a second, I hated that perfect nanny. I wanted to ask Kitty more, but I was aware of El right next to me, so I just said, 'OK – thanks, Kit. Mum did say she'd call later so hopefully she will. I should go now.'

'Are you OK?' said El when I'd hung up.

I nodded.

'It must be weird to see them when you're so far away.' She patted my shoulder and I wondered how upset I looked. 'They're gorgeous. Sorry for barging in. I just came to say – do you fancy a swim? Dad used to say he was going to get a pool here, but he never did and now of course he's run out of money or whatever and it's never gonna happen. But there's a stretch of river down the hill that we go to, and it's actually perfect for a day like this. I haven't been for ages. We can walk – it's about twenty minutes – and then Henry can drive down in a bit and pick us up. If you're, like, rested and don't have any other plans. I'm going, anyway, so no pressure.'

I nodded. 'That sounds incredible.'

We walked through the garden. It was dry, but somehow still looking beautiful. There were lavender bushes in the borders, a fig tree and of course the new shed, which looked ugly next to all the exquisite stuff. It was the sort of shed you'd get at B&Q at home.

The swimming spot was the thing I hadn't realized I'd needed. It reminded me of that first morning in Antibes, swimming with Sophie, before we knew what Eva had done. There was a stony river beach, with grass and plants growing on the banks and trees dappling the water with their shade, and no one else was there. The river was wide. A dragonfly hovered above the surface before darting away, and fish swam around under it. A rope swing hung off a branch. I stepped into the water and submerged myself, first to the shoulders and then dipping my head under and swimming underwater for as long as I could. When I came up, I was a little way downstream, and out of my depth, so I swam back to where El was floating on her back, looking up at the leaves overhead.

'Mum used to bring us here,' she said, without looking round. 'My happiest memories are of this place. Just messing around in the water for ages while she sat right there and watched us and cheered when we did anything and focused on us completely. It was Mum who helped us put that rope swing up, though she was paranoid it wasn't strong enough and had to get a *man* to check it. Men, actually. Two of them – François, the neighbour you met before? – him and his brother. They were way handier than Dad so she got them to help her with the swing and we weren't allowed to tell Dad who did it.'

'His brother?' This was new. I filed it away to add to the evidence later.

'Yeah. Louis moved away years ago. He lives in, like, Brazil or something. Unlike François, who rarely even leaves the village. Hey, it was nice seeing your brother and sister. I'd kind of forgotten what little kids are like. And what it's like to be one. That whole family thing, you know?'

'Oh God! Sorry if it . . .'

'No,' she said. 'It was lovely. I feel like something shut off when Mum died. Like I'd been cut in half. I wasn't a real person any more. I was just made of leftovers. I think if she'd been . . . Well, it was so sudden. One minute I'm homesick at school and bargaining with the universe. You know, saying *whatever it takes for me to be allowed home, please do that.* And then I'm on my way back here because Mum's dead. I thought I'd made it happen.'

'El, that's awful.'

'I mean, I know now that I didn't make it happen. And we *should* outlive our parents. It's worse when it goes the other way. Fritz dealt with it by never coming home. But Henry and I didn't deal with it at all. We just didn't. And although our schools had counsellors and all that, it just . . . Well, seeing your baby brother and sister made me think

197

that maybe I'm thawing out after all. Perhaps I can think about the entire concept of childhood without turning to ice. Coming down here reminds me of being a kid, so I haven't been for ages.'

She took a deep breath in through her nose and flipped over so she was standing next to me. I saw her deciding to talk about something else.

'So anyway,' she said, grinning. 'You and Henry? What's going on?'

I laughed, caught by surprise. I started swimming around lazily, chasing the pockets of warm water.

'What do you mean?' I said it as casually as I could, though I couldn't stop the smile that crept on to my face.

'Excuse me, but you know perfectly well what I mean. The way the two of you look at each other. Hold hands under the table. Are you into him? What happened with that Thorpe boy?'

I didn't want to reply, and yet somehow my mouth did it for me. 'Nothing at all happened with the Thorpe boy. He ambushed me and it was horrible, so we don't speak any more. And yeah. I'm into Henry.' I paused. 'Very.'

'Oh! Well – good, I guess?'

Then we were both laughing.

'I got things wrong with Jonno Thorpe,' I said. 'I thought I was meeting him as a sort of friend because Izzy was busy.' I paused for a second to appreciate the rhyme. 'But turned out he thought I'd been *leading him on* all this time. Henry rescued me.'

El nodded. 'That does sound like Jonno. The thing with Henry, though,' she said carefully, 'is that he's massively conflict-avoidant. My whole family is. Apart from Fred. Brother-Fred. Fritz. He just says whatever's on his mind. The rest of us tread on eggshells the whole time. There's basically an elephant in every room.'

'So with Henry . . . ?'

'He lights up when you're around. He hasn't done that for ages.'

Everything in me leaped. I swam across the river so I was next to her again. 'Has . . . has he had a lot of girlfriends?'

She laughed. 'Henry? What do you think? Fritz would be the one with a thousand girlies hanging off him. Henry's only had one, really. Leonie. She was Swiss and they lasted maybe a year? She was a pianist and they'd sit side by side and listen to classical music like little dorks. But that's it, really. You?'

'Nah. Nothing, really. Nothing to speak of.' I realized I knew almost nothing about El. 'And – you?'

She grinned. 'Oh, I get everywhere, Cat. I'm not really into monogamy. Oh – I'm into girls, though. You knew that, right?'

I hadn't particularly thought about it, but I nodded.

'Yeah. I mean no, but it makes sense.'

We swam around for a while. I was fizzing inside. The words *he lights up when you're around* buzzed inside me. I found the perfect spot for doing a handstand, where there was a sandy bit of riverbed. I practised over and over again, pointing my toes and getting my legs as straight as I could. When I eventually stopped, El was sitting on the bank with Henry, both of them watching.

Henry stood up when he saw me looking at him. He was wearing a pair of red board shorts. I'd never seen so much of his body before, and I liked it.

I watched him pick his way barefoot over the stones to the place where the rope swing was hooked round a branch. Then he was swinging out over the water and jumping down with a huge splash and a yell. I went for the rope swing next, and for the rest of the afternoon the three of us messed around like little children, and I forgot about absolutely everything else.

When we were all exhausted and getting out of the water Henry grabbed me round the waist, and I turned towards him. He kissed me on the lips.

He did it in front of his sister. As I stood there, knee deep in river water, kissing the only boy who had ever made me feel this way, I realized that this was happiness. I wasn't thinking about anything but Henry. His hands on my waist. I held on to him and kissed him back.

'Get a room, you two,' said El, in a nice way.

When we stepped apart, I looked up at him, and he looked down at me and we smiled. He reached for my hand and helped me up the bank.

My clothes and towel were on a patch of grass under a tree and, as I walked over to get them, something changed. It was the sound of a stick snapping somewhere.

I looked up. Was someone else here? All my senses were alert. I held my breath and waited. Henry and El were nearby, but too far to have heard the snap.

I looked around. There were trees surrounding us. Was that a figure? It was. Were there eyes on us? On me? Yes, and I knew who it was.

I grabbed a towel and held it to my body and when I looked back he had gone. However, as I walked to catch up with the others, he fell into step beside me.

'Cat,' he said, his voice low. 'Please – you should leave here. Will you –'

'Wait for me!' I shouted. The other two turned round and waved at us both.

'Hey, François,' said El. She was grinning at him. '*Ça va?*'

No one but me found him freaky. I walked away from him and didn't look back.

Much later, I looked through a window and saw him in the garden, but as soon as he saw me looking he melted away.

21

The days passed happily and I put François out of my mind because he was totally outweighed by Henry. Who cared about anything else? I was obsessed. I had no space for anything but him. I waited, tense, in my room at night, and he knocked, night after night. He came in and kissed me. We hugged. We touched each other, a bit more daringly each night. We didn't have sex, but I really wanted to and we started to talk about it.

'I feel like I'm ready,' I said. I looked at his face. Henry had a smile that I only saw in these moments. The quiet moments when it was just the two of us. The magical, secret times.

'I want to take things slowly,' he said. 'I want you to be absolutely certain.'

'I am!'

He hesitated. 'Also. Sorry if this is a drag, but I'd rather not do it with my father and sister in the house. So – only if you're comfortable with the idea – I thought maybe we could go down to Antibes for a night? Not to the Allens' place. Our house down there.'

'Oh God! Yes, please!' I said, though Sophie and Owen would be back soon, and I wasn't sure when we were going to manage it. We'd find a way.

We held hands all the time now. Fred and El both grinned whenever they saw us. I started opening up to Henry about my uncertainty about the future.

'I don't know if I'll get the grades,' I said one night, 'but, even if I do, I don't think I can go. My mum needs help with the kids, and until this summer it's always been me. I know they've got Summer helping right now, but she'll leave. And Mum has made me feel so bad for going away. We've spoken on the phone a couple of times, but not for long, and it still feels awkward. She needs me at home so I think I'll have to postpone uni anyway.'

He took my hand.

'It's none of my business,' he said, 'but, Cat? It seems to me that those kids aren't your responsibility. And I don't think you should put your life on hold to look after them.' He paused. 'I'm sure they're great, and I hope I meet them one day, but, honestly, they're not your kids. I feel quite strongly about this.' He made me feel differently about everything.

I checked in with Sophie every day, as I'd promised, and she replied from time to time. They were brief replies, but they still sounded like Sophie, and they'd be home soon and I'd have to leave. I told her about me and Henry. She was 'thrilled' for me.

I was having the time of my life.

*

Then, one day, Fred, El and Henry announced that they were going out.

'You're welcome to come with us, Cat,' said Fred, in his affable way, 'but it's all going to be in French and you might not find it interesting.'

They were off to visit El's godmother, who lived an hour's drive away. 'She's nice,' said El, 'but very proper. She doesn't speak English, and it's all quite formal there. Honestly, it's a bit of a duty visit. You don't need to come. I wouldn't, if I didn't have to.'

I agreed that I'd stay home. Over the past week, my world had shrunk down to Northanger. I lived my life inside these walls. It was coming to an end, but Henry and I had talked about that. He was going to come back to Antibes, to stay in their place down there while I moved back to the apartment with Sophie and Owen, and we would just carry on, but with more privacy. We were leaving on Sunday.

'Go and swim if you like,' said Henry, 'but be careful if you do. There can be a bit of a current in that river. Also, the walk back up the hill is better if you have a car.'

'Yeah,' said El. 'Walking is definitely better if you're not walking.'

'No – please don't swim,' said Fred. 'I don't want to be worrying about you, down there on your own, Cat.'

'Of course,' I said, smiling at this man who was a million times more paternal towards me than my own dad had ever been. 'I promise I won't swim. How about this? I'll cook something for dinner while you're gone.' I had no idea why I was saying this: I was a terrible cook, but it turned out we'd finished Maria's food and she wasn't due back until next week. 'So when you get back there'll be . . . supper.' I had never said *supper* before, but it seemed to work.

I stood on the doorstep and waved them off up the drive. Then I closed the front door and walked around the house for a bit, pretending it was mine. I stood in the entrance hall and looked at the guns. They couldn't be loaded. Could they? I kept forgetting to ask Henry. They were just hanging there, held up by slings of material, displayed on the walls. It was a weird vibe, particularly next to the art. I wondered whether this oil painting was by Elisabeth. I loved its bright colours.

Elisabeth.

I had barely thought about her at all, but now that Henry was away from me it came flooding back. I felt as if I was waking from a dream as I stood in the entrance hall and looked up the stairs. When I stepped out of my flip-flops and picked them up, the stone floor was cold on the soles of my feet. When I set off up the staircase the carpet was thick and soft and I walked slowly, wondering exactly where and how she had fallen.

Soon I was at the locked door to her studio. For the first time ever, I tried the door: it really was locked.

I thought about my secret podcast. Izzy hadn't replied to my message from the beginning of the week, but I'd be in Antibes again on Sunday. Did I even want to be friends with her now? When she'd taken Jonno's side so completely? But I wanted to talk about podcasts and the only people I could talk to were either in Dubai, or blanking me.

Then I remembered Aisha. I walked slowly away from the studio door and called her.

'Cat?' she said. 'Hey, girl! Are you all right?'

'Yeah,' I said. 'Yeah. I'm fine. Actually, great. You?'

'Up against it,' she said. 'Kinda hectic. But yeah. All good.'

She sounded stressed.

'I thought you were on holiday? Relaxing? Doing nothing?'

'Yeah.' She was silent for a moment. 'Work caught up, I guess. When you're self-employed, you're never actually on holiday. If something comes up, you do it. When are you back in town? Sophie and Owen must be home soon, right?'

I walked around the house as we talked. In my head, I pretended I wasn't going to do the thing I was definitely about to do. I opened the door to the laundry cupboard, the place in which Henry used to hide. I climbed in. There was a shelf, but there was space for a person, even a tall one, to sit curled up under it. I sat there and imagined being young Henry. I carried on talking. It was a nice place, and being here made me feel close to him.

'Aisha?' I said. 'Can I ask you something?'

'Fire away,' she said, her voice cheerful.

'If you were somewhere where people trusted you and, in fact, where you were fully besotted with one of those people, but there was a bit of a mystery – a thing you wanted to investigate – and it was something totally entangled with your friends' lives and they'd be really upset with you if they knew, what would you do?'

She was silent for a while. Then she said, 'Cat – what are you saying?'

I swallowed hard. I needed to say this.

'It's just that I've found some things here. At Henry's home. It's to do with his mum, who died, years ago. I don't know. I'm in the house on my own and . . .'

I could hear her smiling when she replied. 'Oh, Cat! I . . . Babe, if there's a story, we go for it. You're there on your own right now? Have a poke around. You're only human, and you might actually find something out. If no one knows what you're up to, you're not hurting anyone.'

I was smiling too, grateful for the permission. 'I mean, recording a few impressions for a . . . kind of podcast, but one that no one's going to hear, just a practice one, is OK, do you think?'

'Totes harmless,' she said. 'When are you back? I need to know *all* about this.'

'Sunday,' I said. 'Henry and I are going to the market here, and then he said he'll drive me back to Antibes. I want to know what you've been working on too.'

'Henry, hey?'

'Yeah,' I said. I felt my face cracking into a grin. 'Henry.'

'Well, my stuff is cosmetics reviews, so I think we'll focus on yours, babe.'

We agreed to meet up on Monday, and when I hung up I was just sitting in a dark cupboard. I stayed there in silence for a bit. Then, for no reason, I switched on my phone torch and shone it around. '*You're an investigator like me,*' Aisha had said. '*It's what we do.*'

There were some pieces of paper tucked under the corner of the carpet. I pulled one out with my fingernails. What emerged was an envelope. Blank on the outside, but with something inside it. I definitely shouldn't look at it.

The phone BEEPED in my hand. I gasped, and in a few seconds I was out of the cupboard, on my feet, guilty as hell. It was just a message from Kitty, a clip of all the kids standing in the sea and kicking water at each other.

I had to calm my breathing. I replied with a row of hearts, and reminded myself that I was not here to spy on Henry because Henry was my boyfriend. We hadn't used the words *boyfriend* and *girlfriend*, but I was sure that was who he was. I walked down the wooden stairs by the kitchen and when I realized I still had the envelope in my hand I shoved it into my pocket to return it later.

I felt Aisha had given me permission. I walked into the kitchen and put my headphones in.

'I'm alone in the house.' I hated the sound of my voice in the empty house, so I imagined I was talking to friends. Kitty. Aisha. 'Just me, the cat, and you, my imaginary listeners. It's time to do it.'

I stood in front of the row of keys on their hooks. I looked at the key with ET on its label: I had smiled at the idea of ET the alien, but actually ... ET had to mean Elisabeth Tilney.

There weren't cameras in this house. Were there?

If I was going to panic about the idea of someone watching me, then I might as well give up now, because it would mean I'd never find out anything. I stopped for a second and considered it. Mr Tilney had a laptop, and I'd seen him writing emails, but he didn't seem like a technological wizard, and why would you have your house wired up when you lived alone?

And, actually, he'd left the laptop out. He often did. It was a clunky old one, and it was on the kitchen table right now.

I stopped the recording and walked over to it.

Maybe, I thought, it didn't have a password? I opened it, just in case. The screen came on straight away. Of course it wanted a password.

I typed a few characters, waiting to see how many it wanted before it would let me press enter. Five. I needed a five-letter password. I remembered what Henry and El had said about the 'golden boy' and typed in F-R-I-T-Z.

It didn't work. I tried H-E-N-R-Y instead, and that didn't work either.

What was I doing? Why was I invading Fred's privacy for no reason?

He'd never know. I told myself I'd give the password one more go and then I'd stop.

I looked around. I was hardly going to type in random five-letter words until it let me in. In fact, it would probably lock me out and next time he tried to open it he'd find that out. Could I just say I was trying to look something up?

The cat came stalking across the room. What the hell? I typed M-I-N-O-U, and waited.

And the computer opened up.

Once I was in, I didn't even know what I was looking for. Had I thought there would be a camera feed covering the screen? Of course there wasn't. I had a look at the apps, and none of them showed anything interesting at all. The emails were open, and I skimmed down them without even meaning to. I saw one from a company called 'Provence Immobilier' and another from a company called 'Gorgeous French Homes'. The Gorgeous French Homes one was in English and I read the preview of the message: Hi Fred. Yes, we could get the listing live as early as next week if you . . .

The cursor hovered over it. Then my eye snagged on a name at the bottom of his inbox.

Sophie Allen.

The preview said: Fred. I am so sorry about . . .

That was more interesting. Should I click on the message and read it properly?

No! I had broken into the computer to check for CCTV and I was as sure as I could be that there wasn't any.

I slammed it shut. Why had I even done that? It wasn't my business. I put the computer back exactly where I'd found it and went back to the row of keys.

Again I thought of François, muttering something in my ear, a word that sounded like *bonsoir*. Why had he done that? And then he'd hidden and watched us in the water and I didn't know how long he'd been there and that freaked me out. And he'd tried to talk to me. He skulked and watched and whispered and I didn't trust him.

Although I hadn't seen him for five days, I also thought I had. I'd seen a figure in the garden, twice, and it definitely hadn't been Fred or Henry.

I started recording again.

'Do you hear that? . . . Exactly. There's no sound. Except this . . .'

I carried on narrating as I took the key from the hook and walked to the entrance hall. I sat on the bottom step.

'Everyone is out. I can see them on Find My Friends. They're fifteen miles away, and heading further every time I refresh it. What the fuck am I doing?'

I held my breath and listened to the house one more time. I was about to do something super intrusive and this was my moment. I had to do it now: I might never be in the house on my own again.

The cat followed me up the stairs. She mewed, or whatever it was that French cats said. I, the human Cat, swallowed. Was I going to do this? And why?

That was the whole point. I wasn't going to do anything, or take anything. I wouldn't mess with any of it: I was just going to look. I'd look around the studio in case there was anything else that implicated François. If there was, I'd decide what to do about it. Maybe I'd share the picture with Henry, and let him decide what to do.

'Walking up the stairs. That's what. Honestly, I wish you could see this place. The staircase is massive. Stone, but carpeted, and the carpet's squishy under my bare feet. Still brutal, though, if you fell. The air smells of polish and summer. I know my way around this house – when I arrived here I would never have imagined that. I'm getting a feel for its secrets. Its ghosts.'

I talked myself brave. The floorboards were smooth on the soles of my feet. I walked along, round a corner, down a small flight of steps. Then I was in front of the door.

'This is it, people,' I said. I felt quite stupid talking to no one, but the idea of Aisha, Kitty, maybe even Sophie listening to this made me braver. I kept talking.

I thought of Henry. He was my favourite person, and this was his family home. His mother's room. What was I doing?

'First,' I said, 'is this the right key?'

My hand shook as I put it into the keyhole. It slotted straight in. I tried not to think about the way I was betraying the trust of people who considered me a friend, who had invited me into their home with no idea of what I was about to do. The people I liked more than anyone else I'd ever met. I knew I should turn back now.

Yet I didn't appear to be doing it.

It was only a room. I wasn't going to steal anything. I was curious. Looking. El and Henry would want to know exactly what had happened to Elisabeth. I might be able to help them.

'I'm not sure if you can hear that,' I said. 'It's the sound of the key turning . . . You definitely heard that creak. Wooden door, opening inwards. They probably heard it creaking down in the village.

'It smells musty. Like no one's been in for a while. But here we are.' I paused. Listened for the sound of a car coming back. Nothing.

I took a deep breath. It still wasn't too late to back out.

'Let's do it.'

I stepped across the threshold.

22

Elisabeth's room was dark, and I realized the shutters were closed. I pictured the outside of the house, the two windows that were always shut. This was the room behind them. It was dark and smelled old and dusty. A place that might have been undisturbed for six years.

Even though I knew the window was on the side of the house that overlooked the fields, and that no one would notice if I opened the shutters, I decided to leave them as they were in case I couldn't close them properly again. It was too risky. I shone my phone torch around until I found a light switch, and then I turned it on and stared at the room that was in front of me.

It wasn't just a studio. This was a surprisingly big room, and it had a bed in it, which I wasn't expecting. The bed was covered in a patchwork quilt. There was a pillow, but it was on top of the quilt, in a way that meant the bed wasn't made up.

I touched it. Had she slept here?

A movement made me spin round, terrified, but it was just Minou following me in. How old was Minou? Did she miss Elisabeth? Or had she never known her?

Then I looked at everything else. I had half expected this room to feel as if its inhabitant had just stepped out, but that wasn't the case at all. Apart from the bed and a wooden chair, everything was covered by dust sheets. It looked as if it was filled with ghosts, the sheeted kind. Ghosts with corners. The wooden floor had a layer of dust on it, and I could see that my feet, and Minou's, were disturbing it. I would have to do something about that before I left.

The whole place smelled uninhabited. I saw a few corpses of flies on the floor. They crunched when I stepped on them.

I walked over to a dust sheet that covered something taller than I was, with a pointed top. When I looked under it, it was an easel, with no painting on it. Just an angular wooden frame.

Another ghost was a little table and chair. I pictured the woman in El's photos sitting at it and sketching. Maybe this was where she had made the drawing of François. I shivered, realizing that I only knew what she looked like because of the photos in El's room. There was no picture of her in any of the main rooms, not even on the sitting-room mantelpiece. Henry and Fred's graduations were there, and El's last day of school, but not Elisabeth.

Another sheet covered the thing I had been hoping to find: a pile of art. I hoped there would be more pictures of François here. More notes. El had said Elisabeth always used notes and sketches to communicate. Instead, though, there were canvases of varying sizes piled into a wobbly tower. I sat on the floor and started looking through them. I didn't know much about art, but I was pretty sure these were oil paintings. They were enough like the ones in the hall for me to know they were by the same artist. I looked through them, trying not to feel disappointed. They were mainly pictures of this house and they told me nothing. There it was from the front, the side. The windows of this very room had their shutters open, unlike now. I looked at a painting of the view from the terrace, imagining her sitting out there with her easel and her paints, looking at the view we now saw without her. I wondered whether she and Fred used to have aperitifs there every night. How weird it must have been for her when all three children were away at boarding school. I imagined her looking forward to the holidays starting, to the house filling up again. To the laughter and the arguments and the splashing on the rope swing.

Or maybe not. She'd clearly been happy enough to send them away.

At the bottom of the pile there was a picture of the three children when they were much smaller. This one was a watercolour, with precise pencil lines and pastel colours. It was gorgeous: El was about the age Mia and Joshie were now, Henry was a rosy-cheeked little boy and Fritz looked proud and adult next to them, a perfect son and heir who looked like a prince. She had arranged the three of them in a line on the sofa, with El in the middle. I looked at them all for a while, then photographed the picture.

I realized I should be narrating this as I went, but when I tried my voice didn't work. I didn't want to speak in this room. It felt wrong. I would just talk about it later. I could even do a fake narration afterwards. I didn't have it in me to relate this to an imaginary audience in real time.

I almost missed the pile of stuff under the little desk. It was a tiny pile, containing three sketchbooks.

I put them on the desk and sat on the chair to leaf through. My hands shook as I turned the pages. Every muscle in my body was tense. I told myself there wouldn't be anything in here, but a part of me was certain there would.

The first book was filled with drawings of details. A picture of a vase of flowers. A bunch of tiny grapes hanging from a vine. A detailed study of a hand (maybe Elisabeth's own?). Another hand, this one hairy and definitely male.

Were Fred's hands hairy? I would check, later. I closed the book and pushed it away.

The second book was almost completely filled with sketches of flowers. They were pretty, but boring. Then, towards the end, there was a picture of a man.

It was François.

She had drawn him over and over again. He was holding a cigarette, as he had done at the market, and a glass. He was smiling. Looking thoughtful. He was the man I'd met at the market on Sunday, but a bit different. These pictures were from at least six years ago, and this version of François was, of course, younger. His face was thinner. His hair was a bit different. The essence of him was the same.

Little versions of François covered pages and pages, and then I turned the page and found I was looking at a lot more of the man than I had ever wanted to see.

He was stretched out on what I was pretty sure was the bed in the corner of this room, and he was extremely naked. Naked, and looking at the artist with a glint in his eye.

I closed the book. My breath caught in my throat. Wow: I had *really* not wanted to see that. My stomach churned. I had never seen a naked boy with my own eyes, unless you counted younger siblings, which you didn't. I'd seen bits of porn because it was impossible not to. I'd thought about Henry. Now I was looking at François and I wanted to throw up.

It jolted me out of my trance. How long had I been in here? Where were the family? My hand trembled as I opened my phone and it took me a few goes before I'd managed to refresh Find My Friends.

I exhaled. They were twenty miles away, safely with the godmother.

I put everything back where I'd found it, carefully replacing the dust sheets as close as possible to the way they'd been before. Then I took a dust sheet and used it as a brush, to erase the footprints.

I locked the door behind me and tried to walk in a casual and normal way back to the kitchen where I hung the key on its hook. Then I rushed up two flights of stairs to my room, where I lay on the bed and breathed hard.

Had Elisabeth and François been *lovers*? They must have been. That was not the way you drew someone who was a neighbour and a family friend.

I knew how it went from here. I may not have known a lot about relationships in the real world, but I knew plenty from crime podcasts. Elisabeth had been having an affair with the neighbour. He had probably asked her to leave her husband. She had said no, and he'd killed her. It would have been easy for him to come to the house when Fred was out. I pictured them arguing. Him pushing her. Her falling down the stairs. He probably hadn't meant to kill her.

Or had he? There were those words on the sketch. *He will kill me.* She had known it was going to happen. Had she felt trapped here, unable to tell Fred about her fears? Because how could she tell him?

He had been happy enough to talk to François at the market. He couldn't possibly have known.

And now I knew. And François was interested in me, for some reason. He must somehow sense that I was uncovering things.

I'd be back in Antibes the day after tomorrow.

I looked at the ceiling, breathing hard. Pictured Fred coming home and finding her dead on the staircase. How was I going to keep this from showing on my face when the others got back?

I couldn't sit still. I decided to walk down to the river and swim. Then I remembered that I'd promised Fred that I wouldn't so I looked, instead, for something to cook for dinner.

There was a bowl of onions in the kitchen. Flour in a jar, butter in the fridge. Loads of herbs. I pulled up the onion tart recipe that Sophie had sent me. First, though, I needed to breathe some air.

I walked down the garden, past the fig tree, past the new shed. I could smell the fresh wood of it even as I walked past at about ten metres away.

I stopped and looked at it. A shed was a good place for hiding things. Maybe, while I was feeling so brave, I should have a look in. I'd seen François skulking around here and had a sudden mad thought that he might be living in it. I felt the dry grass crunching under my shoes as I walked over. A bird high in the fig tree squawked at me in a way that made me jump.

I looked around. There was no one there. I tried the shed door but it was locked.

I looked back at the house. I could see my bedroom window from here.

I walked round, and found there was a window in the far end, the other narrower end. I had to stand on tiptoes to look through it and when I did . . . there was nothing in it at all.

Of course François wasn't living in a shed. He had a house in the valley.

Fred had built it, but so far he hadn't filled it up. He was probably saving that job for when he was alone again.

I felt guilty about all the intruding I was doing. I went back to the house and had a long, cool shower, trying to wash away the guilt.

23

I was cooking onions really slowly in lots of butter when my phone started blowing up. It was on the work surface next to me, plugged in. When it pinged four times in a row, I jumped, certain that I was in trouble.

The first message I saw was from Sophie. It just said:

Sorry. Stay where you are darling xxx

That made no sense, but OK. I looked at the other names on the screen. Kitty had messaged twice, and there was one from Mum too, and one from Izzy Thorpe, maybe replying to my apology at last.

Kitty's said:

Wtf is going on? Do you have to come back? Can we help?

I scrolled back to her first message:

Just saw this!!! What?

There was a link to a news article. The headline said 'British couple arrested in Thailand'.

There was a photo of . . .

A photo of . . .

A photo of Owen and Sophie. Owen and Sophie, but looking different. Sophie, always so poised and put together, was all over the place. Her hair was covering her face, and I realized she must have done it on purpose, to shield herself. It was clearly her, though. I recognized her dress, her rings, everything about her.

Owen was looking straight at the camera, and his face was blank.

Thailand? They were in Dubai, but also that was the least of my worries. My hand shook as I held the phone. I clicked on the article and tried to make sense of it.

British couple held in Thailand on drug trafficking charges

Two British citizens arrested yesterday at the Thai/Cambodian border following an investigation have been named as Owen Allen, 55, and Sophie Allen, 42, of Truro, Cornwall. The pair, who are married, are being held in Bangkok as they await extradition to the UK on charges of drug smuggling and false accounting.

The arrests come as Allen Holdings Ltd, a company of which both are listed as directors, has been closed down after a year-long investigation by journalist Aisha Sami.

I put the phone down.

Aisha?

Aisha, who I'd spoken to an hour ago? What had she said? *Hectic with work*? I felt dizzy. *Cosmetics reviews*. That was what she'd said. I made myself focus again. I forced myself to finish reading.

'On paper it looks like a simple import/export operation,' said Sami. 'Bringing art in from all over the world. However, when I started investigating the places where the cocaine and heroin that's currently flooding Europe came from, one trail led me to the Allens.'

Sami's investigation took her to the French Riviera, where the Allens were spending the summer. 'It's a small community there, and when I was able to meet people connected to Mr and Mrs Allen – people who, I would like to stress, had no idea what their friends were doing – my investigation progressed.' When Sophie Allen, a former BBC radio producer who quit her media career to focus on Allen Holdings, and Owen Allen, a former banker, discovered someone was on their trail they fled to Asia.

The pair are understood to have gone initially to Cambodia, which does not have an extradition treaty with the UK. However, Sami was following their movements and is understood to have alerted authorities when they crossed the border to go shopping.

Seb Jackson, a lawyer representing Mr and Mrs Allen, said: 'My clients strongly refute these allegations and look forward to proving their innocence in court. They visited Southeast Asia on holiday, which is not a crime. This arrest is the result of a malicious smear campaign waged by a single individual. We will not be saying anything more about it at this time.'

I read every word of it, twice. I tried to make sense of it. I was the one who'd taken Aisha into the apartment. Had I done this? She'd got chatting to Izzy first and become part of our group, and I supposed it had all been to get close to Owen's business. To bring them down.

I thought of her words to me this afternoon. 'If there's a story, we go for it.'

Then the meaning of what I'd just read hit me. Owen's business was a front for smuggling drugs? What the hell? *Cocaine and heroin*? It had to be a mistake. I clung on to that thought. People got things wrong. I had certainly got Aisha wrong: I had been imagining myself an investigator, but I hadn't had the tiniest inkling that I was being used by someone I'd thought was a friend to get closer to my hosts. Nor that my hosts were drug smugglers, for that matter. I remembered Aisha asking for a tour of the apartment. Pretending she wanted to rent it in the autumn. Asking to use the loo. Hanging back when I returned to the terrace. I was hot with guilt. I'd done this.

It couldn't be right, though: it just couldn't. It had to be a huge mistake. But why had their lawyer said they were on holiday in Southeast Asia when that wasn't true? When they had *already* been on holiday in France? Why had they lied to me about going to Dubai?

And when had Sophie sent me that message? Where was she now?

I remembered the other messages and almost dropped my phone in my rush to read them. Izzy's came first.

Cat!!! did you know?? What's going on and are you ok? Do you have stuff in their apartment because if so you should go and get it out right now.

Did Aisha totally play us that whole time???

A tiny part of me was relieved. Izzy was talking to me again. At least there was that. We'd been fooled by Aisha together. I'd call her in a minute.

Mum had sent a voice note so I pressed play. Hearing her voice, her mummishness, made me step back from the counter and lean on the wall for support. This, surely, would end the weirdness between us.

'Cat. Oh my God. I just saw the news. I know you're with your other friends, but are you OK? Please let us know. You'd better come home. Just let me know you're all right. You didn't go to Thailand with them, did you? I know you didn't, because you video called the kids, didn't you, and they said you were in a big house in France. I don't want you to be caught up in anything. I knew you shouldn't have gone. I can't believe it's true, though. A huge mistake. Sophie wouldn't ... Owen wouldn't ... There'll be an explanation, won't there ... ? Just call. OK?'

I inhaled deeply. Mum was properly panicking. All her words had come out in a big rush. I put the phone on silent, pushed it into my pocket and took some deep breaths. *I knew you shouldn't have gone*: that part wound me up a bit. Other than that, though: my mother was worried about me. I had risen to the top of her list of concerns and in a horrible, selfish way that felt good.

I'd call her back in a minute. I needed to get my head straight first. Izzy had asked if I had things in their apartment and I did. A lot of things. My passport, for one. I'd need to go back and get it. Would Henry drive me?

Could we stop at their empty house, if he did?

Oh God. What would they think of me now? Henry and El and Fred?

Drug smuggling. I kept coming back to that. Drug smugglers weren't like this. The Allens had been so kind to me. So generous. Were my new clothes, my travel tickets, our dinners all paid for by something horrific? It would take me a long time to get my head round it.

Was I complicit? Yes. I looked down at myself. I was wearing my green dress because I loved it and wore it whenever it was clean, and also, in all honesty, when it wasn't. This dress had been paid for by ... drug money. I could feel my phone vibrating in my pocket and desperately wished I wasn't here alone. I needed someone to talk to. Someone real.

I got my phone out again and ignored the messages that I could see were arriving from Kitty again, and Mabel and Izzy. I had loads of Instagram notifications and emails. All I wanted was Find My Friends. Where were Henry and El?

Nearby.

That was where they were. I looked at their dots in the same place. They were about five miles away, on a main-looking road. I refreshed the app: they were a bit closer. They would be back soon.

Then I looked down at myself. I didn't want to be wearing this dress any more. I ran up the back stairs, and up the second set, and stood in my bedroom and changed into clothes that hadn't been provided by Sophie. I didn't have much of that stuff left, but I grabbed a pair of denim shorts from the bottom of a drawer, and pulled on a slightly bobbly yellow T shirt that I'd used to sleep in. That would do. At least I wasn't wearing clothes paid for by . . .

Had they really made all that money from drugs? Really? It did make more sense than art.

I scrolled to that message from Sophie again.

She must have sent it just as they were being arrested.

I scrolled up. It was just voice note after voice note. They were all just Sophie being nice to me. Being effusive. Maybe a bit drunk with Helena. Did she feel bad about what they were doing? No wonder she'd had a drink in her hand most of the time.

I sat on the bed and tried to control myself. This wasn't the time to cry. At some point I knew I'd need to look at what Aisha had uncovered properly, but not now. This wasn't the time for it.

It was the smell of the onions that got me back down the stairs just in time to save them: I turned the gas right down under them and added sugar and salt and more butter. I grated in four garlic cloves like Sophie's recipe said. I took my pastry out of the fridge and tipped flour on the work surface, ready to roll it out.

I rolled, and greased a pie dish that I rooted out, and switched the oven on. I stirred and stirred the onions and seasoned them and kept myself busy until I heard the car pulling up on the gravel outside. I took some deep breaths and pulled myself under control before I walked out of the kitchen, along the corridors, to the entrance hall.

When I saw Henry coming through the door, I ran at him and made him hug me. As soon as his arms were round me, I started to cry. He stroked my back and nuzzled my hair, but I could feel that he was looking at the others over the top of my head.

'Hey,' he said, after a moment. 'What's happened?' I could feel how mortified he was by the fact that I was doing this in front of his dad.

Then I heard El's voice. 'Oh my God,' she said. 'Look at your phone, H.'

All three of them were exactly the people I needed. They sat me down and, when I refused alcohol, gave me a cup of tea-leaf tea with lots of sugar in it. Sugar was definitely my recovery drug of choice.

'I mean, I think we'd all wondered,' said Fred, pacing around the kitchen. 'I suppose I'd heard whispers. Nothing specific. Just that they might have some dodgy business dealings.' He paused. 'I know that our mutual friend Eva was concerned.'

I looked up quickly. He had never mentioned Eva before. Then I sighed, disgusted with myself. I wasn't going

227

to do any more stupid investigations. Aisha had tricked me – she'd chatted to me today and encouraged me to poke around, minutes before her own investigation of my friends went live – and although I supposed that what she'd done was ultimately good (if she was right), I didn't like it. I saw what I had been trying to do reflected back at me. She'd tricked her way into the apartment. She'd used us to find things out. She had done all the things I'd been doing, except she'd done them properly. And then she'd told me to do them too.

I would drop the whole thing. The investigation Izzy and I had not quite managed to start into Eva and then the one I'd taken much further, into Elisabeth: they had both been stupid. They were both over. I was done.

'Really?' I said. 'People knew?'

Fred shrugged. 'I mean, they have that penthouse. And the place in the Alps. And I'd wager that their place in Cornwall isn't some kind of shack, right?'

My voice came out very small. 'They have a swimming pool.'

'Exactly. You just don't make that kind of money from buying up art from unknown Latin American artists, or whatever it was meant to be. You've seen those closed shipping containers? They can hide a multitude.'

I stood up and went to put the tart in the oven.

'I just can't believe I got it so wrong,' I said. 'I had no idea at all. Aisha said she was on holiday after a break-up. She asked to see their apartment because she wanted to rent it off-season sometime. That was what she said.'

'She played you,' said El.

'And there's no shame in that,' Fred insisted. 'You're a pure soul, Cat. It speaks well of you.'

That made me hot with guilt.

'I feel so stupid.'

'You shouldn't,' said Fred. 'Please don't. You must stay here as long as you like. What can we do to help you?'

Idly, I looked at his hands. They were smooth. Barely hairy at all. They were not the hands in the drawing.

'Izzy said I should get my stuff from their apartment.' I thought about it. 'The main thing I guess is my passport.'

'Your passport's there?' said Fred. 'Then yes. We must mount an operation to retrieve it.' He paused, thinking. 'Let's get you there tomorrow morning.'

We all agreed, and I felt warm and grateful. I imagined Henry and me heading to Antibes together. Collecting my stuff and then going to their empty house . . . It made my breathing go strange. All these emotions.

Fred wandered outside, El set off upstairs and Henry hung around. As soon as we were alone, he took me in his arms again. I pressed myself into his body, loving the warmth of him. The comfort, the bulk.

'I'm going to text Sophie,' I said. 'Say sorry for bringing Aisha into their home. I want her to know I'd never do that on purpose.'

'She knows that already,' Henry said, into my hair. 'Don't say it. It just sounds worse if you do.'

I thought about it. I knew he felt me nodding.

'Oh – Cat?' he said, a moment later.

'Yep?' I gave him a weak smile.

'Sorry,' said Henry. 'I know you've got enough else to deal with but . . . was Minou around earlier? She should be agitating for dinner by now but I haven't seen her.'

'No,' I said. 'I haven't . . .' I stopped talking. Then I carried on, trying to style it out. Keep the same casual tone. I held him tighter so he couldn't see my face. 'Haven't seen her lately. She was around earlier, yeah.'

Shit shit shit.

I knew exactly where she was.

Henry nodded. 'She'll turn up. It's just out of character for her not to be right here by half five. She's probably stalking mice or whatever she does. So we picked up a bottle of *rinquinquin* earlier. Dad is so taken with you. He said, "*We'll get it for Cat because she doesn't drink much but she likes that.*" Honestly, he's never that thoughtful. Never. Fancy one? Aperitifs while the tart is cooking?'

I forced a smile. I tried to react in the way I would have done if I hadn't been filled with cold horror.

I took a deep breath.

'That would be perfect!' I said. 'Thank you. That's really lovely of him.'

Henry started taking glasses down from the shelf.

'I'm having one too,' he said. He looked at the oven. 'Can you leave everything for a bit?'

I nodded, and set a timer on my phone for the tart.

'Yep,' I said. 'Sure. Just going to the loo. The tart's going to be twenty-five minutes. I'll see you on the terrace.'

The key hooks were in the corner, and Henry was standing between me and them. I would have to wait for him to leave, take the key without anyone seeing, unlock the door to let Minou out of the studio and get the key back on its hook, at which point I would never do any investigating ever, ever again.

First, I went to the downstairs bathroom and actually did do a wee, for authenticity and because I needed one.

Then I crept back into the kitchen. I could hear Henry and Fred talking about Owen and Sophie on the terrace. El was the danger. Drinks were always at six and she usually turned up a bit late. I checked the time: it was one minute past. I lingered for a moment, then walked over to the keys, reached out and took the one I needed. For the second time that day I dropped it into my pocket, though it was a different pocket. I knew it was visible in the back of my shorts, but you'd have to be looking at my bum to notice it. Henry might see it.

He might feel it.

'Hey!'

I turned round and saw El in the doorway. I picked up a knife and started cutting a tomato. We needed salad anyway, I decided. She took an avocado out of a bowl and held it up, a question on her face.

I nodded and she reached for another chopping board. 'Thanks. Henry's taken drinks out,' I said. 'So lovely of your dad to get the one I like. I'll be there in a sec. I can do the avocado. Don't worry.'

She looked at me for a moment, then nodded and handed it to me. Was I imagining something different in her manner? She had been so friendly: it had always felt as if we had known each other for years even though it had actually only been a week. Actually, not even that. Now I felt she was staring into my soul. It was my guilty conscience. Had to be. Or maybe she thought I had known about Allen Holdings Ltd all along. Maybe she was judging me by association, whatever she said.

She opened a cupboard and took out a bag of crisps, and without bothering to decant it into a bowl took it out to the terrace. I set off, as fast yet quietly as I could.

As I approached Elisabeth's room, I could hear mewing. Poor Minou! I couldn't believe I'd locked her in a room for an entire afternoon. I'd seen her come in too: how had I forgotten her when I left? I remembered myself smoothing over the dusty floor. I'd got rid of her footprints without even checking if she was still in the room.

I'd been too freaked out by those drawings to think of anything else.

I looked up and down the corridor as I pushed the key into the lock. My hand was shaking much more this time: the key's end scratched around the lock so much that I feared it was drawing a picture on the casing, that it was maybe writing my name and my guilt right there.

I gripped it with both hands and forced it in, and then it was turning and the door was opening. Minou shot out like a racing car, zipping down the corridor and round the corner in a way that made me think of Dash and Ethan and their toy cars – the ones you pulled back and let go. I closed the door, locked it and pushed the key back into my pocket.

Checked the corridor: all clear.

In the kitchen, Henry was making a big fuss of feeding Minou, who was shoving her face into an open tin of tuna so wholeheartedly that he had to hold it out and let her eat from the tin before he was able to tip the rest into her bowl. I paused as I walked past, but knew that I needed to get myself outside. I needed to be sitting on the terrace looking at the evening sunlight. It would be easier to appear normal and innocent if I was doing that, and I couldn't put the key back while Henry was in the kitchen.

I paused. Henry was stroking Minou, crouching down crooning at her in a baby-cat language that made me want to walk over and kiss him.

The longer I held on to it, the bigger the risk of them spotting the key was gone.

I palmed the key out of my back pocket and edged towards the row of hooks.

'Was she in the bathroom?' Henry turned to look at me. 'I thought, since she appeared like a bolt of lightning after you left, you must have found her trapped?'

I grabbed the excuse and ran with it, grateful. First, though, I dropped the key on to the work surface, where he couldn't see it, and pushed it as close to the hooks as I could get it so it was under them. I couldn't actually hang it up while he was talking to me, but I'd do it as soon as I could.

'Yeah.' I ran through plausible options as fast as I could and settled on one that I hoped might work. 'Not the bathroom. I . . . I went to my room for something and she was in there. She'd been sleeping on my bed earlier and I guess I closed the door. Or it blew shut or something.'

I realized that I'd inadvertently played a masterstroke. I'd made it sound as if I'd gone to my room for a tampon, and so Henry would never interrogate my story. Sure enough, he blushed and gave me a little smile.

'Well,' he said. 'No harm done. Your drink's out there, so go get it while it's cold.'

Outside, Fred handed me a wine glass filled with pale-pink liquid.

'I'm sorry – the ice has almost melted,' he said. 'I suppose I poured it a little early.'

El shot him a look and I realized that they thought I'd been in the loo all this time. I appeared to have found my salvation and alibis in bathroom embarrassments. I'd take it.

I looked at the horizon for some perspective (but I knew that François's house was somewhere out there so it didn't calm me much) and tried to steady my heartbeat and my hands. *Be normal be normal be normal.* At least, I supposed, I had a reason to be agitated today. They'd think it was about the Allens. Small mercies.

'Thank you,' I said. I held my glass up. 'And, you know, thanks for having me here. It's a total haven. I don't know what I'd do without you right now. I hope your visit was good today.'

'You're welcome,' said Fred. 'As I said – as long as you want. Let's get your passport tomorrow. Make sure there's nothing of yours in there when authorities seize the apartment.'

234

'Do you think they will?'

He shrugged. 'Yes. But no reason for them to take your possessions.'

El leaned over to clink her glass on mine. 'Today was fine, thanks,' she said. 'Let's talk about normal things. I mean, Dominique, my godmother, she's pretty ... I don't know ... old-fashioned? So everything always has to be –'

She stopped talking as Fred stood up.

'Old fashioned!' he said. He clapped his hands. 'Thank you! You're a genius. I knew I didn't want one of these pink drinks. Sorry, Cat – I know you love them, but I'm an old man and I feel as if I'm drinking squash. I'm going to make a proper drink. An old fashioned. I'll see if Henry wants one. Did he find that cat?'

'Yes,' I said quickly. 'He did.'

'Knew she'd turn up. Silly beast.'

'I'll have an old fashioned too!' Eleanor shouted at his back. She turned to me and rolled her eyes. We both sipped our drinks. Everything was fine. I'd got away with the cat thing and as soon as I had my passport I'd book myself –'

'WHERE IS IT?'

The words bellowed out of the kitchen. I had only heard that tone from Fred once before, in a much milder form, when he was arguing with El about the house. His shout now was that multiplied by a thousand. He didn't sound like himself at all. He was a different person.

My heart started pounding in my chest, and for the first time in my life I understood what *weak at the knees* meant. I wasn't standing up, but I felt my legs turning to water.

El made a little face at me, then twisted round to call back into the house.

'Where's what?' she said.

'The fucking key!'

Had I got it close enough to the hooks to make it possible for anyone to believe that it had fallen down? I desperately hoped so.

'What key?' called El. If she'd looked at me at that point, she would have seen it on my face, for sure. But she didn't.

'The key to ... You know!' He was coming closer. I could hear it in his voice. Then he stopped. Henry was saying something. I could hear his tone, but not his words.

'What do you mean?' said Fred. Another muttering from Henry. El started saying something to me, but then Henry appeared on the terrace, flustered.

'Sorry about him,' he said. 'Pretend you didn't hear that.'

My voice wobbled, but I managed to say, 'Everything OK?'

'Yes,' said Henry in a tone different from anything he'd used with me before. 'A key had fallen down. Probably the cat. It's back on its hook now. No drama.'

A couple of minutes later, Fred came out with new drinks.

'Sorry about that.' He was giving a self-deprecating smile: it was the first time I'd seen him looking like Henry. 'My mistake. I thought – well, I thought for a moment that someone must have been into the house, Cat, while we were out. You did say you walked in the garden and

I was afraid somebody might have … Anyway. Doesn't matter. The cat had knocked the damned thing down. Cheers!'

Henry had saved me.

Henry had to know I'd taken the key.

He knew that I'd been into his mother's room.

I wanted to die. All my dreams of me and Henry in the future shrivelled and vanished.

I saw that my aperitif was almost empty, though I hadn't noticed myself drinking it. I swallowed the last mouthful and stared at the glass. There was half an ice cube in there, shrinking as I watched. My relationship with Henry, such as it was, melted with it.

I pasted on a fake smile and stood up.

'Right!' I said. My voice reminded me of something but I couldn't think what. 'I'd better go and get the salad sorted! Dinner will be about fifteen minutes.'

Later, after an excruciating dinner during which no one seemed to be in a mood to talk, though everyone was very kind about my mediocre onion tart, I shut myself away and made some calls. The first was a voice call: I wasn't going to spring another video one on her.

'Cat?'

'Mum!' Hearing her voice was the thing I needed, my annoyance with her from earlier gone. I didn't really care what we said.

'How are you?' She sounded careful. 'I mean, what's going on?'

'I'm . . .' I wasn't sure what to say. I thought of the four children at home. The fact that she was pissed off with me. How would I even begin to explain to her what I'd done? 'I'm fine,' I said. 'I mean, the Sophie stuff. It's all . . .'

'Did you have any idea?'

'No! Did you?'

She sighed. 'My darling. If I'd had a clue, I wouldn't have let you go. You're sure you're OK?'

'I'll come home soon,' I said. The words *my darling* warmed me up as we talked about the babies. As she was telling me what they'd been eating, I realized what my own voice had reminded me of earlier, when I'd been bossy about salad.

My own mother.

For some reason, that fact made me cry.

I video-called Izzy as soon as I'd sorted my face out, and she picked up straight away.

'Oh my God!' she said. 'Cat Morland! Talk to me.'

I hadn't even known Izzy long, but I'd missed her. We settled in to talk about everything, except Jonno. Once we'd covered the Allens (no one knew anything and all the rumours had been totally non-specific) we moved on to Northanger.

'I actually started a project here,' I told her. I dropped my voice. 'But you mustn't tell anyone, OK?'

Later, I waited for Henry. For the first time, he didn't come.

24

I was sitting at the kitchen table, drinking a cup of tea and eating a bit of yesterday's baguette with apricot jam, when Fred walked in, put the kettle on and started fiddling around with coffee filters.

'Ahh, Cat! Good. Just let me grab a coffee and we'll set off. No point hanging around.'

'I . . .' I tried to make sense of this. 'I thought Henry was taking me?'

He looked round, smiling. 'Well, I don't see him around. No, Cat. He's not feeling a hundred per cent today. I said I'd take you down there. I'd like to go and check on the boat anyway.'

Did I actually need to go at all? Couldn't I just get a new passport? Or maybe I could get a bus? I could ask Izzy to go in and get it, now that she was speaking to me again! Helena had to have a spare key.

The way Fred had shouted last night had been scary. I really didn't want to be in the car with him. I could hardly blame Henry, though, for faking illness to avoid the trip. Of course Henry, specifically, didn't want to spend hours in a car with me when he knew I'd been snooping around and lying about it.

I knew there was nothing I could do. Fred seemed to sense my worry and became super friendly as we prepared to go.

'Tell you what,' he said, standing on the doorstep, taking a deep breath of morning air and looking at his car. 'We'll do a *déchétèrie* stop en route. The tip. I'd like to get rid of all the crap and make the car a little less disgraceful. Would that be all right with you, Cat?'

I nodded. I was trying to hold myself together, but I'd messed everything up. Henry knew what I'd done here. I'd taken Aisha right into Sophie and Owen's apartment and left her to look around. Sophie had drunk wine with her! I was complicit in everything that had happened to Sophie and Owen. Aisha must have loved me: I was exactly the sort of dupe a person like her needed.

And then she'd cheered me on to do the same thing to Henry's family, and I'd done it.

If the Allens were really using their business to bring drugs into Europe alongside the art, that was terrible. But I wouldn't have deliberately unmasked them in the most sensational way possible, sending them dashing to Cambodia and ensuring they were arrested and splashed on the front of the papers. I hoped they didn't think I'd done it on purpose. Maybe I should send that message after all. But would they see it?

However, none of that was my immediate worry. I got slowly into the car and Fred slammed the door and walked round to the other side. I did up my seatbelt and looked round in case Henry and El had appeared, but they hadn't.

I supposed Henry had been taking things slowly between us to check if we were compatible, and he'd got his answer in time. We weren't. I was the sort of girl who would steal a key and look through his dead mother's things. He didn't even know that I'd done it for an imaginary podcast. I shuddered. I had to make sure he never found that out. Who even was I?

Fred looked at me with a conspiratorial smile, and I took a deep breath. He had been kind, but I didn't really know him.

He started the engine and sounded the horn three times, and then we were off. Near the end of the driveway, he tossed his phone at me.

'Put music on,' he said. 'Anything you like.' He paused. 'Ideally, something I can hum along to. The passcode is two-zero-one-one. November twentieth. El's birthday.'

I put in the code and looked at his screen. It was an iPhone, a way newer one than my second-hand thing. The photo was a picture of Minou sleeping in a shaft of sunlight. I opened my mouth to comment on it, but couldn't do it. Not after last night. Not Minou.

'What music app do you use?' I said instead.

He laughed. 'The one that says Music on it. Path of least resistance.'

I opened Apple Music and looked at his playlists. It felt far too intimate. He had a playlist called 'E 🖤 classical', and I wondered if it was his dead wife's favourites, or

El's, or maybe even Eva's now I knew they were friends too. When I saw another called 'Car tunes', I opened it in relief. This was regular stuff. Songs to hum along to, as he'd said.

I pressed play on a Beatles tune. 'Here Comes the Sun', one I knew. Fred nodded his approval and soon we were both singing along. We didn't really talk. I began to relax.

After about an hour he turned off the main road. A song came on: it was one I didn't know, called 'Why Does it Always Rain on Me?'. It hadn't rained for ages.

'Skip this one,' he said, laughing. 'It's taunting my garden.'

I picked up his phone, smiling, ready to jump to the next track. As I had it in my hand, a text preview appeared at the top of the screen. The sender was just listed as 'Thorpe' and the few words of text said, No. You should just get her . . .

Thorpe. I didn't want it to be Jonno, but I was sure it was. Fred was far too gentlemanly to refer to a woman by her surname, and Jonno was the only Thorpe guy around. *You should just get her*? Was it narcissistic of me to wonder if Fred and Jonno were talking about me?

I pressed the forward button and the next song started up. At least I recognized Bob Dylan's voice.

Then we were slowing right down and driving through some gates marked DÉCHÈTERIE.

'We just need to dump everything from the back of the car,' he said, driving slowly. 'Sorry. Won't take long.

You don't mind heaving a few things into skips with me, do you?'

'Of course not!' I listened to my stupid voice. All bright and chirpy. 'I can do all of it if you like. It's not too heavy, is it?'

'Indeed it's not,' he said. 'And thank you. I appreciate that. But let's work together. Get it done in half the time and then we can head onwards to the coast. Fancy a trip out on the boat after we've done the day's business?'

'Oh wow,' I said. I didn't want to go out on the boat at all. He didn't reply because he was winding down his window and showing a card to a man, who scanned it with a handheld thing. Then we were allowed through.

It was an incredibly well-organized place. The parking spaces were on a little manmade hill, which meant the skips for the different types of recycling were lower than us so it was easy to throw things into them. We got to work. The boot of the car was long and it was absolutely filled with rubbish. Fred showed me that it was pre-sorted into boxes of garden waste, rubble and non-recyclables.

'Can you take the landfill crap?' he said, putting a box into my hand. 'Just chuck the whole thing down there. I'll do the rubble because it's heaviest. Don't you love these places? So well organized. Cameras everywhere to catch us if we don't recycle properly.'

He pointed, and I looked at the camera. I felt a bit self-conscious. I picked up the box of landfill crap. It was heavier than I'd expected: it was a kind of plastic chest with a lid. I opened the lid, ready to empty it.

'Don't bother, Cat,' called Fred. 'Lob it in. Box and all.'

I felt bad throwing a reusable plastic box into landfill but I did it. I threw it away from me, and as it fell the lid flew open. Blue plastic started to unfurl itself. Brown shapes tumbled down. Stones and things. I didn't think they should go into landfill, but what did I know? It was all gone and I moved on to the next load.

By the time we reached Antibes, the sun was high in the sky and everything was bleached in its bright light. Fred drove to the usual car park and I felt strange to be back here. It was impossible to imagine that Sophie and Owen were in *prison*. Prison in Bangkok: that could only be horrific. What was Sophie wearing? Was she allowed any of her own stuff? In the Bridget Jones film (my only reference point), Bridget had sung Madonna songs with the other prisoners, but I knew it wouldn't be like that. It would be awful. Horrific, particularly for Sophie who loved to surround herself with luxury.

If she loved life so much, maybe she shouldn't have been involved in drug smuggling. That was the little voice in my head.

I double-checked my bag for the keys. There they were. I had found the safe code in one of Sophie's old messages. Fred and I walked together to the big front door of the apartment building.

I'd only been at Northanger for a week, but this building felt like something from a different lifetime. The door was blank and there was no hint of the fact that the lives inside it had been totally upended. Still, a part of me expected it to be a big misunderstanding. I thought I'd find them both in there, smiling at me, offering drinks.

I unlocked the main door, my heart pounding, and was suddenly glad that Fred seemed to be assuming he'd come in with me. I didn't want to go in alone. I pushed the main door and it swung silently open. I stepped over the threshold, and then he did too.

25

The apartment had the atmosphere of a place that hadn't been lived in for a while. No one had made morning coffee lately. Nobody had cooked. The smell of Sophie's various perfumes lingered and that made it worse. It was as if someone had pressed pause, and it was waiting.

I thought of Elisabeth's room. It had been like this, but further into the future. The dead flies underfoot, the dust all over the dust sheets, which I supposed showed they were doing their job.

'Right.' Fred was looking around, and when I saw it through his eyes it just looked normal. The huge piece of art on the wall was the only thing that seemed to jump out at him, and he walked towards it, breathing heavily.

'Well, look at that,' he said, smiling.

'It's nice, isn't it?' I said. He looked around at me as if he'd forgotten I was there.

I realized as I looked at it that it was by Elisabeth. How had I not seen that before? Why did they have an Elisabeth Tilney painting?

'Magnificent.' We both looked at it. I remembered Sophie saying the artist had been a friend and decided not to say anything about it. He clearly made the same decision. 'I'm glad it's all quiet up here. Just wanted to come with you in case you had any . . . trouble. But you gather whatever you need. I'll be right here.'

I nodded, and went to my room. It didn't take long to pack all the rest of my stuff: most of the things I'd left here were the things I'd brought from home, which I'd discarded for not being stylish enough for Antibes. Fuck that. These were the only things that felt real now. I shoved them all into the bag I'd brought with me, then opened the door to the balcony and stepped out.

This had to be the last time I would come here. I leaned on the railing and looked down at the square. There was a long queue for the Picasso Museum: it snaked all the way along the wall and out into the sun, and I wanted to tell people to wait. Come back in a couple of hours, and the line will be half that length. I watched people walking around, heading to the shops, to the beach, to the harbour, and wondered about their lives. This wasn't my world. It had felt like it for a bit, but it wasn't.

I looked at the spot at which I'd tried to kiss Henry that first night. I was glad we'd eventually kissed, happy that we'd had this wonderful week even though I'd messed it up so much that I was sure I'd never kiss him again. I would head home and Henry would . . . do whatever he did next. I blinked hard.

Then I pulled myself together. I stepped back into the apartment and closed the doors carefully, making sure they were locked. I stripped the linen off my bed and piled it up, though there was no point putting it into the washing machine because it would go mouldy by the time anyone was here to take it out. I folded the light duvet and put it on top of the bed, and put the pillows on top of it.

Fred looked round when I stepped back into the living area.

'Ah,' he said. 'Are you done?'

'Nearly,' I told him. 'Just need to hope I've got the right code for the safe. And really hope that my passport's in there.'

'Oh I say,' said Fred. 'Let's have a look, shall we?'

It felt a bit intrusive, going into someone's bedroom while they were in Thai prison. A treacherous part of me wondered if I should be taking photographs since I knew that Kitty, for instance, would like to see in the drug smugglers' luxurious bedroom, but I shut that down fast. If Fred hadn't been here, I might have done it, so I was pleased he was saving me from myself.

The smell of perfume was stronger in here. The bed was made, the sheets tightly pulled up and tucked in. All the doors were closed and the room was tidy. I realized I'd never even stepped over the threshold before: it was spacious and airy with huge windows looking out in two directions, one of them with a sea view.

I walked straight to the safe and put in the code that Sophie had texted to me. 48–29–48–58.

Nothing happened. Shit. My passport was in there and if I couldn't get it out I'd never go home.

I stared at it and waited.

Maybe they'd changed the code. I could hardly call them in prison to find out.

Then Fred reached his arm round me, which felt weird. I froze. Oh God.

But he was just reaching for the keypad. He pressed a button with a green symbol on it, and there was a beep and the safe door clicked open. I sagged in relief.

'Thank you!' I looked round at him with a grin. He was smiling back. Now he actually did touch me, but it was just a hand on the shoulder, and it was reassuring.

I pulled the door all the way open, and there was my passport, lying there, looking all new and shiny and black. I picked it up and opened it to check it was mine, then stuck it into my bag. Thank God for that. Now I could go home, and all things considered I thought I'd better rearrange my flight and do exactly that.

The safe didn't have much else in it. A couple of envelopes, and a few small boxes. I hesitated, then closed the door, locked it by putting the code in again, and heard the mechanism closing.

'I'll just go to the loo before we go,' I said. Actually, I wanted a few more moments in this place. It felt so weird to walk out, and leave forever with no idea of what was going to happen to it next.

'Of course. Actually, me too,' said Fred. 'When you get to my age . . . well. Is this an en suite?'

I left him there and went to say goodbye to my own little bathroom. There were day and night moisturizers in there. Sophie had got them for me, the brand she used, and I put them in my bag to take home for Kitty, who loved stuff like that.

I looked at the huge dining table, remembering all the time Owen had spent sitting there on his computer. What had he actually been doing? How had Aisha caught him? Had she done it when I'd brought her up here?

Could I do that? Could I lie to get myself into a place, all for the sake of a story?

Well yes, I could. Clearly. Did I want to be that person? That was a different question.

I walked around the kitchen, checking for anything that might go mouldy. There wasn't much there. Sophie had emptied the fridge of anything that was going to go off. I put a pack of Petit écolier biscuits in my bag, hearing Sophie saying, 'For God's sake eat them, Cat!' I'd take them back to Northanger and share them, if Henry and El were talking to me.

Then Fred was back and we were going. I locked up carefully behind us. We took the lift down to the ground floor. My head was so full of Owen and Sophie and Aisha and prison and extradition that I didn't notice the man with the camera as we stepped out of the front door. I just turned to make sure it was locked behind us.

Then I heard what he was saying.

'*Excusez-moi?* Speak English?'

I looked round. The man was pointing a properly big camera at me. Snapping away.

I was frozen. He took the opportunity to keep talking.

'Do you know Owen Allen? Do you live in the building?'

Fred put a hand on my shoulder and led me away, talking to the man in fast French. He bustled me round the corner, and then round another and another, winding through little alleys that sometimes felt like parts of people's gardens, until we were somehow back in the car park. We didn't speak until we were in the car, with the doors closed and locked. I exhaled hard. *Fuck.*

'Should have guessed that might happen,' said Fred. 'Well, we got away. Now, if you don't mind, I'll just look in at my place, and then we should get some lunch. Are you hungry?'

I was, but I didn't know what I'd say to him over lunch. I did a kind of shrug, and he said, 'Well, good, because I'm starving.'

His place turned out to be a little house on a street called Boulevard de Bacon, which made me smother a giggle. It was at the other end of town, right opposite the sea and the marina. He parked in a tiny space outside and led me across the road to the water to show me where they kept the speedboat.

'Boulevard de Bacon?' I said, looking back at the road sign and trying to stifle my smile.

He grinned at me. 'I know! I've always assumed it was after the painter, but it makes me hungry every time. Now, where's that boat?' He looked around. 'Hmm. Gone. This can only mean one thing. Or two, but I hope it hasn't been stolen.'

He was bouncing on the balls of his feet as he shaded his eyes from the sun and watched a boat coming towards the harbour from out on the water.

'Well,' he said, delighted. 'You're honoured, Cat. The boy wonder himself.'

I had no idea what was going on. What boy wonder? What was he on about? I shaded my eyes too and stared at the approaching boat. My phone started vibrating in my back pocket so I pulled it out and found a string of messages from Izzy.

Cat – aren't you in the countryside??? What the hell are you doing?? Where are you right now? Are you safe?

Her second message had a link in it. It was a link to the *Daily Mail*, and I clicked it quickly, accepting cookies I didn't want so I could read the story. There was only one line of it, but it was the photo that made my heart stop.

Mystery girl seen leaving alleged smugglers' Riviera apartment 'with bags'

A mystery girl was seen leaving the €1-million Antibes apartment of alleged drug smugglers Sophie and Owen Allen this afternoon, carrying bags of possessions. The mystery girl was accompanied by an older man.

. . . More soon

I stared at it. How had they written an article, or two sentences at least, so fast? And uploaded it to the internet? And put it on a website where it would be seen by millions of people all over the world?

And why?

I looked at the photo that accompanied it. Fred's arm was on my shoulder, because he'd been leading me away from the photographer. But it didn't look that way. The picture had somehow managed to make us look like a couple with a massive age gap. It was horrible. I felt dirty and weird.

Fred was looking at me, a strange expression on his face. 'Cat – did you hear me? Are you all right?'

I knew he hated young people being lost in their phones so I just passed it to him. He glanced at it, scrolled down and rolled his eyes.

'Parasites. Ignore it. Look – here he is. My firstborn. Fred junior, or Fritz as the kids call him.'

'What?'

I hadn't expected to meet Fritz at all. I wanted to throw my phone into the Med, but instead I shoved it back into my pocket and tried to focus. Fritz was here? I followed Fred's gaze to where a speedboat was coming to the marina, and then walked after him, down a jetty to wait.

I wanted to message Henry. I wanted to tell him Fritz was in Antibes, but I didn't. Henry didn't seem to be speaking to me.

Fritz was objectively gorgeous. He looked as if he'd stepped out of *The Talented Mr Ripley*. He was wearing a striped T-shirt and a pair of blue shorts, and with his dark-blonde hair and blue eyes he could have been a model.

However, I was incredibly wary. All I knew about him was the way Henry and El discussed him. The golden boy, the banker. There was a lot they didn't say when they were talking about him.

'Dad,' he said. 'Thought you were at Northanger?' His voice was public school all the way, much more so than his siblings'.

Fred laughed. 'Lovely to see you too, young man. Happened to be in town on a bit of a mission with Cat here, and we were calling in at the house to check everything was all right when who should I see approaching but the son and heir?'

Fritz looked to me. 'Oh! The famous Cat!' He smiled at me and I smiled politely back.

'I am. And you're the famous … Do I call you Fred or Fritz?'

He sighed as he tied the boat up. 'Excellent question, Cat. In my day-to-day life, I'm Fred. What with that being my name and everything. I'm Frédéric, spelled the French way. Mum used to call me Ted to avoid confusion, but no one else does that. Fritz was a name my siblings invented to piss me off so of course that's the one that stuck. Fred is fine.'

'Sure.'

'I mean, what kind of psycho names his child after himself? Could have just called me something else and saved me a world of hassle, but no.'

Fred senior just laughed. 'Sorry. Seemed a fun idea at the time. Look, Cat and I were going for some lunch. Would you join us?'

There was a pause. It went on. I looked from one Fred to the other. Soon the silence was uncomfortable. The tension between the two of them was so strong it buzzed through the air like electric wires.

Then younger Fred shook his head slightly and turned to me. He put on a breezy polite voice.

'You were staying with Owen Allen, yeah?' I nodded. 'Then yes. Let's go for lunch. I want to hear *all* about it. And how are Henry and El? Have you met François?'

I gave him a sharp look at that, but he did just seem to be chatting. Mr Tilney looked happier than I'd ever seen him.

'Everyone's dandy,' he said, 'though it would be better with you there.'

I felt bad interrupting, but I had to say it:

'Can we go somewhere out of the way? I never thought I'd be someone who had to say this, but I really, really don't want to be photographed.'

Fred senior had gone straight back to Antibes today for 'some bits and bobs'. He seemed to view a nearly three-hour drive as basically nothing. We'd ended up having a lunch

26

The next morning, I woke up back at Northanger with one thought in my mind: *I need to go home.* I'd got my passport back, and so I could pack my stuff and get out.

I avoided even looking at my phone because I couldn't bear to see myself as 'mystery girl' again. If I ignored it, maybe it would all go away. However, when I did sneak a peek, I found that I had a million notifications, that my tiny private @catincornwall account had been inundated with follow requests.

Fred senior had gone straight back to Antibes today for 'some bits and bobs'. He seemed to view a nearly three-hour drive as basically nothing. We'd ended up having a wildly lovely lunch yesterday in a random restaurant in a village square, somewhere between Antibes and Northanger. I'd sat with the two Fred Tilneys (Freds Tilney?) and although things had been awkward between them, they'd both focused on me and talked to me as if I was genuinely interesting. I'd eaten a goats' cheese salad and drunk a *citron pressé* and told Fred Jr what I knew about the Allens' business dealings, which was basically nothing. I told him how I'd met Aisha and how I'd taken her into the apartment, and he'd reassured me.

'There's no way you should blame yourself for that, Cat,' he'd said. 'Imagine being the kind of person who suspects everyone around them of being there to fuck them over. Don't ever become that person.' I'd smiled, but the guilt had eaten me up.

I couldn't stop thinking about Elisabeth. Young Fred looked so much like his mother, going from El's photos, that I'd almost felt she was at the table with us. I could see that this was why he was so clearly big Fred's favourite child. He was a bit of Elisabeth, still here. His eyes were somewhere between light brown and green, and they were mesmerizing: his mother's had looked the same in the pictures. Fred had been in sixth form when she'd died. That was very different from being thirteen. I wondered whether he had ever questioned what happened. Then I pushed that thought away.

No. No more of that. It was nothing to do with me and I was leaving it alone.

Fred senior had tried hard to persuade his eldest son to come back to the countryside with us, but he had refused.

'I'm sorry, Cat,' he'd said. 'I don't mean to be rude. Nothing personal. I just don't go there. And Dad knows that so I'm not actually sure why he's asking.' The atmosphere was strange between them again. I felt Fred senior looking at me, and then saw young Fred looking at him.

'Actually, Cat,' he said, without taking his eyes off his father. 'You're welcome to come back with me. To Antibes, if you'd like to spend more time there, see your friends. There's loads of space in the house. You don't need to go to Northanger at all.'

I hadn't known what to say to that. In the end, I'd muttered something about all my stuff being at Northanger, and Fritz had told me to let him know if I changed my mind.

Fred had leaned over to him. 'What are you doing tomorrow? I could come back down and see you?'

Young Fred had shrugged.

'I do need to get home to England,' I'd managed to say. 'If you're coming back, could I get a ride to the airport?'

When I'd gone online to book a flight, though, there was nothing available to anywhere near home until Tuesday. And tickets on that flight, to Bristol, were two hundred pounds, and I didn't have two hundred pounds. I was trying to work out who to approach for a loan. Bill, I guessed. I hoped he'd be OK with that.

So, for now, I was at Northanger. I wanted to see Henry the moment we got home, but he was nowhere around. I went to my room. I didn't see anyone.

When I got up in the morning, I found that Fred had already left, dashing back down to the coast to hang out with the son who didn't want to see him, apparently forgetting my request for a lift. Henry and El were sitting on the terrace, and when I tentatively stepped out there, wearing my green dress because it was the best thing I owned, they both turned and smiled.

'Cat! You OK?' said El.

'Erm,' I said. 'Yes. Fine. Are you?'

'Sorry we sent you off with him,' said Henry. 'I wasn't around. But I honestly thought El would go with you.'

'And I thought Henry would.'

'We didn't mean to send you by yourself.' Henry took a deep breath. 'Truly, Cat? Dad was in a weird mood and we were both avoiding him. Which meant you got the whole day with him.'

'You got papped looking like you were gonna be our new stepmum,' said El. It hung in the air for a second, and then we all burst out laughing. 'Jeez. Anyway, let's go to market. You can tell us all about it on the way.'

I relaxed. We piled into the tiny car with the roof down, and Henry drove us to the market town, while the three of us talked about nothing in particular and I felt the release of not dwelling on the awful stuff. The relief of the fact that we seemed to be friends again. I thought back to those magical days when there'd been nothing but me and Henry. Maybe we could go back there, just for a bit. The sky was blue, the sun so hot now that I had to reapply sunscreen as we travelled. This was my last market day. However things worked out, next Sunday I would be at home.

'I've never had to use sunscreen while I was in an actual car before,' I said. El laughed and so I did too. I was giddy with the fact that I had my passport back and that the two of them were talking to me. I would call Mum again, I decided. From the market. I'd tell her that I'd be back home as soon as I could sort out the ticket. She'd be happy.

259

Soon I'd be back with my family. It was the only thing I wanted.

I needed to start to engage with the world outside this corner of France.

Then ... well, then I could go to uni. The kids were a lot, but, as Henry had said, they weren't mine. The world was open. Rich people's lives were more comfortable with better food and nicer dresses, but they weren't better than mine. I had a family who loved me and I was pretty sure none of them were importing heroin or pushing people down stairs.

I was never going to live a life in which I had a huge house, an apartment on the Riviera or a boat. I couldn't imagine being able to afford a car, let alone a convertible or three cars. I was pretty sure I had already bought the most expensive cheese of my life, so in a sense it was all downhill from here. And I was fine with that. There were things I did want to do – I was desperate to go to Belfast, and so I'd focus all my energies on that. If I got the grades for it, and I had no idea whether I would or not since my revision had been punctuated by childcare, then I would find a way to go.

The market was the same as before except that today my budget was zero. I couldn't offer to pay for the parking. I couldn't buy a drink. Actually, I probably could. One soft drink: that was my limit.

I pretended not to be hungry and skipped the breakfast stop, though I was starving after missing dinner last night. I set off purposefully and then, when I was out of sight, walked around aimlessly. I looked at things, and as these were my last days in France, I took some photographs. I said *bonjour* to stallholders, but I didn't linger for long enough to feel awkward. I walked through back streets, to the edge of the market and beyond. On the outskirts of town, the houses weren't the stone buildings of the centre: out here they were modern and practical, still with shutters, but with apricot-coloured plaster on the outside, in a row, looking normal. There were plastic slides in front gardens, a dog that barked as I went past.

I checked the time often, but everything was moving slowly. I was sluggish and hot. The sun started to give me a headache, and my legs didn't want to move. When I passed the sign that announced I was leaving town (it was the town name, crossed out, a flourish I loved), I turned back.

I sat down awkwardly under a tree to wait and felt something in my pocket as I did so. I pulled it out. It was a piece of paper. An envelope.

Shit. It was the letter I'd picked up in the linen cupboard the other morning, the one I'd forgotten to put back. I looked around, but there was no one anywhere nearby, so I pulled my knees up to shield it, and started to read.

H & E,

Sorry about the fight. I said some stupid things.
I appreciate that.
But think about what I said, OK? I know you don't want to hear it. I don't want it to be true either. Just think about it.

She didn't trip. She was Mum! The most graceful person in the world.

She was pushed. I'm sure I know what happened. I was trying to say it the other night, but neither of you would listen. I'm not writing it down. Call me any time, OK? Please.

F xxx

I read it three times.

Fred didn't believe his mother had died by accident. I wished now that we'd had a chance to talk properly when I met him. He had tried to get me to go home with him. Did he know I was in danger? He had even mentioned François. I shoved the letter into my pocket and scrambled to my feet. This was closing in on me. It was feeling toxic. I needed to get out of here.

I needed to go home. I tried to call Mum, but couldn't get any reception at all.

I set off back to the cafe. I'd get there early and ask for a glass of water, and if they said I'd have to buy something I'd spend my last euros on a *citron pressé* and then I'd try Mum again. I needed to make a plan to get home. I was desperate to hear her voice telling me I was going to be OK, that Bill would transfer the money for my flight. I walked back past the last stall, which was a second-hand bookstall full of things I couldn't read. The next one was selling honey, and I smiled at the stallholder and said *bonjour* while continuing to walk. Then it was cheese, olives, meat . . . and on and on and on.

I was too tired, and too hot, and there were too many people. I was starting to panic when I realized I was next to the alley that led to the meeting-point cafe. I hurried over, ready to collapse into a shady seat.

I shouldn't have been surprised to see François sitting at what I thought of as 'our table', but I was.

I looked around. Maybe Henry was behind me, also tired and fed up. Maybe El was. Perhaps they would come along right now and save me from having to make small talk with the man who I (and, I thought maybe Fritz) suspected had pushed a woman down stairs and killed her.

There were plenty of other people around, but all of them were strangers. I looked back at François. He was sitting with a coffee in front of him and he was beckoning me over urgently.

I walked as slowly as I could. I checked the time: I was nineteen minutes early. The others would be here soon. Could I manage nineteen minutes? I had to. I felt the letter in my pocket. Why had I ever picked it up? Why had I read it?

'Hello.' François was smiling at me. All I could think of was the fact that I had seen him naked. I'd seen him naked and I really, really wished I hadn't, and it didn't even matter that I hadn't seen the real him, because the intimacy of seeing his naked form as captured by his lover was worse.

'*Bonjour.*' I sat opposite him and looked anywhere but at him. He signalled to the cafe owner and raised his eyebrows at me, asking what I wanted. I shook my head.

'*Pas d'argent,*' I said. No money.

'I'll pay.'

I hesitated. But the waiter was standing there and it was much easier to order than not to order. I used my most careful French to ask for an Orangina and a glass of water, and then he left and I was stuck sitting opposite the man I suspected of murder.

'Cat,' said François. 'Look, I speak English. More than they know. I pretend I don't have much because then they speak in front of me.'

I leaned back in my chair, trying to put as much distance between us as possible.

'Oh,' I said. 'OK.'

'When do you leave Northanger?' That was a word that sounded good in French. It was a totally different name: Nort-on-jair.

'Um, soon,' I said. 'The first flight I can get is Tuesday. So then, I guess. If I can get my family to send money for the ticket.' I stopped. We were in a public place. I turned aside and pretended to be reading a text. Actually, though, wanting to be safe, wanting to record whatever he was trying to keep so secret, I started a voice note, and put the phone back in my pocket.

'Why?' I said, speaking a bit more loudly. 'Why do you care what I do?'

He shrugged. 'You need money? I can help with that. You need to go. Now.'

I did not want this man's money. All I knew was that a woman had written down that he was going to kill her, and then she'd died in mysterious circumstances. And now he was interested in me. Even if he was interested in getting me away from here, he was creeping me out.

'You know what happened to Elisabeth,' I said. I stared at him. 'I think I do too.'

We looked at each other for a long time. I forced myself to keep looking. I saw his expression change. He had done it. I knew he had.

'Fred, the old Fred? He's here? At market with you?'

'No,' I said. 'He's in Antibes with the other Fred.' As soon as the words were out, I wanted to swallow them back down. Why had I said that? Why had I told him that the two people who could protect me weren't here?

'Good,' said François, and I felt my whole body shuddering.

'I know what you did,' I said. I felt my eyes fill with tears. But I'd done it now. I carried on. 'I think that you –'

He grabbed me by the arm. I looked around wildly, and was relieved beyond words to see Henry and El moving towards us. They came over and sat at the table, grinning, still mid-conversation. I looked at them. I looked at François. My Orangina and water arrived. I wondered if my fear was showing on my face.

El turned to François. '*Salut, François! Ça va?*'

They talked a bit in French and I turned away from François, to Henry.

'Good market?' I said, trying to be normal. My heart was racing. Henry had told me that this was something people said: *bon marché*. I had not had a good market, not at all, but I hoped Henry might have done. I was desperately trying to keep everything feeling half normal between us until I went home. I didn't want the break-up conversation. But I needed to have it. I needed to tell him everything.

Though I had no idea how to tell him what I'd found out about François.

It was funny. Fred was objectively better-looking, but Henry was the one who made my heart beat faster. He was the one whose body heat, on the chair next to mine, made me want to rip his clothes right off. I wondered whether he knew that.

I relived our kisses over and over again. It was better than thinking about anything else.

'Yeah,' he said. 'It was a nice one. I hope you're hungry because we got a rotisserie chicken and two tubs of potatoes. Dad hates that greasy stuff so we obviously go and buy it the moment he's not around because we're basically still little kids.'

I swallowed down a mouthful of bile.

'Do they taste as good as they smell?'

He nodded. 'Better.' He held up a bag, and as he held it up the smell drifted over to me. My stomach rumbled though I didn't think he'd hear it over the noise all around us. I didn't know if I was hungry or nauseous.

A tiny cat came over and stuck its nose as close as it could get to the bag. Henry grinned and put the chicken bag on the table.

'Sorry,' he said. 'But no you don't, kitty.'

I sipped my drink. I looked at François, begging him to leave now that the others were here. I had no idea what he'd been about to say about the house and I didn't want to find out. Fred's secret note had put the staircase scene into my head and I couldn't stop it playing out in my brain.

François was in Elisabeth's studio, near the top of the stairs. He was trying to persuade her to leave Fred for him. She was saying no, that she loved Fred and her children, that she would never . . .

He shoved her. He hadn't meant to, but he did.

She fell.

I closed my eyes and bleached my brain. Whatever had happened, it had been years ago and it was not my tragedy.

Not. My. Business.

Get away from this man.

I stood up.

'I've got a bit of a headache,' I said. 'I've been feeling a bit weird today, actually. Sorry – do you mind if I go and wait near the car? I'll just sit in the shade or something. I think I've spent a bit too much time in the sun. Feeling a bit . . .' I made a face that I hoped conveyed the right sort of thing. I wasn't even faking it. Not really.

Henry looked alarmed. El stood up too.

'Let's just go! We don't need to sit and drink booze when Dad's not even here. Just like we didn't need to stuff our faces with breakfast. Oh, Cat – you didn't come for breakfast! Have you eaten anything?'

I shook my head. I couldn't tell her I hadn't had breakfast because I couldn't afford it.

She was talking to Henry now. 'We have loads of booze at home. François, come later for an *apéro*?' She turned back to me. 'Seriously – you don't look great, Cat. I mean, you do look *great*, but you don't look well. Don't you think, Henry?'

Henry looked at me with the warmest eyes. A look that I didn't deserve. I melted inside.

'Is this one of those traps?' he said carefully. 'Cat always looks . . . beautiful.'

There was a moment. A hiatus where the world stood still and my body started fizzing inside. We looked at each other and this time I didn't look away. I found I was smiling. He was too. Had he forgiven me for going into his mum's room? If so, he was a million times nicer than I deserved.

Then he was on his feet. 'Yeah. Let's go.' He turned to François and asked if he could get my drink and said he'd pay him back next time. François said there was no need, that he had offered me the drink anyway. Although they were talking fast French I followed that much. Then I had a horrible feeling that Henry reiterated El's casual invitation, and that François accepted it.

I sat in the back of the car, roof on, and found that my head really was pounding. I wanted to hide from the sun. I wanted to curl up in the shade and close my eyes and force all the speculation from my head. I wanted to be innocent again. I closed my eyes in the car so I wouldn't have to talk, and listened to the siblings. They were mildly chatting about nothing in particular in the way that siblings did.

'Wouldn't chicken and potatoes AND cake be a bit much?' said El.

'Not for me.'

'Well, that's because you're a fat, greedy pig.'

'Stop it, El – you love chicken. You love potatoes. You love cake. Don't pretend otherwise. You're better than that.'

A pause. 'You got me.'

27

When we got home, I had to unfold myself from the back of the car, and found my muscles were cramped and aching. I reminded myself that I wasn't actually ill. I had faked this to get away from that horrible man. Hadn't I? The horrible murderous man who was going to turn up later.

Why had he taken an interest in me? I was a house guest and this had nothing to do with him. I remembered El saying that his brother lived somewhere far away but that François barely left the village. It creeped me out.

Henry carried the shopping into the house, and El put an arm round my shoulders.

'It can get a bit much in August,' she said. 'We should have thought of it. We're so used to the madness of Sunday morning. And you should never, ever do the market on an empty stomach. Do you think you're ill, or is it more that you didn't eat anything and walked around in the sun?'

It was time to be honest. 'The second one,' I said. I held back the fact that I hadn't had dinner last night either.

'Good. So, maybe have a cool shower? Oh! A bath! How about that? If we run you a lukewarm bath, you'll cool down really fast. And while it's running you can have a sandwich or, I don't know. A banana? What feels good?'

I agreed to a banana because it was easy, and fifteen minutes later Henry showed me into a bathroom. It was the one with the free-standing bath, on a corner on the first floor. The ceiling was high, and there were windows looking in two directions, both of them out over the countryside. The glass wasn't frosted. Henry saw the alarm on my face and smiled.

'Don't worry. There's no way anyone can see in.'

I looked at him and nodded. There was a moment and I didn't know if either of us was going to say anything.

Fuck it. He wasn't going to. I had to do it.

'Sorry,' I said. 'I'm so sorry about the key. I know I really overstepped.'

He looked away. 'It's OK. Don't worry about it.'

I waited for him to say something more. He didn't, but he pulled me close and hugged me. I leaned into him and hoped he couldn't feel my tears soaking through his T-shirt. When he kissed me, I wasn't expecting it, but it was a light kiss, a butterfly on the lips. It was like our first kiss.

When he left, I pulled the door three times to test that it was locked.

El had been right about the cool bath: the moment I lay back I felt the heat that had been trapped in me dissolving. I breathed deeply and told myself it was all right. I would be home soon. Whatever happened, I was going to be on Tuesday's flight. I'd talk to Mum when I was out of the bath.

I leaned my head back, letting the scented oils El had added to the water coat my hair and make it all greasy, not caring.

Even though Henry knew that I had sneaked into his mum's room, he appeared not to hate me. I replayed our kiss just now. I was greedy for more. I wanted ... everything. I'd lost it, but I wanted it back. And yet I had to leave.

I wanted El back too. I'd never had a friend like her. And Fred, who had been so welcoming to me. But I couldn't squat in this strange haunted house any longer.

I realized I hadn't told anyone that it was my birthday tomorrow. And then it was going to be results day on Thursday. I'd have to engage with my notifications soon. Approve or deny the follow requests on my @catincornwall account. Delete all the messages. I'd have to block numbers. I'd look at the torrent of whatever the hell was on there, and then I'd deal with it.

And once I was home, in spite of everything, I would wish I was back here with Henry. I knew I would. I would long to talk to my current self, the one in this bath right now, and tell her to stop messing around. *Henry has told you it's fine. Believe him. You are never again going to be in a huge house in France with the man who got into your head the first time you met him.*

The man you've kissed. The man who wanted to take you to Antibes, away from his family, so you could have sex. It would have been your perfect first time. It would have been everything, and you've thrown it away by stealing a key.

I managed about ten minutes in the bath before I started to feel actively cold. I let the water drain out while I was still sitting in the tub, and remembered how I used to do that as a toddler, skidding up and down the bath in the last bits of water. When it was empty, I used the shower attachment to rinse the oil out of my hair, and to wash it with a shampoo that was on the shelf next to me, which I immediately realized made me smell a bit like Fred.

When I unlocked the door, I was wrapped in a towel, ready to run up the wooden stairs to the attic, put on clean clothes and dry my hair.

However, someone was waiting in the corridor. My heart leaped. Henry?

No.

François smiled. 'Sorry, Cat,' he said. 'But I have to speak to you. What you said –'

I stepped back into the bathroom. My skin was rising up in goose bumps. He stepped forward so he was blocking the door.

'Excuse me,' I said. I heard my own voice, polite and cold but with a tremble that gave me away. 'Can I get past?'

'Of course.' He stood against the wall and I walked out of the bathroom, the tensest I had ever been. I felt every one of my muscles quivering. In my head I put up a force field, an impenetrable barrier between me and the man Elisabeth had studied and drawn before . . .

'I'm sorry I scared you,' he said, when I was past. 'I didn't realize you were . . .' I looked away so I didn't have to see him gesturing to my towel. It was too intimate. 'I can see you're nervous of me. But you don't need to be. You have it wrong, Cat. This is a dangerous house for you. For everyone. My brother was –'

He stopped as we both looked round. There was a shout coming from downstairs. It was furious; a man's voice, jarring in the quiet. It certainly wasn't Henry.

Fred was back, and he was angry. Really angry. His voice was a roar.

'*Where is she?*'

He was looking for either Eleanor, or me. It had to be one of us, unless it was the cat, which I doubted. I heard him storming around, heard Henry's voice, too quiet for me to hear the words but placating in tone. Questioning.

'Still here? Eating my food, drinking my fucking *rinquinquin?*'

Everything closed in. I felt my head tightening, my vision starting to narrow. Fred Tilney was angry with *me*. Furious. But what had I done? I had, of course, eaten his food and drunk his *rinquinquin*, as he'd said, but he had invited me. Had offered it.

Was it the key? How had he found out now?

I looked at François, terrified. I looked down at myself, at my bare feet, my slightly damp legs, my arms holding the clothes I'd worn to market. I cringed at the realization that I was visibly holding my own underwear, and shifted so it was hidden.

There was a man in front of me who I believed was a murderer. Another one yelling downstairs. What the fuck was happening?

274

François put a hand out to touch my arm, then pulled it back again before it made contact.

'He is an angry man.' His voice was quiet, almost a whisper. 'You don't know him, at all. My brother, Louis? He loved Elisabeth. She loved him. The children were away at school, and she needed to leave. But it's her house. She needed *him* to leave. He wouldn't go.'

I felt my face screwing up in confusion. 'Your brother? But he lives in –'

François was talking fast, urgently.

'No – he, Fred? He found them. And he –'

We both looked round at the sound of a crash in the house.

'I saw her pictures,' I whispered, urgently. I had to be brave here. Should I be shouting for help? Who was on my side? Fred, or François? And where was Henry? For now I carried on whispering. 'Elisabeth's pictures. It was you. She drew *you*. Not your brother. And she wrote . . .' I stopped. I couldn't say it.

I had to say it.

I said it.

'She wrote *Il me tuera*.'

There was a moment of silence between us. I saw François's face change.

'She wrote that?'

We stared at each other. It was silent downstairs now. François took a sharp intake of breath. Then he shook his head. 'That was a picture of Louis. We looked the same. Not twins, but the same. He was less than one year

275

younger. Our mother used to say she'd had the same child twice. Fred found them, Elisabeth and Louis, and . . . It was him, Cat. Fred. She was writing about Fred.'

There was another sudden shout from downstairs.

Was that true? Had 'he will kill me' meant her husband? Would he kill her because of her lover?

All this time, had it been Fred? Or was François tricking me?

I whispered. '*He* killed her? He pushed her down the stairs? Fred wouldn't do that . . .'

François gave a little shrug. 'Cat, he would. He killed her on the stairs. And then I am sure he killed Louis. There was a message saying Louis had gone away, but I'm not stupid. We've heard nothing from him since. Because . . .' He gestured towards the sound of Fred's voice.

'He killed your brother?' I tried to straighten out my thoughts. 'And your *brother* was Elisabeth's lover? Not you?'

My head was buzzing. I knew I needed to move, but nothing was working. I had no idea what to believe.

François nodded. 'Now Fred has run out of money. He needs to sell the house, but he can't, and it's because of what's buried. I've been watching him closely. All the time. And I think this is why he has his new shed. A reason to dig up the ground. He's very scared. Very angry. You have to go.'

As Fred's voice came closer, François's manner changed. He became practical and urgent.

'Why do I have to go?' I said. 'Why is he angry with *me*?'

François looked me in the eye.

'He's angry with everyone, in the end,' he said. 'And particularly with women. I knew, as soon as I met you, that he'd do this. The way he was looking at you.'

I believed him. I needed to go. We had no more time for talking.

'Just go,' whispered François. 'I'll tell him you went to the river. I will take him to look for you, keep him away from the house. You – dress, pack a bag and leave.' He pulled a car key out of his shorts pocket and held it out. 'Take my car.'

'I can't drive.' I regretted the banana, which was churning in my stomach. How had I ever been too hot? I was shivering, chilled to the bone. Could I drive, if I had to? How hard could it be? I could make it down the drive, probably.

No. Of course I couldn't.

Fred? The kind, welcoming dad who wore a Christmas jumper in August. The man who'd helped me to retrieve my passport and who'd sheltered me from the paparazzi. I couldn't make it make sense. My head was a jumble.

'So you must walk,' said François. 'Keep as hidden as you can. Keep your phone with you. *Prends soin*,' said François, and I realized this was what he'd said the first time we met. *Prends soin*. Take care. Not *bonsoir*. He'd been worried about me from the start.

Fred had moved away from the entrance hall and we couldn't hear him any more. François patted my bare, damp shoulder, and I swallowed hard and nodded. I had no idea what was going on, but I knew that I needed to run.

'I'm so sorry about your brother,' I said. 'I . . . I think I had it wrong.'

'I'll keep him talking. You get out.'

I hurried up to my room, and François went in the other direction. I dressed quickly in the green dress and felt in the pocket for Fritz's letter. It was evidence.

I realized that young Fred must know, or at least suspect, that it was his dad. That was what he'd been trying to tell the others. It was why he refused to come here. Not just the bad memories. I could call him for help.

I put stuff into my bag, but I realized I couldn't stay long enough to pack everything. I needed to grab the essentials, whatever they were, and leave. My phone was the only thing that really mattered: it went into the bag. I took care not to look at the screen. My passport was still in my bag pocket from the visit to Antibes and I double-checked it was there. I had my purse, for all the good that would do right now. I shoved the mug for Mum between some clothes as well. I took the drawing of Louis too, the first one I'd found, and slid it down the side of the bag. It might be evidence.

Book, charger, headphones.

In the bathroom, I grabbed my toothbrush, toothpaste and sunscreen. Then I ran back to the bedroom and put on my trainers, the ones I'd worn to travel to France, because I had no idea where I was going from here, but it was likely to begin with running through a vineyard.

I crept to the top of the stairs and listened.

He was still in the house.

'Do you think I'm some kind of moron, Lafitte?' he said. 'You're trying to get me to the river so you can get her out of the house. I'll tell you what: why don't you mind your own fucking business for once? Do you know what she's done?'

What had I done?

I could hear his breathing coming closer as he came up the stairs to the first floor. He was on the wooden stairs, the ones from the kitchen. I stood at the top of the attic stairs and looked from side to side. There was nowhere to go. No other exit. All I could hope to do was to get to the other stairs before he found me. Get to the main stairs, get down them and leave through the front door. I could do this without coming face to face with this man who had been nothing but kind to me, and who now, for some reason, hated me with a passion that I didn't understand.

I took a deep breath. I had always kept myself in the background, watched other people, tried to be kind and helpful and fit in. I'd never been able to stand up for myself. I had always known it was my job as a girl to be nice. I had been nice. I had evaded the spotlight my whole life, and I'd found my excitement in podcasts. I'd pictured myself as the brave investigator, solving cold cases. I'd imagined myself doing that, while staying firmly in my comfort zone, being dutiful. Being nice. Agreeing with people.

Whatever this man thought I'd done, I knew the truth of it. I had gone into a locked room in his house. I'd tried to find out what had really happened to his wife. I'd stolen a letter. Those things weren't ideal, but they didn't deserve this.

I took another deep breath.

I didn't know how to protect myself. If anything happened to me, how would anyone know?

My friends were in the house. I tried to shout for them. 'El! Henry! François!'

My voice came out quietly. It was more of a croak than a shout.

I set my phone to record, put it in my pocket and ran down the stairs, ready to dash out of the house.

28

I made it to the top of the main stairs before his fingers grabbed my arm and pulled me back. Fred and I were face to face. I was closer to him than I had ever wanted to be. I could smell coffee on his breath. I'd never really liked coffee.

'Out of my house.' His voice was low and menacing.

I tried to pull away.

'Sure.' My voice was stupid and childish. I tried harder. 'Let me go then.'

I looked at the fury in his eyes and thought of Eva Santoro. Everyone assumed she'd killed herself, but had she? I had no idea what had happened to her, but she had been his friend. He might have killed three people. More.

And he wasn't letting me go.

We weren't alone, though. El was just behind him. I flashed a look and saw confusion on her face. When our eyes met, she looked away quickly. For the first time, I could see that, when it came to it, her loyalty to him overrode everything.

'Dad?' she said. 'Dad – what are you talking about? What has Cat done?'

He didn't look at her. He was focused on me. His face was strange. He didn't look as if he hated me any more. He looked as if he was obsessed, instead. Like he wanted me. He looked greedy.

'Sneaking around,' he said. He almost smiled. 'Did you know she's been investigating us? Making a fucking podcast. About your mother's death. That's what she's doing here.'

His fingers dug into my arms. I opened my mouth to tell El that he'd got it wrong. To say no. I am not doing that.

But I couldn't, because what he was saying was kind of true.

I felt the fight going out of me. He knew.

'She went into your mother's studio to poke around. She's no one! First the Allens took her in and she fucked them over. Putting that so-called journalist on to them. Then we take her in and she does the same to us. She pretends to be all sweet and innocent, but you can't trust her.'

Most of that sounded really bad.

I watched El's face. She looked as if she was in shock. She turned and shouted, 'Henry!'

Not everything he'd said was true, though . . .

'I didn't know she was investigating them!' My voice was louder than I'd expected. 'I thought she was on holiday. And if she *was* investigating, she seemed more interested in talking to me about Eva. You know, your friend? Eva Santoro? I saw her just before she died. She was making plans for the next day. It didn't feel right.' I looked at the expression on his face. I could feel the stairs behind me and tried to shift around. I thought of Elisabeth. Of her art studio, that lovely watercolour of her children. François's missing brother. The weird B&Q-style shed. François, lurking in the garden next to it. Watching.

Her tragic fall down the stairs with, officially, no witnesses.

I changed tack.

'Let me go home,' I said.

He scoffed. 'Home.'

I wasn't having that. 'At my house,' I said, 'no one pushes anyone down the stairs. If anyone wanted to leave, no one would kill them to stop them.' My voice was clear. I managed not to let it wobble.

My words enraged him. His grip tightened on my arm. He dragged me back to the top of the stairs.

I looked down.

François was in the entrance hall downstairs, and when I saw the look on his face I understood that from the moment he'd known I was staying here he had tried to help; he didn't think it was safe for anyone who wasn't family to be in this house, least of all a young woman. He knew what had happened to his brother. He knew who had done it. I guessed it had been impossible to prove or to know the specifics, but he had known. What had he said? He needs to sell the house and he's scared?

'Go, then,' said Fred. He was tall and strong and I didn't stand a chance against him.

There was no sign of Henry. 'El!' I shouted. She took a step back, her face closed.

'Dad! What the fuck is happening?' She said it, but she didn't try to stop him. She didn't tackle him, or move in any way. She literally stepped back to let him do whatever he wanted.

I looked around again for Henry, who was nowhere.

'Henry!' I yelled it as loud as I could. Fred laughed. Even El made a scoffing sound. No one said the words *good luck with that*, but it hung in the air. In fact, the only person from this family who would save me was Fred junior, and he wasn't here. I looked at the stair carpet. And suddenly wondered if it was there for more than safety. Was it hiding something?

François seemed frozen, but when our eyes met he set off up the stairs towards me.

'I know what you did to the last woman who tried to leave this house,' I said, and as I tried to pull away, Fred Tilney pulled his arm back and then shoved me, letting go of his grip on my arm and propelling me down the wide staircase. I tried to grab the bannisters as I fell, but didn't manage to catch hold of anything. Even as I was falling, though, I was relieved. Lots of people fell downstairs. Almost all of them were OK. And these stairs were covered in thick carpet.

El would see it now. Everything would be all right.

I had a soft landing thanks to a combination of the carpet and François, the man I'd thought a murderer until a few minutes ago. He was a little way up the stairs, and he grabbed me before I landed. He got in the way of my fall and the two of us tumbled together down the last part of the staircase, landing with a horrible crash and causing a fiery pain in my knee on the stone tiles of the entrance hall. My knee was twisted and had bent the wrong way, but knees could be fixed. We were alive.

Fred was looking down at us. His face was unreadable, as if he was in a different world.

'You killed her.' I needed him to admit it in front of El. 'Your wife. You did, didn't you? François has always known it.' I glanced to him for backup. 'He tried to warn me. This was her house. She wanted *you* to leave, and you didn't want to go. You pushed her down the stairs and made sure she died. Then you killed Louis too. You killed both of them.'

I thought of the shed. I looked at François, who was pale and woozy. Had he hit his head when we fell? He had thought Fred had installed the shed as an excuse for excavating the garden. That meant . . .

'You buried Louis's body in the garden.' I sounded confident, even though I wasn't. 'Then you started to think about selling the house, because you couldn't afford to keep it, could you? I saw your emails: you had loads from estate agents. One said your listing could go live next week. However much El hated the idea, you knew you didn't have enough money to stay here. But you couldn't sell a house with a body buried in the garden. So you had to dig it up. And you got a new shed so you had a reason to do that.'

The silence stretched out. The next person to speak was El.

'Is this true?' she said, quietly.

'Of course not.' Fred's voice was almost a whisper. I wondered how much El had known. How complicit was she? How enmeshed?

He turned his attention back to me, grinning now. He skipped down the stairs, full of energy. He was a different man from the mild dad who had greeted us in his Christmas jumper all those days ago. I shuffled away on my bum, realizing that I had properly hurt my knee when I fell and that getting away might be harder than I'd thought. We needed to go in François's car.

I looked to François. Why wasn't he talking? We were in this together. I needed him, and his car. I needed him to get me out of here.

'Well, if that nonsense had any truth to it,' Fred said, striding across the hall, 'then what did I do with this supposed body? Check the garden! Be my guest!' He was radiating energy. He looked delighted. He actually rubbed his hands together.

I thought of the garden waste in the car.

The trip to the tip.

'You put it in the car,' I realized.

'Hmm,' he said, with a chuckle. 'Well, if that was true – and it's not, El, just to be clear – but, if it was, who would be on the *déchèterie*'s cameras lobbing it into the landfill waste, I wonder?'

He was practically dancing.

I remembered the plastic box. The lid opening as I'd thrown it down. The flash of blue tarpaulin, unspooling. Brown shapes falling out. I felt my stomach churning. I was going to be sick. I had to look away and make an effort to breathe.

'El?' I said.

'Cat.' Her voice was flat. 'None of this is real. He makes up stories. Says all kinds of things. You should just get out.'

'So you, Cat, are as complicit as anyone,' said Fred. 'Did you think I didn't know you went into the studio? Can you guess how I knew that?' He paused, waiting, until at last I shook my head. I couldn't look at him, but I was aware of him pacing around. He walked over to the furthest wall, thank goodness. I felt his eyes on me but kept mine on the stair carpet. Blue, with a darker blue pattern. I saw the dust on the carpet strands.

'I suppose that when you let the cat out you didn't check inside?'

I thought back. In my panic about Minou, I'd just needed to let her out. I hadn't been in again since then: I had actively forced myself not to think about it, to stay away.

He laughed.

'The cat shit was a giveaway, Caitlin. I knew the cat hadn't knocked the key down. Of course she hadn't. It doesn't happen. I can also tell when my son is lying. So later that evening I went in to check, and when I saw that she'd been locked in there it fell into place. I was in two minds about you at that point. Curiosity is natural, I supposed. A

287

bright girl, in the house on her own: I could see why you'd want to look around. A locked door is an intriguing thing. I'd have been in there like a shot myself. Maybe, I thought, we were kindred spirits. I was ready to give you a bit of leeway. You had access to the Allen place, and I was keen to get in there too, have a nose around – two nosey parkers together. Teammates. I thought making you dispose of the body for me would be a good payback. A bit of insurance. Pulling you into my little world. You like it, don't you? My world.'

He was hooking something down from the wall. It was, of course, one of the guns. I had never asked Henry if they were loaded. They couldn't be, could they? That would be massively illegal. But so was killing people.

I looked at François, who was trying to shift himself into a sitting position. His eyes were a bit weird, and he was rubbing his head. He hadn't reacted to anything that had happened since we fell even though he'd been waiting to confront Fred for years. There was something really wrong.

I looked at Fred, who was fiddling with the gun as if he was about to kill us in the most casual way. I realized that this was what he did. He killed people. I had no idea what he'd done to Eva, if anything, but I would never forget her body, floating in the water. I thought of Elisabeth, realizing who he really was, and Louis, trying to help her get away.

'El?' I said. She was halfway down the stairs. I looked at him again, then back up at her. She needed to stop him. Or was she in on it too? 'El – François needs to go to hospital. I think he hit his head.'

I saw her looking at her father, then back at me and François. Fred was clearly prepping to shoot us, and I had no idea if it was a bluff or not.

'Dad.' She cleared her throat and said it again, louder. 'Dad!' When he looked at her she continued. 'I don't know what the fuck is happening, but you need to stop. You have to fucking stop this. Right now. You've scared her. OK? Job done. Of course you didn't kill Mum!' Her voice broke and she turned away, rushing down the last few stairs to kneel next to François. They started speaking in French: I understood that she was asking about whether he was hurt, and where. He seemed to be trying to talk, but nothing that made sense came out.

We all looked at Fred.

'Don't worry, El,' he said. 'You're right. It's bullshit, but it's going to be easier if you give me a moment. Why don't you step outside? Let me deal with this and we'll pretend it never happened, like we did before. With the nanny. Cat wants to go travelling. She's so upset about what she did to the Allens that she needs to get away. François is heading off to South America to visit his brother.'

I stopped breathing. He was going to do this. He was casually telling his daughter that he would kill us.

'Dad!'

There was a long silence. El and Fred were staring at each other.

'Dad,' she said. 'Please don't.'

'Darling girl. It's the only option, but I'd hate for you to be upset. So just go down to the river or something. Like I said, they're about to leave.'

'Henry!' she yelled, but there was no answer.

El was upset, but I knew she was basically on her dad's side because if she wasn't she'd have called the police by now. But at least she was still here. She hadn't left us like Fred had told her to.

Fred laughed. He seemed genuinely relaxed and happy.

'He'll be in his cupboard, Eleanor. Where he goes when it all gets too much. How did I produce such a pathetic specimen? Thank goodness for you, dear girl.'

I pictured Henry curled up in that cupboard, avoiding the confrontation, and the idea almost made me smile, though it wasn't at all funny. I'd had no idea how messed up these two were. How complicit.

'He's such a twat,' said El, and Fred nodded.

'You thought he'd ride in and rescue you, Cat,' he said. 'Didn't you?'

I nodded. I still hoped he might.

I stretched my legs and arms, and held on to the bannister to stand up. When I put pressure on my right leg there was a sharp pain in my knee, but otherwise I was all right.

I stood up and looked at Fred. He didn't shoot me. That was something. He was weighing the gun in his hands. This felt like the moment. I needed to get out. I needed to get François out.

'Let us go,' I said. My voice was wobbly, but at least I managed to look him in the eye. 'Let us go and we won't tell anyone. Please.'

Fred smiled. He moved the gun so it pointed not at me, but at François. I understood, then, that he was offering to bring me into the fold. He would make me a part of his twisted world. He had already started the process by making me throw Louis's bones into the tip, on camera. Now, he would kill François, and I would become like El and Henry. I would be in his corner, compromised and dirty.

I'd made a lot of mistakes, but I wasn't going to do this.

'El,' I said. I watched her face, sensing that this all hinged on her. 'Stop him.'

She gave me a look of panic.

I lunged towards Fred as best I could. My knee almost gave way but I got there.

A gunshot rang out.

29

I sat outside the house, on the doorstep, and made myself focus.

Police.

My phone was still recording. I stopped it and got the keyboard up on the screen.

It wasn't 999 in France. It was 112. Sophie had told me. I put the numbers in: 1–1–2. I thought of Sophie. When she'd picked me up at Nice airport, neither of us had had any idea that both our summers would end with the police. Her, arrested. Me, escaping a murderer. I'd been worried, at one point, that nothing was going to happen this summer. That I wouldn't have a story.

Someone answered. I tried to talk in French, but it didn't work. The woman on the end of the line spoke a bit of English, and after what seemed like hours I managed to convey to her, through my shock, that I was at Northanger Vineyard, and that there was a man with a gun.

That a shot had been fired.

That I didn't know what had happened after that because it had been too confusing. I told her I'd got out. She said they were on the way. She told me to find a safe place, if I could. To wait there. I hung up and looked around.

Where *was* Henry? I got his number up on my phone and pressed call. It rang. I held the phone away from me, listening in case there was a phone ringing anywhere nearby. All I could hear were birds, and the quiet ring sound from my own phone. When it went to voicemail, I hung up.

El was entangled in everything her father had done. I could see that now. Maybe it wasn't her fault: she'd grown up with the mess. Fritz had escaped. But what about Henry? What did he know? What did he think? And where was he? Was he, even now, grabbing a gun and coming after me? Maybe Fred would convince him that getting me out of the way was the only way to deal with this.

Had Fred shot François? I didn't think so (plaster had fallen from the ceiling), but I wasn't certain. El had rushed to him and shouted at me to go so I had.

Could I go back in? Should I? I couldn't leave François in there, injured. But the police had told me they were coming and that I should hide. I looked around for a hiding place.

The shed? Too obvious.

I wasn't in any position to walk down to the water, or to the end of the drive. I couldn't climb a tree. Could I hide under a car?

A memory surfaced from the first time I'd met Henry. He'd said there was a bush on the driveway at home, with a hiding place in the middle – he had made it sound like a den. We'd laughed about it and I'd told him about hide-and-seek at my house. A bush with flowers on it, he'd said.

A place to hide. To get away from things. To escape from home. That was more meaningful, now that I knew what he was hiding from.

I set off along the drive. I had about five euros and I was in the middle of nowhere with a serial killer and a sore knee. The man who had tried to save me might be dead. My friend had known all along what her dad was like, and she had happily let him take me out for the day alone. Also, I'd just told her that he'd murdered her mum, so I could understand if my well-being wasn't her priority right now.

Henry, the one I would have hoped to depend on – my boyfriend? – was nowhere to be found.

My knee hurt more with every step, but I kept going. Urgh, the drive was so long. At least I was walking towards the direction the police would be coming from. It was the middle of the afternoon, and I could feel myself sweating, turning to see if Fred was behind me every couple of seconds.

There was a bush ahead of me and I hoped it was the right one. The flowers were pink, the ground below it littered with dark petals. I pulled some twigs apart and started to crawl inside. I moved awkwardly on my knee and yelled out loud with the pain.

And then I yelled again, because someone was already there.

It took a moment for me to understand what I was looking at. Who I was looking at. We stared at each other for an eternity before he spoke.

'Hey, Cat.' His voice was dull.

'What are you doing here?' My voice was sharp. Accusing. Henry was lucky I wasn't attacking him. He'd left me with his dad! My breathing was coming faster. My eyes filling with tears. Half of me wanted to yell at him. The other half wanted to fling myself into his arms for comfort.

'What are *you* doing here?' He didn't really sound interested.

I climbed in. We had to talk. I needed to understand. But I didn't get a chance, because as I crawled into the den, he crawled out on the other side of the bush. And then he was gone.

So that was Henry.

I didn't bother to go after him. I couldn't anyway, with only one working knee. If he was running away, or back to his dad, I wasn't going to chase him. I looked around the den instead.

There were some empty beer bottles that looked as though they might have been there for years. Henry had told me about this place as an entertaining tale, but I wondered now what, or whom, they had been hiding from.

It was the best hiding place I had. It wasn't ideal because Henry knew I was here, but it was better than being out in the open. While I waited for the police, I took my phone out. I was calling Mum before I even consciously decided to do it.

She answered after six rings, just as I was about to give up.

'Cat! Oh thank God. Are you OK? What's going on?'

'A lot.'

I felt her switching mode straight away. Understanding, just from those two words, that things were really, really wrong.

'Where are you? What can we do?

I closed my eyes and started to talk. I sat inside that bush and told Mum everything, right up until today. Until now, this moment.

'Right,' she said. 'Where are you right now? Have you called the police?'

'Yeah,' I said. 'They're on the way.'

'Good. Shall . . .' I couldn't hear what she was saying, because of the sound of a car engine.

Someone was coming up the drive, but from the wrong direction, going away from the house. I thanked whatever gods were out there for the fact that the dress I'd been wearing all summer was green and camouflaged. They would have to be looking very hard out of the window at the right moment if they were going to see me in here.

I looked out between leaves. It was Fred's car, but El was at the wheel. She was driving fast, but I caught a glimpse of François leaning on the window in the back.

And now I was stuck almost completely alone in the middle of nowhere with a furious killer who had just shoved me down a stone staircase and fired a gun. The police would be here soon. Please.

I turned my attention back to Mum.

'Oh, Mum,' I said. 'That was the car leaving.' My voice was low now. I was pretty much whispering. 'It was El and François. She must be taking him to get help.'

296

'Sit tight and wait for the police.'

'They'll be here in a moment. I'm sure.' My voice sounded scared. I told myself to fake it, and to inject the confidence I didn't feel. Should I have thrown myself out of the undergrowth and got El to pick me up? Of course, but it had happened too fast. 'I should never have come here.' I thought about it. 'I should have stayed at home. You were right. It's my fault for thinking I could do this.'

Mum sighed. 'No, Cat. No. You can't say that. I'm sorry I was so unfair to you. You deserve adventures. But now I'm getting you out of there. What if I got a taxi to come and pick you up? They could take you to the police station. Just get you safe.'

'I think I need a hospital,' I said, 'actually.'

'Your knee?'

'Yeah.'

'OK. The house is called Northanger Vineyard? I'll find a cab. Stay exactly where you are. OK? I am sending help.'

After a few minutes, I heard engines, and sirens. I heard cars approaching, and passing me. Then another car that stopped next to my den.

I closed my eyes and tried to find the energy to crawl out of my hiding place. I needed to see the police. They had to understand just how dangerous Fred was. He was in the house on his own, unless Henry was with him, and he'd be ready to tell them a story. It would be a story about me attacking him. About François and me turning on him. In his version, I was sure, the two of us would have gone wild.

And they'd believe him. He was authoritative, and I was just a teenage girl.

I needed to move. I was trying to shift around so I could get out without too much damage to my knee, when I heard a voice, and then there was a rustling sound and the leaves were pulled apart. I looked up, expecting a *gendarme*, and I saw . . .

Jonno Thorpe.

The last person I wanted to see.

Well, not the last, but definitely top five.

'She's right here,' he said, and I shrank away from him, wincing at the pain. I had no idea what Jonno was doing here. I thought, wildly, that he might be working with Fred. I remembered the message on Fred's phone, from 'Thorpe'.

'No,' I whispered. 'Don't tell him. Please don't.'

I was in a bush with a knee that didn't work, and he was standing over me. If he was here on Fred's behalf, I was fucked.

He saw something in my expression, and his manner changed. He spoke in a gentler tone.

'Hey, Cat,' he said. 'It's OK. We're here to get you home. On your mum's orders.'

'My *mum*?'

I levered myself out of there and sat on the grass, stretched my leg and prodded it. It hurt a lot. I blinked a few times to get my eyes used to the sudden sunlight and looked down the drive. There were two police cars in front of the house.

'I have to talk to them first,' I said.

'Yes,' said another familiar voice. 'And you have to talk to us too. We've been so worried about you, Cat. I didn't mean to tell Fred about your podcast. I'm so sorry.'

'Izzy!' I looked from one of them to the other. 'How did my mother . . . Anyway, can you drive me back to the house? I need to talk to the police.'

As Izzy drove the car slowly up the drive, I sat in the back and tried to make sense of their arrival.

'How did she manage to send you to me?' I said. 'And how did you get here so fast?' It made no sense at all.

'Second one first,' said Jonno. 'Isabella here was feeling pretty shoddy. She has a bit of a thing for Fritz Tilney. I mean, me too. Who wouldn't? Dreamy. So she was hanging around him this morning.'

'We were on the jetty by their house,' she said. 'Sitting there dangling our legs like movie people. I loved that he wanted to talk to me, but he only wanted to talk about you, because he was pretty fucking worried, Cat. He wanted to know if we should come and get you. I told you you'd been looking into things at Northanger. Making a podcast. He asked if it was about his mum, and I said it was, and I told him you'd been into her studio. Anyway, then we heard someone behind us, and Fred was there. And he'd heard. He said '*how interesting*' and tried to get more info from me, but I didn't have any. Legitimately didn't. But then he sped off.'

She stopped the car next to a police car and turned round in her seat.

'I felt terrible. It was just something about him. He's invited me over here enough times, so we thought we'd just turn up. Make sure you were OK. You know.' She paused. 'Fritz is here too. He's with the police.'

The heat was oppressive. Nothing was moving and the air was crackling with electricity.

There was a sound. Another gunshot. It reverberated around so we couldn't tell where it had come from.

We all looked at each other, and waited.

30

Hours later, Jonno, Izzy and I were sitting in a cafe with my leg up on our table's fourth chair. It was late in the day now, the time that Sophie had once called 'the golden hour', and the shadows outside were long. We were in the market town. By now it was so familiar, but it was quiet and empty today. We'd come to a random cafe on the main street. Jonno and Izzy were trying to get me to eat. They'd ordered a load of food and I hadn't listened so I supposed I'd find out what it was when it arrived.

I'd explained everything to the police. I needed to go back and finalize my statement tomorrow, but Izzy had got them to agree that I could do it in Antibes. So, as soon as we'd eaten, I was going to go home with them. The idea of their lovely big house, of its safety, was keeping me going.

I looked at Jonno. I had no idea what I was thinking or feeling now apart from that I needed to go home to Cornwall. I didn't care that most of my stuff was at Northanger.

'Stay as long as you need,' he was saying. 'Our mum's already talking to yours. We'll get you home when the police are OK with you leaving the country.'

'We've still got a bed made up for you,' said Izzy, with a little smile. 'Remember? In my dressing room.'

'Thank you.' It was taking all my energy not to cry. I was done with all of this, every bit of it.

'Are you eighteen yet?' said Jonno.

'Oh my God!' said Izzy. 'Is it your birthday? Fuck, is it today?'

'Tomorrow.'

The police had taken Fred Tilney away after that second gunshot, which had, it turned out, been aimed at himself. He'd missed because the police rushed him and stopped him, and when we'd seen him leave he was laughing. It was the creepiest thing. A vision that I knew would haunt my dreams.

Then I'd spent ages telling them everything that had happened, with the Thorpes and Fritz helping translate. Fritz had stayed with the police: he said he had a lot more to tell them. He said he'd been trying to get them to listen for years.

When we were allowed to leave Northanger, Izzy and Jonno had driven me to the hospital while I checked in with Mum, and they'd translated again and waited while my knee was scanned. Luckily there didn't seem to be anything horribly wrong, though I'd been sent away with a knee brace. They'd tried to give me crutches, but I hadn't taken them because I didn't want to have to take them back home on the plane. I could walk in a lopsided way with the brace on.

'OK,' said Jonno. 'This is quite a way to end your childhood. Spend your birthday with us. Have some cake.'

'Sugar always makes you feel better, right?' said Izzy.

She was right.

'OK,' I said. 'It does. Yes. Thank you.'

The waiter put four dishes down on the table. A basket of bread (I took a piece before he'd even put the next thing down), a goats' cheese salad, a plate of charcuterie and a bowl of round slimy things covered in sauce. They were inside shells. They looked like . . .

'Are these *snails*?'

Jonno shrugged. 'You said once that one of your brothers tried to eat one. So I thought you should probably give it a go so you can report back.'

I looked at Jonno. Maybe I'd got him wrong. He had paid attention to things I'd said.

He saw me hesitating. 'Or if you don't want to, even better. I'll have them. Love 'em.'

'Personally,' said Izzy, 'I think they're gross. Like snot. But see what you think.'

'You'd have to have eaten snot to know that,' said Jonno, and I felt myself smiling for what felt like the first time in ages. I used the little fork that came with them to pull one out of its shell, and held it up.

My stomach churned. I wasn't ready for a snail. I held it out to Jonno, who opened his mouth, and I fed it to him. He patted his tummy in exaggerated pleasure, and I grinned and ate a piece of tomato.

'See!' Izzy was triumphant.

Jonno took a deep breath.

'Cat – I realize none of this matters now, but humour me. Hear me out. I do realize I behaved like a twat. Izzy thought it was hilarious.'

'Can confirm,' she said. 'Though it took me a while to stop blaming you for dashing off with Henry T, Cat. Sorry.'

'She's taken the piss so much. About the fact that I was so bad at asking you out that you didn't realize it was a date, and then when I did manage to get you to meet me you left with another man. A man who took you to a murder house.'

His lips were twitching. Then mine were too.

'When you put it like that,' I said. 'Oh God. I wonder if they've found Henry. They must have, right?'

We all looked at each other. When we'd left, the police had been searching for him. I'd told them to start with the linen cupboard.

'Hope so,' said Izzy.

'Were you two, like . . . ?' said Jonno. He made a kissing face and hugged himself, rubbing his own sides. 'Honestly! You can tell me.'

I hesitated. There was no point not telling the truth.

'Yeah,' I said. 'We were. Sorry, but yeah. I was massively into him. We never slept together, though we were . . . I thought he was adorable. I thought he was my boyfriend. It turns out I don't know him at all.' I'd tried to call

Henry again, but he hadn't answered. It had gone straight to voicemail. 'You two used to be friends, right?' I said to Jonno.

He nodded. 'We were at school together. He was cool and then his mum died and he went really, really weird. So I just stopped being mates with him and told everyone he was a twat?'

'Fucksake, Jonno,' said Izzy. 'The poor guy! He'd lost his mum! And it now seems pretty likely that his dad killed her. And he's trying to make sense of his life while being a teenager at boarding school. That's what he needs. You telling everyone he's a twat.'

He raised his hands. 'I know! I know! I'm sorry. Poor Henry, but also I hope the police get him and make him tell them everything he knows.'

For a moment I pictured Henry, handcuffed. In a police station, looking defeated. In spite of everything, a part of me wanted to hug him.

'So. Next up: Owen Allen. Did you know?' said Jonno.

'No. No idea. What's been happening? I haven't looked at the news. Not since I started seeing myself in it.'

'Oh, Cat!' said Izzy. 'That picture of you and Fred. I absolutely freaked when I saw it. He's been messaging me for ages. Inviting me to stay at Northanger. Like – no thank you!' She paused. 'That photo. You really looked like a couple. I hated it. It looked like he was getting his claws into you.'

'Honestly, at that point I still thought he was nice.' I paused, remembering my car journey with him. 'Did he message you that day? Did you reply saying something that started with . . .' I tried to remember. '*No. You should just get her* . . . Something like that?'

Izzy nodded. 'Yeah. He'd asked me again if I fancied coming to visit since you were staying. I'd always found him so incredibly creepy. I said he should get you to call me instead. He didn't reply.'

'He has you saved in his phone as Thorpe,' I told her.

'That'll be so no one knows he's creeping on a teenager,' said Jonno. 'And you know what else?'

I leaned forward. 'What?'

'Right. All this comes from Mum. In total confidence. She's going to tell the police, but meanwhile don't tell anyone. You won't put it on a podcast or anything?'

'Jonno!' That was Izzy.

He smiled. 'Don't worry. I didn't think you would. Just checking. So: it turns out he'd been blackmailing Sophie. He has no cash left. Like literally none. He's only got the house, which has no mortgage on it or anything. But he likes to live the high life and he doesn't have any money left to pay for it. So he's been hanging out on the Riviera targeting rich women.'

'He didn't.' I stopped, then forced myself to say it. 'He called Sophie to tell her about Eva when I first arrived. She was really shaken to hear from him and didn't want Owen to know he'd called. And then I saw an email from her on his computer. She didn't . . . have an affair with him?'

'Mum said she didn't. Sophie was friends with Elisabeth, and I can't imagine she'd have jumped into bed with her widower. But apparently he was trying to get her to leave Owen. She was never going to, so then he dug around until he found out about their dodgy business stuff and blackmailed them for a while.'

Izzy jumped in. 'Er, hello! You saw an email from Sophie on his computer? What did it say?'

I thought back. 'I only saw the start of it. It said she was sorry about Eva, I think. I was honestly more worried about snooping round the empty house at that point. I was only checking the laptop for a camera feed or something.'

Jonno made a face. 'By the way, Mum reckons it was Fred who tipped Aisha off in the first place.'

'Fuck!'

'She says the police are already looking at him for Eva,' said Izzy. 'Honestly, our little "what happened to Eva" podcast could have been on to something, if we'd got it off the ground. She went out on a speedboat that night. Then she's dead the next morning. She'd recently broken up with him, so he was pissed off that he wasn't getting his hands on her cash.'

'Shit.'

'So, all in all, when we got the message from your mum, via your sister on Instagram, saying that you needed urgent help, there was nothing in the world that was stopping us coming to save you. And we were almost at Northanger anyway.'

Jonno and Izzy had come to help me. Henry hadn't. Henry's flight was a knife to my stomach. Jonno was braver than Henry. Better than Henry. Jonno was my friend.

He paid the bill and stood up, offering me a hand. I took it. Izzy took my other one. We left the cafe arm in arm.

'Antibes?' said Jonno.

'Antibes.'

PART THREE

PART THREE

31

Truro bus station was the same as it had always been, and I smiled despite everything as the coach pulled in. It was sketchy, with a few people drinking beer from cans and a group of moping teens looking as if they were plotting something.

I thought of myself, earlier this summer, and my own plotting.

I stepped down and took a deep breath of Cornish air. It wasn't sunny. I didn't need to worry about reapplying sunscreen or covering my head. The sky was cloudy, but it wasn't raining, and the air was warm. I pulled my little backpack over my shoulders, and set off for home. I was not going to cry. I was not going to feel like a failure. I had all my stuff from Antibes. I had left a few things at Northanger, and I was fine with never seeing any of that again.

I remembered that Kitty had wanted to go away with the Allens instead of me. If she had, she'd have spent the summer on the beach with an ice cream. She wouldn't have been drawn into drug crime and murder. She would never have gone to Northanger. She'd have been the Allens' perfect guest, and if Jonno had been interested in her she'd have been delighted. When everything went wrong for Sophie, Kitty would have stayed with the Thorpes. She'd never have gone anywhere near Northanger.

I didn't get far up the road because my knee had already been complaining on the bus from Heathrow. For most of the way, I'd had two seats to myself, and when I'd managed to put my leg up it felt much better, though I had to keep an eye out because if anybody came down the aisle and jolted it I was in agony.

Mainly, I'd just sat there listening to podcasts and waiting. I wasn't so keen on the true-crime ones any more. I thought it might be time to move on. The true-crime stories were people's real lives, their actual tragedies, and I had already been complicit in thinking about making horrible complicated situations into entertainment. I cringed when I thought of my own 'podcast voice', the breathy growl I'd cultivated, in imitation of Aisha, back at Northanger. Those days were over. The podcasts I'd been listening to now were different. Informative. One about screenwriting. One about politics. They were interesting. Who knew?

The main thing I'd been doing was occupying my mind, because when I didn't have someone talking into my ear I found myself falling down those stairs. I saw François, his eyes rolling in his head. I saw Henry, running away from me. Fred, laughing.

When my limp got worse, I sat on the low wall in front of the museum and took out my phone. Against all odds, it still had five per cent battery. I pressed the name of the person I most wanted to speak to in the world.

I'd spent my eighteenth birthday hiding in the Thorpes' back garden, covered in sunscreen, with Izzy or Jonno for constant company. They'd poured me champagne and fed me food and just stopped me being alone with my thoughts. I'd spoken to Mum, and to Fritz. Izzy had screened out everyone else.

Helena had sorted everything out. She'd made sure the police were fine with me going; they'd only agreed yesterday afternoon, and she'd booked me on a flight to Heathrow first thing this morning. I hadn't told anyone but Mum that I was coming back today: I wanted to surprise them. But because Mum hated surprises I'd told her, and asked her to keep it secret from the kids.

I yawned as I waited. If the wall had been a bit more comfortable, I'd probably have fallen asleep. It was funny, I thought, how you saw places in a different way when you'd come from somewhere else. Before I left, Truro had just been the way things were. It was home, and it contained school, college, friends, family, Primark, the library and the cinema. Now everything stood in contrast to something else. It was urban after Northanger, and the weather felt cool and humid. If I'd been to, say, the Arctic, it would have felt warm. I laughed at myself. That wasn't really very insightful. I was overwhelmed with relief at being back. Finally, I wasn't an outsider trying to work out how to behave. At last I belonged.

The car pulled up in front of me sooner than I was expecting, and there she was, parking in the bus stop, leaning across to open the passenger door, unencumbered by other kids. I limped across the pavement and climbed in. We looked at each other and then she lunged forward for a hug, and I was crying.

'I'm so sorry I was grumpy when you left,' she said, stroking my shoulder. 'I just knew how much I was going to miss you, but it wasn't fair. I've regretted it every single day. Look at your leg! You poor thing. And it could have been so much worse!'

'It could have been,' I said, 'but it wasn't.'

A bus sounded its horn, and she gave a wave out of the window, indicated and pulled out.

There was one thing that had been on my mind, and since we were almost never alone together I thought I'd say it now.

'Mum?' She looked at me, eyebrows raised, then quickly back to the road as a group of pedestrians were wandering down the middle of it. 'Sophie said at the start of my trip . . . I mean, you don't have to answer, but Sophie said something had happened when you were younger. And . . .'

'You were wondering what it was?' she said. She smiled and reached over to touch my good leg. 'Oh. Thanks, Sophie. Well, it's a bit of a story, and I'll tell you. Not today, but it's probably time I opened up a bit. You're an adult now after all. There was a reason I ended up in a relationship with your dad.'

Then we were home. I stared at the house. It looked normal. There was no sparkling sea view, no balcony. No fields of vines, no miles-long drive. Thank God, no huge staircase.

I looked at Mum and grinned. She unlocked the door and gestured for me to go in.

The first person to notice me was Josh, who came bounding at me and crashed straight into my legs. Ouch. But worth it.

'Cat!' he shouted. 'Cat, Cat, Cat! It's Cat!'

I heard a voice – Summer's – from the sitting room next door.

'Can you see a cat, Josh?'

I scooped him up and carried him through.

'He can,' I said. 'Hi, Summer. Hi, Mia. Hi, Ethan. Hi, Dash. So I came home. Mum just picked me up.'

Summer looked at Mum mock-accusingly. 'You said you were dashing out for milk!'

My mother shrugged and laughed. I wasn't jealous of her ease with Summer, but it rankled a tiny bit.

They were all watching TV. Summer looked a bit guilty to be caught putting the telly on to have a rest, but then she grinned and stood up. She was taller than I'd realized when I saw her on the screen. Much taller than me. She hugged me.

'Cat! Welcome home! It's lovely to meet you in real life.'

Dash and Ethan peered round at me. They looked the same except that one of them had longer hair than the other. I had to concentrate for a moment to work out that it was Ethan.

'Oh, hey,' they said together, and turned back to the TV. I picked Mia and Josh up and sat down with them squashed on to my lap. Mia grabbed a lock of my hair and tucked it into her fist, sucking her thumb and using it as a comfort blanket. Josh put a hand on my cheek.

Mum sat down next to me and put an arm round us. She hugged me. She hugged the three of us.

'Come through and tell me everything. Tea?'

I stood up, bringing Mia with me.

'I'll make it,' I said. Being home was a warm blanket. I knew there was a lot out there that I was going to have to deal with very soon indeed, but, for now, all that mattered was that I was back.

32

British 'serial killer', 62, arrested in Provence

A British man, arrested in France earlier this week on suspicion of the murder of his wife, is being linked to at least two other deaths, French police revealed yesterday.

Frederick Tilney, 62, was seized at his multi-million-euro home near Barles, Provence, on Sunday, and is being held in police custody in Aix-en-Provence. A twenty-one-year-old man and a nineteen-year-old woman were also arrested, but later released on bail.

General Tilney is understood to have served in the British armed forces before marrying a French woman and settling in Provence, where his three children were born. His wife, Elisabeth, died in 2019, aged 49. Tilney has now been charged with her murder.

The alarm is thought to have been raised by a guest who was staying at the house. The property's extensive garden is currently being excavated.

More soon . . .

I read the article, ignored all the notifications and handed my phone to Kitty. The two of us were sitting on my bed, hip to hip, reading off the phone together.

'You were right.' She put my phone in her pocket and looked at me, shocked. She had slicked her hair back into a bun with ribbons in it, and was wearing a white dress that Izzy would definitely have worn too.

I held her gaze. 'Turns out that in real life, Kits, murder is totally fucking grim.'

'You OK?'

I thought about it. *Was* I? It had been a lot, but I'd come through. I was a mixture of bruised and something else. Relieved. A tiny bit proud because at least I'd done this. I'd messed a lot up this summer, but ultimately it was me who'd called the police on Fred Tilney. I'd suspected the wrong man until the real one pushed me down the stairs, but I'd got some things right. Elisabeth had been murdered.

The newspapers were restricted in what they could say about the case, but I was beginning to see that Elisabeth, Louis and Eva might only be the start. I remembered Sophie telling me about one of Helena's nannies, years ago, who had vanished. Sophie had just framed it as a *sometimes weird things happen* story, but now Izzy said the police had been asking questions about her after going through everything at Northanger. I remembered Fred's words to El: '*like we did before. With the nanny*'. What else had he done over the years?

I would have to go back to France for the trial at some point, and I wasn't looking forward to that, but at the same time there was a small part of me that knew I was going to see him in a courtroom and hold eye contact and give my evidence, and that although it would be terrifying it would also be amazing.

Kitty stood up from the bed. She was looking after my phone for me, because, now that I was back, I was doing a digital detox. Kitty passed on messages from people I actually wanted to talk to (Jonno and Izzy, mainly, and Fritz, who had a lot to say). She deleted everything else. Although she wouldn't say it, I could see that she was loving her new role.

'Ready?' said Kitty. She was at my side all the time, because when I was alone I fell apart.

I wasn't, but I nodded.

'Let's do it.'

We had to go to a different part of college today. It was the part where you went for university-level courses and I'd never been in the building before. Like the rest of the college, it was newish, carpeted, and had white walls and an institutionally clean smell that was clearer today, probably because there hadn't been any students here for a while.

Kitty and I walked in behind a group of other people. College was massive and there were loads of people I didn't know. I had dressed as low key as I could (very low key indeed) in blue jeans that were baggy enough to hide my knee brace, and a black T-shirt. Trainers, loose hair.

'Hello! Welcome!' said a woman with a lanyard. I didn't know her. I didn't want to see anyone I knew today; I wasn't ready for any of it. She told us where to go for the results, which had already been out for a few hours, and Kitty and I looked at each other.

'Showtime,' she said.

We walked into a much bigger room, which had a line of tables staffed by people who were in charge of results envelopes. I needed to go to the middle table, with my mid-alphabet surname. I was starting to head there, nervous about what was coming and with no idea about what decision I'd make, when I heard footsteps running up to me.

Adrenaline surged. I knew it couldn't be Fred, but a part of me was constantly alert. I knew that if he was free he would kill me, and that was a feeling I was going to have to learn to deal with. I thought I might need some kind of counselling at some point, because his laughing face, when the police took him out of the house, was in my head all the time. I swung round ready to defend myself, but it was . . .

'Mum!'

She skidded to a halt next to me.

'Have you got them yet?'

'No, Mum. I thought you weren't coming?'

'Me too, but then Bill said, "*Why aren't you going?*" And Summer was taking all the kids to the beach this morning, so I thought, actually, why aren't I? You're always so independent that I assumed you didn't need me. But I wanted to come and support you. Is that OK?'

I let her hug me. I felt myself relax. Mum was being amazing. She was in a better place than she had been for years. I kept getting glimpses of how things used to be, when it was just me and her.

'Of course,' I said. 'Here we go.'

The three of us walked up to the table, and I gave my name. The woman behind the table flicked through the envelopes, pulled one out and handed it to me with a smile.

'Good luck,' she said. I noticed it trembling in my hand as I walked away.

'What do you need?' said Mum.

I looked at her. This was the woman who, as far as I was aware, wanted me to stay at home. Until recently, I'd thought she'd be happy if I failed everything. She didn't even know my plans.

'What do I need for what?'

'For Belfast.'

There was a moment of silence.

'How,' I said, 'do you know about Belfast, Mother?'

'Of course I know about Belfast, Caitlin.' She took a deep breath. 'For one thing, Sophie told me before you went away. She told me how important it was for you. That's one reason I was so moody. I knew she was right. You have to go, darling. None of this is your responsibility. We're hardly the only people with small children. We're fine. I promise.'

I felt myself lighting up from the inside. 'Really?'

'Really.'

'I'll come over after college,' said Kitty. 'Every day, if you like. I'll help.'

'I know you will, darling, but you have your life too,' said Mum, and I stared at the envelope. My future was in here. It suddenly mattered.

'I need an A and two Bs,' I said. My voice came out as a whisper.

Kitty got impatient. 'Come on, babe. Want me to do it?'

I held it out, then changed my mind and ripped it open. I pulled out the paper and unfolded it.

English: A

History: A

Psychology: A*

I stared at my grades. This was far beyond anything I'd dared to hope for. I felt my face changing, smiling at the future that was in front of me. I had finished college. I had aced my exams. I would go to Belfast.

Kitty snatched it from my hand.

'Oh my GOD!' she shrieked. 'You got As and shit. You genius. You could go to fucking Cambridge like Jonno!'

A woman standing nearby with a camera spun round.

'Are you going to Cambridge?' she said, giving me an assessing look. 'I'm from Cornwall Live and . . .'

I thought of Cambridge. For one thing, I hadn't applied there, and for another I wouldn't have gone anyway. Plus, I did not want to talk to a journalist.

'No, sorry.' I took a deep breath. 'I think I'm going to go to . . . Belfast,' I said. Belfast. A new place. A new adventure.

The woman smiled. 'Congratulations,' she said. 'That sounds interesting.' Then she turned away. She hadn't recognized me. Hadn't taken her chance to interview the unnamed (officially, though totally named on social media) girl who had brought down the serial killer. She'd missed her story.

Thank God for that.

Mum hugged me.

'I'm so proud of you,' she said. 'You do know that, don't you?'

That afternoon, we sat in the back garden because it wasn't raining. Almost everyone was there: Mum and Bill, the four twins, Kitty and Mabel and Summer. The children were running and toddling around, and I was sitting with the three girls. I thought of Sophie for a moment. I wished I could tell her my news.

I hadn't heard from El, and I'd blocked Henry. I had so much to process there and it was easier to delete him from my life. I had no idea whether he'd tried to contact me or not, but also I was certain he hadn't.

Summer had magicked up a cake at the Allens', since she was still staying there. The police hadn't asked her to move out, though they had apparently searched the place from top to bottom. The cake was so big that Bill had driven over to pick her up on his way back from work. It had four layers and was covered in chocolate icing, with 'Congratulations Cat!' iced perfectly on the top. She'd allowed Dash and Ethan to cover it in sprinkles, which meant it looked both upmarket and adorable at the same time.

There was a plastic table on the patio outside the back door, and Mum made a big show of carrying the cake out. There was no clutter in the way today: someone had made sure it was all clear. I sat back and let myself enjoy it. I had passed my exams. I was going to Belfast. For now, I was home.

Being the centre of attention wasn't my favourite thing, but here it was different. I was lucky to be surrounded by so many people who loved me. Who didn't push people down stairs, didn't sell drugs, didn't take women out on boats to drown them.

I took a deep breath. I blinked hard. I would take this over Northanger a million times over.

I took a bite and turned to Summer.

'You are amazing,' I said. 'How did you learn to do this? Do they teach you this at nanny school?'

She shook her head. 'Nah. I just love baking. Always have. I was actually on *Junior Bake Off* when I was a kid. Seriously. You can see it on YouTube, I think.'

Mabel put her arm round Summer's neck and pulled her close. 'You can't leave, Summer. Please stay with us forever. You're too perfect.'

She didn't pull away. 'I wish I could. I'm going to miss you all so much. It's been a wild summer with you guys.' She gestured to Dash, Ethan, Mia and Josh.

Josh climbed up on to her lap and tried to grab her piece of cake. I watched them, mildly jealous as always. He reached over and took hold of my face, smearing it with chocolate icing.

When I heard a theatrical cough, I thought it was Ethan or Dash messing around. Then I saw that they were both eating, silently focused on cake.

I heard his voice before I looked round. Every muscle in my body tensed.

'Er, sorry!'

I couldn't move. No. I did not want this. Did not want to see him. I was frozen.

Without turning round, I knew that Henry Tilney was here.

Everyone else was looking at him so in the end I had to. He was standing by the side gate.

'I did knock and ring the bell, but there didn't seem to be . . .' He made his *awkward* face. I was so over that.

Henry Tilney was here, in our tiny overcrowded back garden in Truro. I didn't want him here. I had left his world behind. He hadn't been there when I'd needed him to save my fucking life, so he didn't get to be here now. In fact, I had climbed into a den to hide with him, and he'd left me to it.

Bill, who had been sitting on the grass with Mia, stood up.

'Can I help?' he said. I got up too.

'This is Henry,' I said. 'Henry – what are you . . . ? Are you even allowed to leave France right now?'

I saw his Adam's apple move as he swallowed. 'Er. Yes. I am. I needed to see you and I couldn't get hold of you by phone.'

I looked him in the eye. 'I blocked you.'

'But I can still see you on Find My Friends. Whether you consider me a friend or not, it seems that particular app didn't get the memo. I could see exactly where you were and so, in the absence of any other ideas, I decided to come and ask in person whether you would please consider talking to me.'

I stood up.

'This is everyone,' I said. I went round the garden pointing at each of them in turn. 'Bill, Mia, Ethan, Dash, Mabel, Kitty, Summer, Joshie and Mum.'

'Hi, Henry,' said Kitty. Everyone else said hi too. All of us, apart from the kids, knew exactly what had happened. What he had done, and what he hadn't done. There was a tension in the air: I had no idea how to handle him.

Then Mum stepped in and smoothed it over.

'We're celebrating Cat's A levels,' said Mum. 'And having a late birthday party for her. Would you like some cake?'

She disappeared into the house and came out with a plate. None of our plates matched. The only thing at this table that was made from Provençal glazed pottery was the mug I'd got for Mum at the market that first week, which had somehow survived the fall down the Northanger stairs and everything that had happened since. She loved it.

My thoughts were interrupted by Summer, Kitty and Mabel. They came over to me, one on each side and one in front.

'Want us to get rid of him?' said Kitty.

'We'll throw him out,' said Summer.

'We'd enjoy it,' said Mabel, who was fourteen and tough. She paused. 'He's taller than I thought.'

I looked at Henry. He looked back and there was a flash of such desperation in his eyes that I changed my mind.

'No, thanks,' I told them. 'I think it's OK. I'll just see what he wants.'

Henry and I went into the house. I took him to the living room and sat down. The room was small, and crammed with a sofa, two armchairs and a coffee table. I took an armchair to be sure he wouldn't sit next to me, and put my leg up on the table. Henry sat on the sofa and shuffled awkwardly. He looked at me, and then away. He wouldn't quite meet my eye.

I knew that he and El had been arrested and then let go. Neither of them had done anything, as far as I knew. He hadn't witnessed anything, that day at least, unlike Eleanor. I'd tried to get in touch with François, who was in hospital with concussion, but had only been able to send a message. He'd replied asking if we could talk as soon as he was a bit better. Helena had organized flowers from me.

I hoped Henry wasn't going to tell me that François was dead, that another person had been added to Fred Tilney's tally. That the man I had thought was a killer had died saving me.

I almost spoke a couple of times, but then I remembered that I'd blocked him. He'd taken me to a killer's home. François had helped where Henry, my actual boyfriend, hadn't.

'Cat,' he said. I shot a glance at him, but he was looking at the wall. 'I mean, sorry, first of all. If that begins to cover it, which it doesn't.'

'Mmm,' I said. 'It really doesn't.' I had kissed this guy. Many times. We'd done more than that. We had walked hand in hand through the market, had messed around in the river, had talked late into the night. We'd been planning a trip to an empty house, for privacy. We'd been a couple.

I'd had no idea that he was enmeshed in horrors beyond all understanding.

I waited for him to say more.

Eventually, he did. He seemed to be telling it to the carpet in a small voice.

'We had a nanny when I was small. Au pair, I guess. Jeannie. She was from New Zealand and I loved her. Adored her totally. I felt like she got me, and she didn't think I was boring because I was less cool than Fritz and less fun than El. She thought I was OK as myself.

'Then one day I saw her and Dad in the garden. Kissing. They didn't know I'd seen. I was about seven and I freaked right out.'

'Did you tell anyone?'

'You know me. Of course not.' He gave a self-deprecating laugh. 'And about a week after that she'd gone. She'd left a note to say she'd had to go back to New Zealand because her mother was ill. But I knew it wasn't right. She'd never have gone without saying goodbye to me.

'When I got older and remembered the kiss, I thought it must have been that they were having an affair and my mother found out and that was why Jeannie left overnight. But then I started to wonder.'

I stared at a picture on the wall, a school photo: the older twins side by side. 'What made you wonder?'

I thought he wasn't going to answer, but then he did.

'I guess it was a lot of things,' he said. 'Little things. Mainly the way my mother changed.' His voice cracked. A part of me wanted to comfort him, but I didn't want to touch him in case it stopped him talking. 'She'd been so brilliant. Like El said. Always focusing on us, always the one who was there. But we watched her shrink more and more. Avoiding him. He'd get angry. So angry. That's why I'd hide in the cupboard. El always made sure she was his favourite so she'd feel safe. Fritz was the one who used to fight back. I had no idea about Mum and Louis, not until last week, but it makes sense.' He met my eyes. 'So. Yeah. A part of me knew Dad was awful and sensed that something bad had happened with Jeannie, but mostly I was in denial.'

His face crumpled, and he turned away. 'I'm so sorry. I ran away and hid. I hate being this guy. As soon as I heard Dad shouting and saw François trying to protect you, I realized. I'd known it for ages, but I couldn't face it.'

He stopped. I put a hand on his shoulder. 'About your mum?'

He looked away. 'I knew really that she didn't just trip and fall down the stairs. Fritz had been trying to tell us for ages. I remembered that Dad used to flip out, like he did with you, when she was alive. From time to time. It was why we were kind of OK with going to boarding school, because home could be so dreadful. And we all knew that Louis was in love with her, and I'd kind of let myself believe that he'd been so devastated when she died that he moved away forever.' He wiped his eyes with the back of his hand. 'Like I said, Fritz has always known, but we never believed him. It was easier not to. François took it upon himself to keep an eye on us, because he knew that was what Mum would have wanted. Him and Dad were polite to each other, but under the surface they detested each other. It was always bubbling, always going to come to a head at some point. And I think when François met you he got instant alarm bells. So many people had gone missing around Dad. So many women. François was scared for you. I think he felt he needed to do something this time. He wasn't going to let it happen again.'

'He told me to take care,' I said, 'that first time. At the market. He whispered it into my ear. I had no idea what he was on about.'

'I'm sorry I'm so useless. I have no idea how to be better.'

'Henry – have you ever had therapy?'

'No.' The silence stretched out. I didn't break it. 'I know I have to. And I will. It's hard to face it. The horrors of it all. Things I'd never really admitted I knew, on the front pages of the papers. El's gone back to Berlin. You're here with your gorgeous family and I'm glad you are. It's hard to go anywhere in France without everyone knowing exactly who I am. I was arrested and let go and . . . now what do I do? Who even am I?'

'You need Fritz. Go to him. You have to. He's at the house in Antibes.'

'You're in touch?'

I nodded. 'We are. He's worried about you.'

After a moment, Henry continued. 'While you were standing up to my father, and El was trying to get her head round what was going on, and François was actually saving you, and then your mum and Kitty were sorting out Jonno and Izzy to rescue you . . . I couldn't do anything. You saw me – I even ran away from you. It's a devastating thing to find out about yourself. I couldn't do a thing. The girl I loved was going through the exact same thing as my mother, and I couldn't find it in myself to stop it.'

He'd call me *the girl he loved*. For now, I filed it away, but I'd think about it later.

He took a deep breath. 'I needed to see you to say sorry. I didn't mean to hijack your party and make you watch me crying.' He wiped his eyes again. I found a tissue in my pocket and passed it over, but I'd already used it to wipe chocolate icing from a baby, and so it just made his face a lot worse. I leaned over, licked my thumb and cleaned the icing off.

Our faces were close together.

I'd wanted to kiss him from the first time we met, but now I didn't. I had too much else happening, too much to get my head around.

He leaned in a tiny bit. I leaned back. He nodded.

'Come back to the garden,' I said. 'Come and meet everyone properly. I promise you, it'll be fine.'

He sat on the sofa for a moment longer.

'Yes,' he said in the end. 'If they won't all hate me, then yes, please. I'd like that. You'll have to tell me all the names again. I'm afraid my brain is all over the place.'

33

September

Kitty and I were sitting in a tiny studio. We were both wearing headphones and Kitty was playing with the controls, though I wasn't sure she completely knew what she was doing. I had a script in front of me and I was terrified, but ready to go.

She gave me a thumbs up. I took a deep breath and read the words off the page in front of me. It was time to do this.

'Hello, people,' I said. 'And welcome to the podcast. This is episode one of *Lies We Told This Summer: how I went on holiday and caught a killer*. It's the only time I'm going to be telling this story and I am not open to interview requests. This is it, people. So keep listening. I'm Cat Morland. Buckle up. It's a wild ride.'

This was it. My real podcast, the thing I was actually doing.

It was Sophie who had suggested it.

Yes, Sophie was back – and Owen. After they were extra-dited from Bangkok, the Allens had hired what seemed to be every single one of the world's best lawyers, and after a couple of weeks in prison over here they'd been released on bail and were back in Cornwall, lying low. They weren't out of the woods yet, but they were acting as if they were.

They were saying Fred Tilney had framed them, but I was done with being complicit in things and had turned down her offer of production help.

I was sure their story was bullshit. Owen had spent the whole summer buried in paperwork, so I couldn't see how he'd been unaware of the fact that his company was a front for moving massive amounts of drugs across the world in shipping containers. Still, Mum and Bill were a lot less suspicious than I was. They were relieved to have their friends back for the moment, delighted that it had all been 'a mistake'.

Kitty and I had hired a studio in town, and we were making it work together, without Sophie – just the two of us, with a bit of advice from Aisha. Aisha and I were actually in touch again now. She lived in Dublin, and we were planning to meet in Ireland when I was over for uni in a couple of weeks. She'd been investigating the Allens undercover and had played us all, but somehow I didn't think I was in a position to hold it against her.

I can't believe I missed everything else that was going on, she'd written recently. I was out there investigating undercover, and I missed the effing serial killer. And he was the one who'd contacted me in the first place to tip me off about the Allens. So basically I was played by a murderer, and then my targets bought their way out of trouble. FML.

I went back to my script.

'So,' I said. 'My hot summer in France began late in July, when I flew to Nice to stay in Antibes. I'd never been away from home. I was scared.'

'You really were,' said Kitty. 'Remember how nervous you were, that morning you left?'

Here, we were going to insert the clips I'd made, before I left home. I hated the sound of my voice on them: I'd tried so hard to sound like a professional podcaster and in reality I just sounded like a try-hard wannabe. Still, at least we had a lot of clips. I'd made plenty of recordings. Quite a lot of them were definitely not seeing the light of day.

I stepped in with the next line.

'And then, the next morning, I was recording my impressions when this happened . . .'

This time, we played it out loud. I sat back and listened.

'So,' said my voice. I cringed. 'Here I am. Living my hot summer. I'm in Antibes, in the old town, and I'm standing in front of the Picasso Museum, next to a statue of a person poised on the edge of the ocean, looking out at the Mediterranean. There are boats and swimmers down there. The sun is shining and there's literally not a cloud in the sky. I'm new to this world and I feel like I've stepped into a different universe. A place I knew from my phone, but I'm here. I've stepped into Instagram. You see . . .'

My voice changed. This was it.

'Sorry. That person in the water? I'm pretty sure it's a woman, and I think she's in a dress. I'm way up above and I don't quite know if I'm . . . I mean, from here you'd think . . . You'd think she might be . . . in trouble.'

Then there was a long pause. I remembered that spiralling feeling of horror.

'Shit. I need to find help. Right. I'm going to find somebody who – Oh! Oh, um, *excusez-moi*.'

Then Henry's voice was filling the studio. I closed my eyes. Poor Henry. I hoped he was going to get a ton of therapy and come out of it all right. I hoped that one day he'd meet another girl he liked, and that he'd be ready to open up. I knew, though, that it wasn't going to be me.

'You speak English?' he said.

'In the water. Down there, I think there's someone in trouble. You see – just there? In the greenish . . .'

We heard Henry gasp.

'Oh. I see. Ah! Erm . . . Stay here. I'll get help.'

My first conversation with Henry Tilney. A conversation in which, it turned out, I was telling him something he had already known. It was now clear that Eva had ended her fling with Fred and gone to London for a few weeks. As soon as she was back, he'd invited her for a 'no-hard-feelings' drink on his boat. Then, the next morning, she'd turned up dead.

Henry had suspected his dad for years, but he was so entangled with his father's crimes that he hadn't known what to do. He'd been a part of it by doing nothing. I wasn't going to be the person who made him better. I couldn't.

Fred had had a beard at that point, and I knew now why I'd had that feeling that I'd seen him before. He had been the bearded man who'd approached Henry and me in Antibes, as we walked home after our night on the dance floor. Henry had stopped him, but I thought he'd watched us from a distance. No wonder Henry hadn't wanted to kiss me. What with me being drunk and his dad watching from the shadows, it couldn't have been an enticing prospect.

Then I'd seen him from my balcony. I'd gone out there, drunk, to look for Henry, and I'd just seen a bearded man staring back at me. A serial killer.

Kitty was looking at me. Waiting. She saw I needed a prompt.

'So that was Henry Tilney's voice,' she said.

'Yes,' I said. 'That was the very first moment I spoke to Henry Tilney. The point at which everything began to unravel.'

I looked at Kitty. She looked at me. I shifted around in my seat, leaned closer to the mic and started to tell my story.

Acknowledgements

Thanks first of all to Ruth Knowles, who was totally up for the idea of a book that added murders to a plot stolen from Jane Austen. Ruth, our nine books together have been a dream. Thank you to Amina Parchment-Youssef for being my new editor: I'm excited about everything that's coming next.

And huge thanks to the amazing team at Penguin who, as ever, make things happen in the most incredible way. Shreeta Shah, Charis Lowe-White, copy-editor Sam Stewart, proofreaders Debs Warner and Mollie Schofield, and thanks for the amazing cover design to Kim Ekdahl and Lauren Maxwell.

Thanks to Steph Thwaites, and everyone at Curtis Brown, and to Zosia Knopp and everyone at Tall House Creative.

India Stringer: huge thanks for your perspective on all things Norland Nanny. The children who have you caring for them are very lucky people.

Copy-edits of this book were done while I was on a writing residency in Krakow: enormous thanks to the National Centre for Writing in Norwich, the Krakow

Festival office and the UN Cities of Literature Circular Residency for the opportunity. It was a magical month.

Veronica Henry: thank you for letting me borrow your fictional town of Barles, even though the things that happen in the countryside outside my version are a bit less wholesome than the events of your gorgeous book, *One Night at the Chateau*.

Thanks to Natalie Hart, writing buddy extraordinaire, and the wider Cornish creative community that is so supportive and joyous. Including (but not limited to) Helen Tiplady, Simon Harvey, Bryony Partridge, Ed Rowe, Keith Sparrow, Clare Sparrow, Wyl Menmuir, Anna Wilson, Naomi Jones, Julie Sykes, Jodie Matthews and many more.

Thank you to my fabulous siblings Adam Barr, John Guzek, Theo Merz and Stella Merz, and to Bridget and Nigel Guzek and Charles Barr.

Sending particular love to my dear friend Silvia Salib and the lovely Bess Fox.

To my children and stepchildren Gabe, Seb, Charlie, Lottie and Alfie, thank you for being endlessly brilliant and also for proving quite spectacularly that parenting does not in fact become more straightforward when the kids grow up.

And thank you to Craig for everything, always.

What if you meet
that perfect stranger
again – and again.

Ghosted

EMILY BARR

AUTHOR OF THE GLOBAL BESTSELLER *THE ONE MEMORY OF FLORA BANKS*

LIES FROM THE PAST HAVE BEEN BURIED FOR YEARS –
NOW THEY'RE BEING DUG UP . . .

THIS
SUMMER'S
SECRETS

EMILY BARR

AUTHOR OF THE GLOBAL BESTSELLER *THE ONE MEMORY OF FLORA BANKS*

It was the perfect love story – until it definitely wasn't . . .

A GIRL
CAN
DREAM

EMILY BARR

AUTHOR OF THE GLOBAL BESTSELLER *THE ONE MEMORY OF FLORA BANKS*

TWO GIRLS GET ON THE TRAIN.
WHEN THEY GET OFF,
NEITHER IS WHO THEY SAY THEY ARE.

THE
OTHER
GIRL

EMILY BARR

AUTHOR OF THE GLOBAL BESTSELLER *THE ONE MEMORY OF FLORA BANKS*

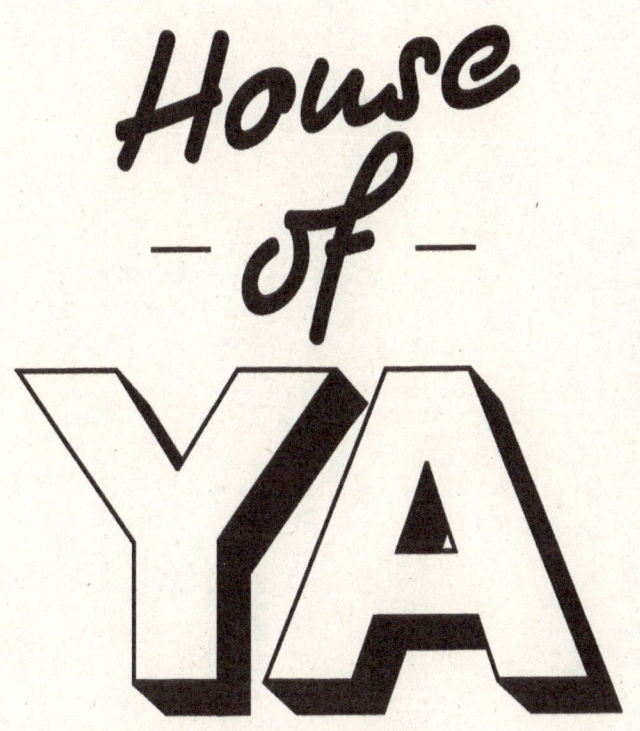

HOME IS WHERE THE BOOKS LIVE

Discover your next read @houseofya